W9-ACR-736

i
am
Gold

i
am
Gold

Bill James

THE COUNTRYMAN PRESS
Woodstock, Vermont

ISBN 978-0-88150-951-9
Library of Congress Cataloging-in-Publication Data
has been applied for.

Published by The Countryman Press,
43 Lincoln Corners Way, Woodstock, VT 05091

Distributed by W. W. Norton & Company, Inc.,
500 Fifth Avenue, New York, NY 10110

Printed in the United States of America

10 9 8 7 6 5 4 3 2 1

Chapter One

2009

One of the notable things about Iles was he'd get very upset at the death of any child, but especially a child who'd been shot. He gazed at this lad on the floor of the Jaguar, and Harpur could read the self-blame, anguish and despair in Iles's face. It had happened on his territory, and in day-light – that's how he would think: a damned affront, a stain; someone, or more than one, monkeying with him, with *him*, Desmond Iles.

Usually, the Assistant Chief's face didn't say much at all. He could do terrific, almighty, disturbing blankness, except, of course, when he went into one of those twitch-ing, loud, lips-froth fits about his wife and Harpur, though that had finished aeons ago. Looking in at the riddled boy through the gap where the window should have been, Iles seemed near to weeping. The boy's stepmother, dead in the driver's seat, would also register with him, certainly, but his main reactions and grief were for the child, Laurent.

Sometimes – not now, no, not now – Iles had quoted to Harpur a saying from one of his famous literary figures in the past: 'Grief is a species of idleness.' Very snappy and cool and clever-clever, but wrong for Iles today, wasn't it, sir? The ACC did a lot of heavy reading and came out with plenty of quotes, now and then fairly sane.

Detective Chief Superintendent Colin Harpur reached the scene at about the same time as the first armed

1

response car and an ambulance. Iles arrived a couple of minutes later. It was the kind of incident the ACC would want to attend personally. He'd find it symbolic, foully symbolic, a sign of possible general breakdown, and on his plate. Laurent Shale's sister who'd been with him in the back of the car seemed unhurt, though her school clothes, forehead and hair were splashed with his blood. Harpur had opened a rear door of the Jaguar and lifted her off the floor and out. Ambulance people declared Laurent and his stepmother dead at the scene, or they'd have been removed at once, too.

A woman paramedic had taken the girl from Harpur and sat with her on the low front-garden wall of a house along-side the Jaguar. She wiped the girl's face with a dressing pad and tried to talk some comfort. 'Her name's Matilda,' Harpur called.

'Is it a mistake, Col?' Iles said.

'In what sense, sir?' Harpur said.

'Did they expect Mansel Shale to be driving?'

'We do know he generally did the school run.'

'And the car's recognized everywhere,' Iles said.

'It's the kind of school where parents are expected to roll up in at least a Jaguar. Manse is hot on that kind of thing – attention to tone.'

'So, Shale must be away talking to an importer, or getting shriven at some abbey, and the wife deputizes,' Iles said. 'Hasn't this family heard about not sticking to the same route? Manse is not in some ordinary, safe career, after all.'

The ACC and Harpur spoke across Laurent's body. Harpur stood in the road. He hadn't closed the Jaguar rear door after bringing Matilda Shale out and he bent now towards the interior of the car and Iles. The Assistant Chief was on the pavement. The near-side rear window had been shattered by a bullet and he crouched with his head through the space. He was in uniform. He'd reverted lately to that *en brosse* cut for his grey hair, copied from Jean

2

Gabin in an old film on TV. His admiration for Gabin came and went. There weren't many people Iles admired non-stop – the poet, Alfred Lord Tennyson, the French revolutionary politician, Robespierre, and the ancient, toughie British queen, Boudicca, sometimes called Boadicea, though not by Iles.

'The second wife of Mansel? A wedding not long ago?' Iles said.

'Naomi. The first one – Sybil – cut loose.'

'They can do that, Harpur.' But, perhaps because of the special situation, Iles didn't turn mad or high-decibelled this time.

'Well, yes, I've heard something along those lines,' Harpur said.

Chapter Two

Of course, there'd been a build-up to all this. It began just over a month ago. One point about Mansel Shale was he knew nobody could see the future, including him, but back then – say more like five or six weeks than a month – yes, back then he'd had this strong idea he'd get killed soon: like shot in the head, most probably, though maybe garrotted.

But, he also had to think, perhaps that's all it was, a strong idea. A strong idea could be a stupid idea. Strong didn't mean sensible. Some madmen became very strong *because* they was mad, requiring straitjackets. It might be the same with certain ideas: powerful but crazy.

As a matter of fact, one evening around that time his son, Laurent, had been told at school to study an old poem about this sort of topic and they talked it over. The poem had a dog in it, and showed people could make a total mistake when guessing who'd die. In many ways Shale regarded poetry as quite worthwhile. Undoubtedly, all sorts liked it, with or without rhymes, stiff covers or paperback. Poetry could tell you things. Manse would not deny this.

But, naturally, he'd realized that if he spoke to other experienced folk in the substances trade about his fear of getting killed they'd say immediately, 'So, hire a body-guard, or bodyguards.' It would be their reply even if Manse admitted his worry could be foolish and panicky. However, people in the dog poem had turned out to be foolish and panicky, and Manse would hate to look the same. That was not right for someone in his position at the head of a top-class firm.

The poem had mentioned that a very good man, but not named, got bitten by a mad dog in Islington, London. Most probably in them historical days Islington had all sorts. Anyway, neighbours and friends went into a true flutter, because they believed the man would die of them bites. No. The complete opposite. The last line of the poem stuck hard in Manse's head. 'The dog it was that died.'

And this was the thing, wasn't it – there might be a lot of doubts about who was actually going to get it? Manse could guess that if he used these arguments with others in the trade they wouldn't listen, they'd just say again, 'Get a bodyguard.' Here's how they'd see it:

(a) in the snort, smoke and mainline trade, slaughter was always a danger for the boss of a rich, pusher company such as Manse's, so maximum self-protection made sense. And,

(b) a business leader like Shale, who knew the scene and its vibes so well, could somehow *feel* if special peril was around, even though out of sight. That being so, to take notice of such signals also made sense.

Therefore (a) and (b) together said, Pay a heavy, or heavies, to keep you safe. That sounded simple. Bodyguards had been trained to wipe out all who tried to attack their chief and, in any case, to put theirselves between him and the bullets or garrotting or Samurai sword. This was what bodyguarding *meant*: you guarded someone else's body – such as, say, Manse's – not your own. Good fees covered this fine flair. You could either pick someone or more than one from your private organization to become a bodyguard, or bodyguards, or you could go to an agency. Almost all bodyguards was men, many black. Sex equality hoopla didn't seem to work in this occupation yet. Nobody said it was not fair to women that only men could get murdered guarding someone else, male or female: think of the Queen or Madonna.

5

Laurent said the final words in that poem, 'The dog it was that died', came in this strange order so the dog arrived bang at the start and gave a terrific shock. Ordinary language wouldn't do. For instance, if the poem ended with, 'But, to everybody's astonishment, it was not the man who died but the dog', we'd have to wait until word number fourteen for 'dog'. But the poem put *The dog* right up front, to really hit you, when you'd reckoned the *man* would die from the very serious fangness of them bites, most likely causing rabies or fatal rips.

This was what Laurent thought, or what his teacher had told him to think. Manse wondered. The poem had a title, 'Elegy on the death of a mad dog', so you knew where the story would go. 'Elegy' *and* 'death' – a doubler. He was pretty sure only deads got elegies. How could you be surprised? Did the dog get poisoned by biting the man, regardless of him being so good? Did he have something rather murky in his blood that killed dogs? There would of been plenty of blood, some swallowed by the animal, probably. Manse felt confused, especially when he tried to get some message from that poem for the present. And what good was poems if they didn't help us now?

Way back, he'd had a great bodyguard, Neville Greenage, black, late twenties, but he went to Yorkshire or Austria, somewhere like that, to start his own operation. Later came Denzil Lake, originally from Hackney, London, white, dead now, owing to extensive gunshot damage to his mouth-throat-skull area, with suicide a possible, no question.* No question. Denzil had some stress. Well, he had a lot of stress. Understandable. Eventually understandable. He turned out to have been, for God knew how long, one of the most heartfelt and treacherous sods in ongoing commerce, and some thought the two-timing needed for this wore the rat right down, destroyed him. Manse had trusted Denz. Mistake, soft mistake. Deeper

* See *Easy Streets*

6

checks should of been done. His parents and family in Hackney didn't seem very much at all.

In the homework poem, perhaps the dog knew it would die of big madness soon and wanted to show it still had life and could do the kind of thing dogs did *because* they was dogs, and which *made* them dogs, like biting people – the way someone with a weak heart might go skiing or running the marathon to prove they could, though they couldn't, and dropped dead on the slopes or track. Many questions regarding this poem did trouble Mansel, but, just the same, people *could* mess up when forecasting a death, and he thought he probably had it wrong about what would shortly happen to him. He must not give in to madness and shadows. He still worried, though. Garrotting he regarded as deeply Continental and sick.

It delighted Manse to find Laurent studied ancient, truly useless stuff like that infection poem. If you paid the rosy fees charged by private schools, recession or not, you'd hope for far-out items like aged poetry and similar. Ordinary lessons, such as the multiplication tables, or mortise joints in a woodwork class, you could get any-where. Manse had both the children, Laurent and Matilda. Clearly, their mother didn't want them hanging about her when she did any of her flits. Sybil was more or less settled in North Wales the last he heard with a roofer or optician or snooker table salesman or vet – that kind of employ-ment. Of course, quite often Syb wanted to come back, but after the divorce he'd married again, and this made a definite difference. He had to consider Naomi and would of considered her even if he didn't have to. Manse hated casualness towards people – some people.

After Denzil Lake, he had felt nervous about employing anyone else in that bodyguard job. Manse tried Eldon Dane for a while, but he didn't seem right, and Eldon went back to selling, especially at discos and raves. He had a grand gift for discos and raves, perhaps inherited and in the genes, though there wouldn't of been many discos and raves in his father's time, and none in his grandfather's. Bodyguards kept very close to you. Well, obviously – their bodies had to be in place to guard yours. That might be OK, if you could totally believe in their loyalty. If you couldn't, though . . . If you couldn't, if they'd been worked on and turned by some smart and filthy enemy, they was in a great spot to do damage. The greatest. Didn't an Indian politician get assassinated by her own bodyguards? As a matter of fact, Manse could not speak Hindi, but he fancied he heard her yelling in the local language, 'You are paid to look after me, not this!' And they'd reply with some big-time political statement, probably, and cry, 'Nothing personal!' So, Manse hesitated to replace Dane, drove the Jaguar himself, went without a holstered chaperon, thank you.

Not just the Jaguar. The car was pretty well known on this territory. He'd use one of the smaller vehicles sometimes, including a van, hoping to stay unnoticed: a very basic ploy he'd adopted for years, even when Denzil drove, and not something new, because of the recent death fear. Taking the children to Bracken Collegiate, and bringing them home, gave him the most worries, of course. He could not use a van or dinky car for that kind of trip. This was a school where parents came in the big BMW, or a Mercedes or Lexus or 4×4, the 4×4s with mud streaks on them to show the family had paddocks. Matilda and Laurent would be ashamed if they had to climb out of or into the back of a beige van, however new. They'd never said so, but he thought they might of already been on the end of some snoot and snidenesses from other kids, and even the staff at Bracken, because of Manse's particular career. He knew unholy rumour about his firm drifted around the town, not all of it fully correct, and none of it provable in court, even with witness protection.

If you picked private education you had to put up with occasional shit. Mostly, it was envy, especially now. The teachers and the pupils saw that Laurent and Matilda had big, steady money behind them. A recession couldn't hurt Manse, not badly. The opposite. The 50 per cent tax on high earnings wouldn't touch him because he didn't pay tax, except on minor income from a next-to-nothing, legal, cover business he owned – haulage and scrap, the usual folderol. How could he pay tax on his chief business earnings when they didn't exist, not officially?

On account of that 50 per cent, several big companies had shifted their headquarters overseas where tax was lower, so they could attract better staff. Manse didn't need to go abroad either to recruit or sell. Some commodities people had to have regardless of a slump, people in this city like all others. For such troublesome days they might even need more help to relax. He felt bound to supply. A mission and duty. Manse had brought some prices down, but only by 5 per cent maximum. The result? Turnover up. Profits in line.

Laurent and Matilda said some children had been moved from Bracken and sent to state comps because daddy, the estate agent or accountant or advertising exec, was having it grim, such as out on his one-time money-bags earhole and down the Jobcentre. The big BMWs and Mercedes and Lexuses and 4×4s still rolled up, though not so many of them now: doctors, dentists, undertakers, cut-price clothes shop directors, MPs, car-boot sales landlords, Tesco management, takeaway owners, still did all right. They kept their kids at Bracken so they could become doctors, dentists, undertakers, cut-price shop directors, MPs, car-boot sales landlords, Tesco managers, takeaway owners one day, and get through the next crisis – or maybe this one if it dawdled.

Whatever the situation at Bracken, Manse wouldn't give extra problems to Matilda and Laurent by using a van, or even the Audi or small Peugeot. On these journeys he had to risk the Jag. He made sure they both rode in the back. Obviously, rapid automatic fire in a thorough, arcing burst could take in them as well as him, and even a single hard-nosed bullet might travel right through Manse and hit the child immediately behind. You couldn't ask kids to wear helmets and flak jackets over or under their blazers. It would look like Belfast in the bad times. He'd told them in a vague sort of way that if anything seemed to go wrong on the school trip they should get down at once on to the floor. They hadn't asked what 'go wrong' would mean, so he supposed they knew.

They'd always been savvy. To some extent this pleased him. But he also felt sad they *needed* to be savvy about matters such as a possible street ambush on the school run, with anything up to twenty or thirty rounds flying. Should a childhood be like this? Because he was who he was, he notched high earnings for them to help enjoy, but he also brought peril. And, so as not to scare them too much, or add to their shame, he added to the peril by driving them on many term weekdays in the Jaguar, very vigilant, and chatting in as easy a style as he could manage about all sorts, though not that skip-around wanderer, Syb, their mother. Occasionally Laurent and Matilda used the bus for school, but this unsettled Manse and he would certainly not allow it to become a known habit.

He had a Heckler and Koch 9 mm, thirteen-shot pistol in a shoulder cradle under his jacket on the Bracken run. He wondered whether the children knew this, and hoped they didn't. It could seem bad for a simple school shuttle – like Belfast again. He varied their routes. They'd spot this, naturally, though they never spoke about it to him. If you were a kid you accepted as ordinary the kind of life you'd been given because you didn't know anything else, not from the inside. A leopard cub or young starling would grow up doing the things leopards or starlings did, because that was what they was, the leopardness or starlingness being all they had.

He thought he remembered from Sunday school a Bible verse, 'Can the leopard change its spots into stripes or oblongs or zigzags?' – the answer being, 'Are you fucking

10

stupid?' – though not spelled out. He felt glad the children accepted tricky conditions as normal, but also, again, he was sad that they had to. When they grew up, would they think they must go a different way to work every day, even if they was only librarians or hairdressers? Manse didn't necessarily want them in his sort of retail. This was not a role like being a king, where the boy kid had to take over finally, because that's how it worked with kings.

Of course, now and then he might be away, seeing bulk people or London lawyers or constructing an alibi. Once, when Manse was absent from the city for a few days, that cheeky, sarcastic prat, Iles, had suggested he must of gone on a sacred pilgrimage or retreat to Santiago de Compostela, being so pious and saintly. Naomi insisted on doing the trips at these times, although Hubert V.L. Camborne or Quentin Noss from the firm could of taken the duty.

It always troubled Manse when Naomi did the driving. The Jag was the reason still – too easily recognized, but necessary. He would always leave it for her. In a rush, some hired thugs might see the car, assume he must be at the wheel, and shoot before they realized their error. They probably wouldn't care much anyway. As they'd regard things, it was only Manse Shale's woman, so why fret? And children, possibly.

Chapter Three

Iles remained with his face and head into the car, staring at Laurent. Harpur didn't often get much silence from Iles, but he got some for two or three minutes now. Matilda with the woman paramedic behind came around to Harpur's side and also stared at her brother, but through the open door. 'You should be sitting down, dear,' Iles said, eventually.

'She wanted to see,' the paramedic said. 'She cried and was shaking for a time, but –'

'A parked silver car over there,' Matilda said, and pointed. 'Most likely a Mondeo. Automatic fire. Well, obviously. Just before he was hit, Laurent said, "It has to be that twat, Ralphy." Those were the words. I think he meant Ralph Ember, the one they call Panicking Ralph.'

'We've heard of him,' Harpur said.

'Oh, really?' she said. 'When you lifted me from the car you got some of Laurent's blood on your ear.'

Harpur brought out a handkerchief. She took it from him, folded it and rubbed at the smudge. She returned the reddened square. 'Laurent had seen something, someone, he recognized?' he asked.

'I don't know that. I don't think so,' she said.

'Why would he say . . . what he said?' Harpur asked.

'A guess. So many tales around our school – about a war. Ralphy Ember against dad. Turf. That's what they call it, isn't it, "a turf war"?'

'Yes,' Harpur said.

'You know about all this already, don't you – the substances, the turf? I mean, I'm not grassing dad up.' She was about thirteen, fair-haired, long-faced, guarded, thoughtful, off-and-on confident. She had blue eyes which for most of the time looked to Harpur very challenging, as though she expected lies from anyone talking to her and also expected to see through the lies. He was used to eyes like this in his own daughters, Hazel and Jill.

'Mr Harpur keeps a keen watch on the commercial scene. All right, he wears deeply awful clothes, and I can tell they make you uneasy, Matilda, but he's no write-off,' Iles said. He withdrew his head from the window space and stood straight.

'One man in a Mondeo,' she said. 'Or maybe a Toyota. Balaclava. Black or navy balaclava. I couldn't look for long. I had to get down.'

'You did right,' Iles said.

'Dad told us – anything unusual on the school run, get down,' she said.

'Lately?' Harpur said. 'He told you this lately? Why? Had something happened to trouble him?'

'Laurent – slower to do it, get down, I mean,' she said. 'He wanted to see.'

'Oh, God,' Iles said.

'Up in Bracken Collegiate we get some dirty stuff, both of us,' she said.

'Dirty stuff?' Iles replied.

'Sneering. That kind of thing. "Daddy's a super-pusher, isn't he, Matty, dear?" They sneak up, mutter it at you in break time or whisper it in your ear, even during a class. *Especially* during a class. "So what does that make you – an under-pusher? He fights other super-pushers, doesn't he? Massive Manse against Big Panicking Ralphy. Baron battles. But they keep the stuff coming. Where *would* we be without them?" And I get similar at the riding stables and archery club. The word's around.'

13

'We'll have to talk to you properly, soon,' Iles said. 'One of our women officers.'

'Yes, dad's been jumpy lately,' she replied.

'Jumpy how?' Iles said.

'You know – jumpy. Like he knew there could be peril. Well, I expect he always knew there could be peril, but he seemed to know it stronger than ever lately.'

'How could you tell?' Iles said.

'Maybe my stepmother didn't really understand about things,' she replied. 'I'm not sure. It was hard to find out what she knew and thought. And I don't think dad could explain properly. It might have scared her or disgusted her. Yes, might. Our mother – our *real* mother– went off. He didn't want that to happen again. But now, this.' She nodded towards Naomi Shale.

Iles said: 'Here's Inspector Fleur Coulter. Go with her in the car now, will you, Matilda? You'll want a change of clothes and a bath. She'll take you home. Will you be able to get into the house?'

'We have keys.' She corrected that then, her voice shaky for a moment. 'I have a key.'

'Can you reach your dad?' Iles said.

'They'll hear in the firm what's happened. Someone will ring him. Not Hubert V.L. Camborne. He's with dad, doing the driving and bodyguarding. Maybe Quentin Noss will make the call.'

'Would you prefer if I or Mr Harpur rang him – told him?'

She thought about that. Perhaps it was inbred not to give police more than you had to, and inbred to be so composed now. 'Better if it's Quentin,' she said. 'Dad wouldn't like it – wouldn't like it if I left it to someone from outside. He doesn't trust many people. Definitely he doesn't trust either of you. You're police. But most of all he doesn't trust *you*, Mr Iles. I've often heard him say that. "ACC Slippery", he calls you. '

'Mr Harpur and I have daughters, so we know how

helpful girls can be to their fathers. We'll take your advice and leave it to someone in the firm.'

'Daughters? Another story around Bracken was you fancied one of Mr Harpur's. The older one, Hazel, but not old enough, all the same.'

'Tell Inspector Coulter everything you saw, would you, please,' Iles replied, 'from the first moment you noticed the parked silver car.'

Chapter Four

Going back to them moments when Manse first started feeling he might get killed, he had definitely decided he would not want a vulgar, newsy funeral with black horses and black plumes fixed in their head bridle. Showiness Manse loathed. He hadn't thought it right to discuss this kind of dark matter with Naomi pre-death, but he hoped she'd realize from knowing him pretty well by now that he hated nearly all display, although Sir Winston Churchill's funeral, seen sometimes in TV documentaries about history, didn't seem too bad. But, obviously, Manse knew he himself would never get a gun-carriage.

Also, his art worried him. He had a lot of paintings at home, many what was known as Pre-Raphaelite, from a span in history, and with brilliant colours, especially girls' hair and clothes. He really loved these works. But imagine his estate had to be probate-valued, suppose he got popped. It would be sickening if a scholar came in and said some of them, or even most, was fakes, and worth next to nix, not a couple of million. Manse would look a bonus-package fool then, for getting killed, *and* for spending big money on duds that he hung on his walls, causing visitors secret, superior giggles. He wouldn't like his children to grow up thinking he had been a full-scale idiot, and not having all that much to leave them, the art being a joke.

The only art expert Manse knew was a picture dealer, Jack Lamb, who lived out in that country mansion, Darien. No point in asking Lamb to check the paintings because

Manse had bought most of them from him. He wasn't going to say, 'Glad you asked, oh, yes, I slipped you a phoney there, Manse, for six hundred grand, if I remember right,' was he? And then: 'This lad I know does Burne-Joneses Tuesdays and Thursdays. It's one of his, and one of his best, as I recall.'

You didn't quiz Lamb too much about where he got the items. Suppose you did, he'd reply things like, 'Many's the collector after this one, but I knew it would be so right for my good and discriminating friend, Mansel Shale.' Or, 'Yes, you're correct to sense it's heavily, even madly, discounted, Manse, but I like to think long-term, and look after my steady customers. Ultimately, this always pays off in my business.'

Manse had considered going to the City Museum and asking if he could commission their Pre-Raphaelite wallah to come to the house and do a valuation. But there was two snags about that, wasn't there? First he, or she, might recognize some of these paintings as being on a police missing list. Second, how would you know he or she was straight? Working in a museum didn't make someone honest. He or she might say some was fakes, and offer to get real ones as replacements, so as Manse would not look a cunt when dead. Then this trickster would go off with the paintings, which might really be genuine, and bring Manse other Pre-Raphaelites to hang where they'd been, these being fakes. Manse would have to pay him or her a fortune for these, so he or she would clean up twice, by also selling the others, maybe to Jack Lamb.

Of course, art was how he and Naomi met, on visits to a gallery a couple of years ago. He'd admit it must be quite a step for her, from discussing pictures to finding out something about the kind of commodities career Manse had. Although art really grabbed him – some art, anyway – it couldn't be his complete life, could it? She had to realize he could only buy good art because he earned good money

17

at work. You did not get paid for looking at pictures, unless you was Anthony Blunt, and think what happened to him.

If Manse mentioned to Naomi that she should take different approaches to and from Bracken Collegiate with the kids when he was away, he knew she found it a pain and frightening and difficult to understand. He didn't think the children would explain to her. Some matters, such as the swap of school run roads, just happened, that was all, like a leopard being a leopard or a starling a starling.

'But why, Manse?' Naomi had said, the first couple of times he'd asked her not to stick to the same trundle.

'People notice if you start a pattern,' he said.

'Which people?'

'Oh, yes, they notice.'

'Does it matter?'

'They'd know the timetable.'

'Who would?'

'If you get samey. They see the car in the usual place, usual moment, morning or afternoon.'

'Who do?'

'That's enough for them. They think, "Right. We'll be there." They expect it to be me, you see.'

'Who do?'

'I can show you on the map new ways to go. Like them signs, "Diverted Traffic". Only a few extra miles and minutes. We don't want to make it easy for them, do we, Naomi? They could be watching.'

'I still don't know who *they* are.'

'We mustn't make it easy for them, must we?'

Chapter Five

Harpur watched Iles. The Assistant Chief had pulled his head out from the cabin of the Jaguar, but still gazed down at Laurent. The paramedic took Matilda away. Most probably, Iles would be continuing large, Assistant Chief-type thoughts about the symbolic meaning of this outrage – its significance as a pointer to savagery and moral disintegration throughout the country and perhaps the Western world. Although he used to make fun of a previous Chief here, Mark Lane, because Lane saw vast implications in any big crime on his ground, now Iles seemed to suffer from the same cosmic twitch.

But, as well as this wider view, Iles would also have formed a detailed picture of what had happened here and how. This might be what Assistant Chiefs and upwards brought to the job: they did global, they did nitty-gritty, too. Or, Iles did, anyway. He could see the core of a situation more or less instantly, and then would know where to place it in the great, overall context of things. As only a detective chief superintendent Harpur didn't have to mess with contexts. He specialized in actuality and in guesses at it. He knew he'd better try to work out a version of the actualities here. Soon, Iles would return from general focus on the universe, and his part in it, and order Harpur to speak a step-by-step scenario of how he saw these sad events and the lead-up to them.

In fact, perhaps he'd already begun to swing back towards the particular. 'Manse Shale went up to Hackney,

London, for Denz Lake's funeral, didn't he, Col, a while ago – after Lake's termination by double-barrelled mouthwash? Was it two Astra pistols doing deep throat with him?' Iles said. 'Some said suicide, didn't they?'

'The trip to Hackney is the kind of high-management gesture Manse would always make, sir. Nobody's more committed to the duties that come with supreme rank. When he gets a title, his escutcheon motto will be, *Noblesse oblige*. Pinched.'

'We ran surveillance on Shale at the time, yes? This would be 2007. March?'

'Not surveillance. We had information.'

'From?'

'Yes, certain information,' Harpur replied.

'Who went with him?' Iles said.

'It obviously required some travel and at least a day's absence from the firm, but this would not deter Manse. He'd feel compelled to show respect as chairman of the companies. Suicide or approximate suicide – a tragedy either way.'

'I saw some of the reports, didn't I?'

'I like to keep you in touch, sir.'

'Is that right?'

'It's routine.'

'Is that right?'

'If an Assistant Chief is Assistant Chief (Operations) he should obviously be kept informed about operations.'

'Logic I love, Col,' Iles said.

'Thank you, sir.'

'Shale was in private discussions post crem, I think.'

'With a brother of Denz, and a cousin.'

'Separately?'

'One to one.'

'Did the one know about the other one?'

'Sir?'

'Was the brother aware Manse talked privately with the

20

cousin and was the cousin aware Manse talked privately with the brother?'

'I have nothing on the content of these conversations,' Harpur said. He waited for more questions, hoping he could then work out the direction of Iles's thinking. But the ACC went silent now, his face unreadable, his mind possibly back among those vaster, staff officer issues. What did this shot boy and his shot stepmother and their shot car indicate about the state of the planet and the Assistant Chief's responsibility for it?

So, Harpur entered his own realm: the actual. Clearly, the street – Sandicott Terrace – was part of that. It would lead up to the main Landau Road and a further straight, four-mile drive to Bracken Collegiate. She could probably have joined Landau Road and the direct, swift-flowing traffic sooner. The route through Sandicott Terrace and other minor streets was most likely a deliberately complicated roundabout course to guard against ambush. But no good.

'A parked silver car over there,' Matilda had said. 'Most likely a Mondeo. Automatic fire.' The Mondeo had been waiting for them. Sandicott Terrace was ideal for the attack, short, narrow. The Jaguar would be moving slowly as it turned into the street and possibly slowed further as it pulled out to pass the parked Mondeo, or, possibly Toyota. Then, up would come the automatic pistol, and the blast would take in the Jaguar's windscreen, Naomi Shale, the passenger window and the boy in the back, not quick enough at getting down on account of curiosity: 'It has to be that twat Ralphy, or someone hired by him.'

Fully automatic pistols could be very inaccurate. The force behind the bursts tended to make the gun jump and fire high. But the distance between the two cars here would be minimal and some bullets were sure to spray the Jaguar. Its driver took hits and, out of control, it mounts the pavement on the wrong side of the street and is stopped by one of those low, front-garden walls, destroying half of it, but not more because the car had little speed. Iles was standing near the wall wreckage now.

At first, Harpur did think of the setting as perfect for the onslaught, but doubts came. For one thing, the Jaguar might have veered the other way, left instead of right, and hit the Mondeo, perhaps making it undrivable, cancelling any getaway. And then there was the timing. The scheme seemed to have been to let the Jaguar come alongside and open fire through the lowered Mondeo driver's side window. Even though the Jaguar might not have had much pace, the shooting would need to be very quick, more or less instant. Did that explain why Naomi Shale was hit instead of Manse? Iles had suggested error. Yes. There'd be no chance to correct a misidentification. In fact, only the Jaguar might have been identified. The driver was assumed to be Manse because he usually drove the Jaguar on the school run and elsewhere. Had this been a sloppily planned and casually organized attack, its main calculation that some fraction of a machine pistol's volleys at next to no range, car-to-car, was certain to hit? *Spot the Jaguar. Have the Jaguar abreast. Fire. Leave. Get to the motorway. Job done.*

Of course, there were people on their doorsteps now. Perhaps one or two had seen something, if they'd been looking out on to the street when the shooting began. Harpur would get them all interviewed, but didn't expect much. There might even be cell phone pictures. Tapes closed off both ends of the terrace. Four officers erected a tent over the Jaguar. Iles came around the back of the car and joined Harpur. 'How do you visualize things, then, Col?'

'Well, I'd say –'

'You'll be worried about the route.'

'Well, yes, sir. How would –'

'How would they know they should wait for the Jaguar in a back street chosen to fool them?'

'It's difficult to –'

'She's probably the sort who wouldn't like being ordered by Manse to vary things. New wife, has to establish herself.

Hoity-toity. But she accepts there could be some point to what he says. So, she does get off the big road and treks through suburbia. To work a bit of self-assertion, though, she keeps the varying to along the same ground every time, so the arrangement is half Manse, half her. This procedure has been noticed, borne in mind, perhaps during previous absences by Shale.'

'Do you know her to be that kind of woman, sir?' Harpur said, and realized at once he'd tripped. Oh, God, what a sodding mistake.

'They're all like it, Harpur. They hate being what they call male-constrained. They'll break out from the well-ordered and proper, as of right.' Iles's voice galloped and skitted towards a scream. 'But I hardly need to tell *you* this, do I, when we've all heard how you in your fine, inhuman, destructive fashion –'

Harpur's mobile phone called him. Iles swung a fist, trying to knock it from Harpur's hand, but he'd expected this, of course, and had made sure he'd tightened his grip. 'I suppose you've got some way to set that off your fucking self to save you when a conversation gets awkward, concerning women,' Iles said.

Harpur took the message. 'The Control Room says we have road blocks in place, sir.'

'A woman, such as my wife, apparently normal and well placed, will suddenly decide she –'

'We've closed ten miles of motorway in both directions.'

Iles came back fast from his agony interlude, as he usually would, like someone emerging from a *petit mal* blackout: 'Let them know we're dealing with a machine pistol, Col. That's a lot of wild fucking fire power.'

Chapter Six

When those personal death ideas first came to Manse he did think for a while about his own funeral and the art, but he had also tried to push the worries away. Jitters, he decided. They'd pass. But, as well as this, he naturally wondered who would want to do it, if people really came to finish him. He could not discuss this with Naomi, or with other top members of the firm. It seemed to Shale that Naomi didn't understand all the details of his profession, and he would prefer it to stay like that for now. This was a lovely, kindly, intelligent woman. She deserved to be screened off from the quirkier sides of Manse's activities. He wanted her to shop and buy interesting handbags and shoes.

Obviously, that would not be her total existence. She had many genuine capabilities. But he'd like her to concentrate on the handbag and shoes side for now, anyway. Naomi had only recently become a full part of his life, and didn't know some of the folk who might want to smash Manse – hadn't even heard of them. It would be foolish to bring such people back into focus.

Also, if he mentioned to some of the major members of staff that he had these unexplained, unexplainable, dark fears, they'd think he was breaking up, coming to pieces. They'd think it because they hoped it. *Dear Manse is pissing down his leg.* They'd love this. That's what being staff *meant*, major staff especially – henchmen and women who spent three-quarters of their time scheming a takeover. They'd act sympathetic, yes, and probably recommend some psychiatrist or mood pills or high grade snorts, but one or more of them might decide Manse had gone frail, into hopeless brain decay, and could be shoved out of the leadership and replaced. So, although he reassured himself often that these panicky ideas were . . . panicky only, he decided he ought to make a private list in his head of some who might like to see him killed – that is, additional to staff people and his long-time business associate, Ralph W. Ember.

In many ways the end of Shale's chauffeur/bodyguard a while ago was only to be expected, but it definitely gave him certain anxieties. Did his own worries about death have to do with what happened to Denzil Lake? Denz had family. The dossier on him said his relatives and chums might be pretty roughhouse, based in the borough of Hackney, London, and familiar with weapons. These could be the sort of people who would not accept that Denzil had done himself, and come looking for those they thought did do him, or ordered it. Yes, or ordered it. Why, why, why, should they doubt it was suicide? London people could be like that – twisted, nosy, uncooperative.

Denzil had been found with the barrels of two fired pistols in his mouth, and the ruination of his face, head and throat was exactly what could be expected from such a well-aimed double blast. Wasn't a gun in the mouth a very usual type of suicide? Didn't it seem obvious that if he put *two* pistols into his mouth, not just the one, he wanted to be sure everything went OK, that is, his death? Belt and braces. But, of course, some smartarses thought it would be nearly impossible to pull both triggers at exactly the same time, and, if he didn't, he'd be too damaged or dead from the first shot to fire the second. That was their line. Also, they said the recoil would of flung at least one of the pistols away from the body, not left both between what was left of Denzil Lake's teeth. Manse regarded that argument as troublemaking and unnecessary.

Then, the fucking coroner's court decided on an 'open verdict'. That is, it *might* be suicide, or it might not. Untidy.

Feeble. Lawyers told Manse it meant the court couldn't be sure Denz actually intended to kill himself. Well, if you'd been shown up as a total traitor, and then put two loaded guns in your mouth, wasn't that enough to prove you wanted to end it, and had a perfect reason, such as guilt and shame for betraying Manse and his business?

Naomi did not know about Denzil and the rather swift way he had to be removed from his appointment in the firm. This was one of those historical aspects best left alone, in Manse's opinion. He had not even met Naomi when Denzil decided to pass on like that. Manse later had thoughts about his own funeral, but he also went to Denzil Lake's, ten days after death. Well, of course. For a long while Denz had acted as his true aid and protector. Only a few knew what a disgusting secret enemy he'd been under all that loyal show. And at the funeral things had struck Manse as reasonably OK. Funerals could be very perilous gatherings, even more than weddings or christenings. 'Show me families, I'll show you spite.' Manse had hatched this saying after several very poor experiences.

But here the family and friends had seemed all right, and ready to believe Denz had finished himself, or ready to behave as if they believed it. He was known to have a fondness for off-beat handguns, so that to put a pair of Spanish Astra .38s in his mouth, and not just the one, chimed well with his fads. People at the funeral told Manse they sympathized with him over the loss of a brilliant and even noble employee and mate. Manse had replied with similar good remarks, but to do with Denzil as a wonderful son, father, nephew, drinking pal. There had been a couple of chats at the gathering after the cremation absolutely unconnected to mourning, but, as far as Manse could work out at the time, they were not bitter or dangerous or hate-laced. No, the reverse, really.

Manse would of thought it disgraceful if people at a funeral spotted the outline and bulge of a pistol under his made-to-measure dark suit jacket, and he'd chosen only a small, .22 revolver, not the 9 mm H. and K. And it was totally unneeded. Of course, he had no proper bodyguard any longer because Denz was gone in that sudden, extremely absolute way of his. For the funeral, and only for the funeral, Manse did take Hubert V.L. Camborne with him, from the outfit. Manse realized that to bring a bodyguard could be regarded as just as crude and insulting as going armed. But Hubert had been quite a friend of Denzil, and might rate as a mourner. Manse told Hubert to give out full sadness, at least at the beginning, not actual blubbing but pain in the face.

Naturally, Manse did some wondering about him. Maybe a pal of Denz must know what a piece of rot he'd been. Might Hubert be part of that rottenness? Manse made himself hope he wasn't, but you never knew who these people had contact with and spoke to, for example, even to police, such as that sly bugger, Harpur, so smart at herding informants. Some risks you had to put up with. At those conversations with a couple of Hackney people after the crematorium, Manse had deliberately not insisted Hubert should be present. He could stay at the bar. This made it look as if he had no guard role. Hubert, too, carried only a small pistol, not at all drawing attention to itself.

In Manse's view, the style of the funeral was OK, although in London. Manse and Hubert had gone up in the Jaguar. Manse arranged for Quentin Noss to take the children to and from Bracken Collegiate. It would have to be in the Audi this time. Manse's older sister would move in and look after Matilda and Laurent while he was away.

Shale had offered to pay for the funeral, as a gesture towards one of his prominent ex-personnel, plus £500 into the kitty for drinks and snacks afterwards. But the Hackney lot wouldn't have it. They stated Denz was *their* boy and all the costs had to fall on them. The costs didn't fall too hard: it was a very ordinary turn-out, no horses with plumes and no wreaths as big as bandstands, perhaps because Denz had spent most of his career away from

London, and wouldn't be widely known here. Anyway, Manse liked the ordinariness. The service and crem trip had seemed quite tidy – foul, gutter-looking people, most of them, but able to behave tame and reasonable now and then, such as the send-off for Denz. Manse felt glad he and Hubert had made the big journey in tribute. Shale agreed deeply with the vicar's text today. It said nobody was without sin. So true of Denzil Lake, the fucking ratting bastard in his economy box.

Denzil's body had been released by the coroner after some sort of basic inquest, but then much later on came the full thing, and all the so-called evidence and rubbish from experts – also so-called – leading to the open verdict. It was after this that Shale began to feel matters might change up Hackney way. Maybe people there would take a different view of Manse and what had happened to Denz. So, thoughts about his own possible death began to give Manse bother. Why did they have to bring up at the second inquest all them stupid views re pulling the two triggers at once being impossible, and the flimflam about recoil?

No, there'd been nothing awkward and snotty like that at Denz's funeral. In fact he'd been aware of a special, respectful regard for him from several in the main, ugly, grieving group. This showed itself best in private talks at the after-crem drink-up and buffet. First, Denz's brother, Egremont, wanted a confidential few words. Later, one of Denzil's cousins had also approached for an intimate chat. These meetings were brief but could definitely be described as sort of constructive. Manse felt that built into them lay a true recognition of his distinction, power and reliability.

The conversations had a terrific sameness, although they took place separately and could not of been overheard. The thing was, Egremont told Manse it would be a sweet, natural, even holy move if he took over the late Denz's position in Manse's firm, following the death. Half an hour afterwards, Lionel-Garth Field, the cousin, mentioned to

Manse the same idea, but, of course, about hisself, Lionel-Garth. Each said this arrangement would help honour and maintain a precious and esteemed family link built by Denzil with Mansel and Mansel's business company. There would be what Lionel-Garth called 'continuity' despite the abrupt withdrawal of Denzil.

Both Egremont and Lionel-Garth assured Manse they wouldn't object to moving out of London with their households to join Manse's operation. Lionel-Garth said he'd have no worries about education for his children because he'd heard that the school where Manse's son and daughter went, Bracken Collegiate, did a fair job. Egremont pointed out that *his* son was away, boarding at Charterhouse, his public school, and a shift of domicile from London would not affect him.

Manse listened to both with what he regarded as outstanding politeness, a decent, unmocking smile often in place. Naturally, he would never consider taking either of the sods into his firm. He wondered if Denz had let the people in Hackney think his position with Manse was executive level or even boardroom, not caddie. Egremont and Lionel-Garth probably imagined a lovely salary and fine bonuses would flow. But Manse was not interested in one or the other for even a nothing job like Denz's, although the firm did need to expand because of upped sales after a grand marketing campaign, especially of coke.

Them two came from the same bloodline as Denz, and Manse had seen what that could do. The genes factor might be weaker in Lionel-Garth, but some traces of it must exist, enough to turn Manse off. However, he quite enjoyed these interviews because they'd shown that people here regarded him as someone worth trying to butter up, and who had a definite right to go on into the future for a while. Life Manse regarded as worth hanging on to hard when possible, and clearly too good for a jerk like Denz.

Manse liked to dossier the main people he met. He carried a small recorder and would speak his impressions into it as soon as he could. 'Egremont Lake, about thirty-eight, younger brother of the late Denz. Hackney tribe. Big-jawed, narrow-eyed – blue – about six feet tall, 185 pounds. Face square, nose never broke or if so very sweetly surgicalized, skin pale, but not jail-pale, pale like he's sent the blood to a safer place in his body, such as elbows. Voice half smarm, quarter threat, quarter ordinary. Suit suitable, dark, double-breasted, nearly a fit, buttons too big, like trash bin lids. Shoes proper black, a good shape, not made in Vietnam. Cockney accent with some smoother bits, maybe learned from his son in the public school. No scars (or, hidden by the same surgeon). Hair dark, full quota, no grey, layer-cut with a slim oblong hanging over left fore-head – so fetching. Nimble enough. Some sudden silences in the sales patter, which could mean true sadness about Denz.'

And then the cousin: 'Lionel-Garth Field, slobbier than Egremont. Grossish face. Deep slabs of fat under the eyes and porking out the cheeks and neck. Like a "Before" pic-ture in one of them colonic irrigation brochures. Much gut. Five feet six or seven, early forties. About same weight as Egremont. Fast talk, and plenty of gasping from the effort. No clothes could really make a job of him. Jacket taut on the flabby shoulders and trousers tight on calves. Crimson and cream training shoes, just right for a funeral. Stout lips that seemed to fight each other like two snakes when he got excited. He got excited when he described what he could bring to the firm. He broke that into bullet points – (a) energy, (b) man management skills, which included women, (c) the common touch, when needed, (d) account-ancy flair. Mousy hair receding. Bald spot.'

Chapter Seven

The elderly couple whose low, front-garden wall had been half destroyed came out from the house and stood on their bit of lawn staring at the tented Jaguar. Iles said: 'We'll get the damage repaired immediately. Mr Harpur has a note-book.'

The woman shrugged. 'It's not of much consequence. But those poor people in the car – terrible.'

'Yes, terrible,' Iles said.

'Is there rhyme or reason to it?' the man said. 'You're a high officer. I can tell from your uniform. Not coarse material and you seem unruffled. So, what is your view?'

'Some people have their own rhyme and reason,' Iles said.

'Yes, another way of life, and now it has forced itself into ours,' the woman said.

'It's Mr Harpur's and my job to prevent that,' Iles said. 'We've failed you, unforgivably.'

'I've noticed that Jaguar passing by the house once or twice lately, a woman driving and those two happy-looking children in the back – Bracken Collegiate blazers,' the man said.

'She was new to things,' Iles said. 'She hadn't learned proper practice. Or not how important it is.'

'Who?' the woman said.

'We can't really blame her for that. She'd come from what you called "another way of life",' Iles replied. 'There are special requirements here.'

'Do you mean it was wrong to drive up or down this terrace?' the woman said.

'Sometimes it was right, sometimes it was wrong,' Iles said.

'But surely she should be able to drive where and when she wishes, as long as it's legal,' the man said.

'Yes, she should,' Iles said. 'I repeat, we've failed you. And failed her and the boy.'

'I've heard people say the police have lost control of the streets,' the man replied.

'It hurts Mr Harpur, ' Iles said. 'He's a street person.'

'That would suggest some other . . . well, some other force has taken them over, an evil force,' the woman said. 'This is not civilization as we used to know it.'

'Civilization has always been a bit hit-and-miss,' Iles said. 'Think of Adolf. Enjoying *lieder* one minute, fixing piano wire toppings the next.'

'But the little girl is all right, isn't she?' the man said. 'We watched from the window when she was lifted from the car.'

'A brave child,' Iles said. Two police photographers arrived and entered the tent. Iles and Harpur moved out into the middle of the terrace. 'The old lady saw the significance of this, Col.'

'In which respect, sir?'

'Civilization. Its break-up,' Iles said. 'That "evil force" she spoke of. It invades, assaults, knocks down their little sheltering walls.'

'*We're* here to shelter them,' Harpur said. 'We're a *police* force. We haven't been knocked down.'

'Often in my prayers, Harpur, I say, "Thank you, God, for Col and his stupid fucking optimism."'

'What does *He* say?' Harpur's phone rang again. He told Iles the message: 'Three of our cars have cornered a silver Mondeo in North Bewick. The driver, white, male, late twenties or early thirties, abandoned the car and ran to a charity shop. He carried a machine pistol. He's still inside the shop. Possible hostages.'

'Is it the charity where you get your garments?'

Chapter Eight

As a matter of fact, Manse Shale first met Naomi the day after Denz Lake's funeral. Obviously, this helped cheer him up following a definitely sad occasion, no matter what a vile two-timer Lake had been. Funerals were funerals and bound to be a bit morose around the edges. Shale spoke for a while there with Denz's parents at the after-party, as well as them conversations with Egremont and Lionel-Garth. By praising Denz and his work for the firm, and for Manse personally, he tried to comfort Mr and Mrs Lake. He regarded this as a considerate thing to do, and Shale often liked to act with kindliness, even to their sort. Also, he said how guilty he felt for never seeing what inner suffering Denzil must have been battered by, suffering that would lead him to suicide.

'Don't blame yourself,' Mrs Brenda Lake said. 'Denzil always spoke so well of you. Cornelius will confirm this.'

'I would never have believed he was the type to do it,' her husband said.

'None of us can know fully what others might be going through mentally,' Shale said.

'He was a sensitive boy,' Brenda Lake said.

'True,' Shale said. 'This is what I mean by hidden inner suffering. Some are *too* sensitive for this life.'

'It's the only one we fucking got,' Cornelius replied. He was crafty-faced, mid-height with thick grey hair, flimsy-looking spectacles, about sixty, his body a bit twisted to one side, like he'd been put on the rack in one of them old castle torture chambers somewhere and as an extra joke they hadn't quite equalled up the stretching.

'If he'd but shown he needed help I or one of his pals might have been able to bring support,' Shale said. 'Would certainly have tried. Also the firm's Personnel Department will sometimes employ a counsellor at an hourly rate, but free to staff.'

'Denzil never liked to complain,' his mother said, 'even as a child.'

'"Stalwart" is a description I and others would apply to him,' Mansel said. 'Yet below that steady surface who knew what turmoil? Perhaps only Denzil himself.'

'Were the pigs on to him for something?' Cornelius Lake replied. 'This can upset many, them bastards banging the door with their sneers and questions and bright white sergeant's stripes in the middle of the night. You got to learn how to deal with that. I've told him, time and again. "Denzil, get unemotional," I used to advise him. The point is, kill yourself and they've had a little victory, haven't they?'

'I know he would regard it as a wonderful tribute that you should travel so far to say goodbye today,' Brenda Lake said.

'What else could I do?' Shale said.

'Or some women giving him a rough time?' Cornelius asked. 'Spreading themselves via the night-spots, while pretending he's the only one, and he finds out. Heartbreak. He's got the Astras handy. He's down, down, down. He wants the end of it all.'

'Your staff are so fortunate to have such a leader,' Brenda said. Bulky, erect, mild-voiced, she touched Manse's arm for a moment in congratulation.

'Colleagues like Denzil made leadership easy,' he said. 'Their loyalty, skill and strengths.'

'I don't say all women are slags,' Cornelius replied. 'Think of Brenda here or . . . well, there are definitely other unflighty ones about. But things have changed from when we were young, no question. Women are looking around for what will give them a perfect future. That's what I mean by spreading themselves, including abroad, the Commonwealth. They feel entitled. That's a word heard a lot these days – "entitled". They're making up their mind. To some of them, Denz might not have looked like the best they could do once they got to know him, and found out more about him, especially if he was catching shit from the law and due to catch more. All right, he had the big job with you, but some women are funny. She could be thinking, how long's it going to last if the police are already on to him? He'll be celled for maybe years and she'll have to start it all over. So, try someone else now. Things like this might build up in Denz's mind, and that's when he gets the Astras out of the drawer.'

'Often Denzil would speak in a very worried, concerned way about the behaviour of Sybil, your wife,' Brenda said. 'I trust you don't mind me speaking of this.'

'Spreading herself,' Cornelius said.

'And Denz praised your determination to give the children, Matilda and Laurent, sort of double love, so as to make up for what was missing from their mother,' Brenda said.

'She didn't do anything with Denz, did she?' Cornelius said.

Mrs Lake gave a small nod towards Shale's shoulder: 'Cornelius and I take it as a true mark of respect and, yes, affection, that you're carrying only a very small calibre pistol today. Likewise your thug.'

'It's the least we could do,' Manse said.

'Not Astras, are they?' she said.

'That would get up your nose I should think,' Cornelius said.

'What?' Shale replied.

'If she was giving it to Denz,' Cornelius said. 'This could make you very angry with both of them. Any man would feel the same, his wife banging an associate. I could understand that.'

'I gather she's more or less settled now – shacked up in North Wales, Rhyl way?' Brenda asked.

'The children loved Denz,' Shale replied. 'They were very upset when they heard he'd taken that route. They'd have such fun together sometimes. Jigsaw puzzles, French cricket, darts. He had a lot of tolerance.'

'And not at all vain,' she said.

'The reverse,' Shale said.

'He'd come up from only a very lowly job in your organization to such a brilliant spot, yet he remained at heart the same, approachable, ordinary guy,' she said.

'Well, yes,' Manse replied.

'The sensitivity we've spoken of – perhaps it made him secretly despair for the state of the world,' she said. 'The ice-cap melting and obesity problems in some countries, yet starvation elsewhere.'

'No note from him,' Cornelius said.

'This is what makes it deeply tragic,' Shale replied. 'It is as if he felt himself so much alone – nobody to explain himself to.'

'We haven't been told very much about the people who found him,' Cornelius said.

'Friends. An awful shock for them,' Shale said.

'That's another word. It covers quite an area,' Cornelius Lake said.

'Which?' Shale said.

'"Friends",' Cornelius said.

'Members of our company,' Manse replied. 'We like people to feel they are more than just workmates – that there is a bond between them. A community.'

'This would be pushers, enforcers, lookouts, that kind of thing?' Cornelius asked.

'Such a bonding of staff is perhaps the greatest asset any firm can possess,' Shale replied. 'Priceless. It is at least as important as money in the bank.'

'Did he have trouble with the bank?' Cornelius said. 'He could be a bit of a spender.'

'Generous. Unstinting,' Brenda Lake said.

'Them banker bastards – they pile it up for theirselves in all sorts of dirty ways, but jump on anyone who got even a small problem with his account,' Cornelius said.

'Sybil's living with an industrial door manufacturer, isn't she?' Brenda said.

'That kind of thing,' Shale said.

'And you – you don't think of a new partner?' Brenda said, with a gentle smile.

'But I suppose there's not many women industrial door manufacturers about,' Cornelius said.

The pub where the get-together took place when Denz had gone was pretty good, in Shale's view – dark wood panelling, small, shaded lights fixed to the wall as well as main overheads, tiled floor near the bar, easy to swab, and booths. In fact, Manse did not mind Hackney as a district too much at all. He recognized that people had to live somewhere, and this made Hackney and such a pub necessary. It seemed to him the right type of place for Denz to come from, and the right type of place for his family to live now, such as Cornelius. You wouldn't want this brigade in some of the other more famed parts of London, except on days out. And, he'd admit it to himself, Manse did feel quite glad late in the afternoon to leave Hackney and its crew.

Luckily, there was an exhibition of Pre-Raphaelite paintings in a private Mayfair gallery, and tomorrow after lunch he'd get to that. He and Hubert would stay in London overnight. Manse wanted to see his lawyers in the morning, to do with the divorce and his will. Clearly, these were connected now Syb seemed to have been content somewhere else for nearly a year. Manse always used London lawyers for his specially important business. They were most probably the best. And he would of hated to reveal any of his exceptionally personal matters to a solicitor he might play golf with at the club back home.

Chapter Nine

2009

One of the other notable things about Iles was that for a while in a crisis he would generally follow the proper, official, OK'd routine for coping, but might then suddenly and inexplicably chuck this and take to methods of his own. Often, these were extreme and/or crazed and/or doomed and/or dangerous. Harpur wondered from the start whether this might happen at the charity shop siege.

Oh, God, yes, he'd wondered. He knew Iles. He'd watched the career of Iles, paralleled the career of Iles. Recurring streaks of frantic egomania would probably help stall him for ever at Assistant rank. This was very high – one big notch higher than Harpur's – but not the top. He'd never make Chief. Harpur thought Iles probably recognized it. He needed somebody to control him, or try to. He needed a context, but not one created by him. He needed a hierarchy, where he could figure at second or third, but not first. Of course, the Home Office prized originality in a Chief and even some ego, though maybe not the kind offered by Iles. Occasionally, he would murmur his title to Harpur, giving all the creepy, hissing serfdom of the 's' sounds : 'I am the very model of a modern Asssssisssssstant to His fucking Eminence, Col.' Iles hated Chief Constables, of course, but couldn't do without one.

The guidance for running a hostages and siege situation was detailed, graphic, founded on previous cases here and overseas, and concerned above all with patience, psychological subtlety, communication: supremely, with patience. 'I am Gold,' Iles told the armed response teams' chief inspector who'd commanded the charity shop siege until now. Harpur and Iles had driven over from Sandicott Terrace. Whoever ran an incident took the code name 'Gold'. It meant, What I say, you do. It meant Supremo. It didn't necessarily go to the most senior officer present. Iles might have been ready to observe only, leaving the chief inspector as Gold to get on with it. Or he might have told Harpur to take Gold.

But this was Desmond Iles. He didn't know how to observe only. He did know how to delegate, but wasn't keen on that if the job looked big. The charity shop job looked big. Iles would regard it as a natural and inevitable move for him to go Gold on arrival, as it was a natural and inevitable move for a caterpillar to turn butterfly.

Chief Inspector Clive Lyndon gave his summary. 'We had two officers after him running when he quit the car but he grabbed a woman on the pavement and put the machine pistol to her head, then dragged her into the shop. We stopped pursuit, for her safety. We think possibly four hostages, sir, the woman, the manageress, plus a voluntary worker, female, and perhaps a customer, we think male, spotted by Sergeant Pardoe through the window during the chase on foot. Fifteen officers in place, six front, six back, three on the roof opposite, all armed. The roof contingent and two officers front and back have sniper rifles, the rest Glock pistols or carbines. We don't know his ammunition state, nor whether he has an additional weapon, weapons, under a topcoat. There's an intermittent telephone link and the negotiator has talked to him twice. Or listened to him. It's mainly threats to the hostages and a demand for uncontested exit for him and one hostage. He says he'll release the rest immediately then and the other one later. He doesn't quantify "the rest". Our estimate of four as total is not confirmed. He's pulled two display rails of clothes across the window to obscure what's happening inside.' They stood behind Iles's car.

'Accent?' Harpur said.

'Not local. Could be Lancashire – Manchester?'

'A famous hire-for-the-day hitman agency there,' Iles said. 'Its sales slogan, "We aim to please."' Two ambulances, two dog-handler vans, a fire engine, a catering wagon, and more police cars pulled in.

Lyndon said: 'The manageress, early fifties we're told, sensible and cool, married with teenage children. Mrs Beatrice South. The woman he took from the street, thirties, jeans, denim jacket, desert boots, holding a carrier bag – perhaps out shopping. The gunman, thin, about five foot nine, maybe late twenties or a bit older, dark jacket, fair-haired – a lot of it – brown cowboy boots. The car was stolen in Preston a week ago. Nothing aboard to give us an identity.'

'He's shed the balaclava, has he? We keep on talking, Clive,' Iles said. 'Do nothing to scare or anger him. Don't press for a name. Offer food and drink, to be delivered by an unarmed officer. Attrition, gradualness – essential here. Almost all similar previous situations prove it. He'll probably know he's messed up – hit the wrong people, including a child. He might feel he can't do any worse. So, why not knock off a hostage or two? Don't panic him into that sort of neat, slaughterous logic.'

'We're offered use of a psychologist, sir,' Lyndon said.

'Oh? Not some twat called Andrew Rockmain, is it?' Iles said.

'It could look very negative later if you've rejected him, sir,' Harpur said.

'What do you mean, "later"?' Iles said.

'Later,' Harpur replied.

'If people get killed here?' Iles asked.

'Later,' Harpur said. 'We should try everything.'

'Rockmain?' Iles said

'Including Rockmain,' Harpur said. 'You don't want a *Guardian* headline, "Police chief spurned psychologist help in fatal siege."'

'I'm *not* the Chief,' Iles said.

'Journalistic licence. You're head of Operations. This is an operation. You're Gold.'

'I agree with Mr Harpur, sir,' Lyndon said.

'Who the fuck asked *you*?' Iles replied. 'Rockmain has a green corduroy suit.'

Chapter Ten

2007

In the morning after Denz's funeral Shale went to see his lawyers at their offices near Lincoln's Inn. He left Hubert to get on with whatever he wanted to and gave him a couple of hundred for expenses and so on. You had to be thoughtful with them. Bodyguards operated at special closeness to you. They could be fucking dangerous.

Manse often used to think that if he hadn't chosen a career in commerce he might have liked to be a lawyer himself. The many big volumes they had to keep handy to remind theirselves of old cases must be very heavy, but Manse knew a lad who could have put up extremely strong shelves, using sapele wood and Rawlplugs. What impressed him about lawyers was they knew there was not just one kind of truth. They realized it had a lot of aspects. They was not tied down and stuck on to one narrow sort. It was their job to look after the side of truth that suited their client best, because the client was paying them.

Of course, the other side's lawyers would be doing the same for *their* client. Truth depended on where you was looking at it from. The lawyers looked at it from where their client wanted to look at it, and would be ready with many arguments, in court or by letter. This could be very helpful for a client. Manse believed absolutely in being helpful to people when it was not stupid to be helpful to them, and if you was their lawyer, obviously it would not be stupid to help them. This could get your partnership well known and make it a success. To be helpful to them was why you was their lawyer, wasn't it?

Naturally, Manse had to adjust the truth a certain amount, anyway, before he dealt with his lawyers. It would not be clever to let them know where his main money came from, or much about it at all, really. They thought the haulage and scrap metal firm produced his income. Or they *pretended* to think it. They did not want to be told the reality, did they? Certain tough and kinky rules cooked up by the law chiefs governed their game and they had to be careful which kinds of business folk they took on to their books, fearing taint. Too much truth could be . . . too much. They'd probably heard 'haulage and scrap' mentioned by quite a few of their customers and would never laugh or even smile at it. You expected this kind of considerate treatment when you was paying the sort of fees lawyers wanted, especially London lawyers. It was all based on so much an hour, or not *so* much but *very* much an hour. Manse would write the cheque, though, and never niggle. He needed them. He felt more comfortable knowing they was there and screwing him the way top lawyers did to folk throughout the centuries. You could not get safe, and stay safe, cheap.

The lawyer he had to see was a woman and black. Manse did not mind. He felt they should be allowed to get on if they was good enough. That is, women, white or black, and blacks, women or men. He thought she took a reasonable interest in the parts of his life he had come to talk about, namely, the divorce and his will. He found it strange in a way to think of her ancestors in, say, Jamaica or the Congo, ages ago, and now producing this woman who would look into some of the most important matters of his personal self. Those ancestors could never of imagined one of their descendants might one day be taking a detailed scan of Manse's private situation. She was probably brought up in this country. She didn't have an accent, except London. But, obviously, her roots would go back to somewhere else.

She was about thirty-two, wearing light-coloured glasses and an engagement ring and wedding ring, so she should understand OK about divorce. The light-coloured glasses didn't spoil her looks. In fact, they seemed just right to show she was a lawyer, not a waitress somewhere. Manse would certainly never try any moves with her, though, because it would be not very appropriate, considering what he'd come to see her about. And, in any case, she had the rings. They might mean something. The engagement ring had two square diamonds at least half a centimetre by half a centimetre, and most likely genuine. The wedding ring was wide and pale. The paleness did not mean it was low grade gold. Manse had heard that Welsh gold had this whitish tinge, and the Royal Family liked it. Her husband might also be a lawyer and they could have quite a decent home somewhere with a fair whack of money going in. Good luck to them. If she had children she might be able to pay a nanny, ethnic or not. This was how things was changing in Britain. Why not? To quite a degree Manse believed in change and equal chances.

She had some papers in front of her on the desk. She said: 'They're asking for a one-off payment of two million to your wife, to complete the divorce, Mr Shale.'

'That's the kind of figure I thought they'd come up with.'

The room was big. Manse would not say *too* big, though some might consider the size of it showy. Most probably it could be called a suite. One side had a big table with nine chairs around. It must be for conferences, proving she could call people here and they'd have to come. Eight of the chairs was ordinary, straight-backed office furniture. At one end of the table, though, he noticed a much larger chair, with arms to it and a high back. This must be where she sat when she organized one of her meetings. Manse thought she deserved it if she had done all her law exams and brought in a lot of fees to the company, Crossman,

44

Fenton and Stuckey. She was Fenton, Joan Fenton. He would of been pissed off if they had given him less than a partner. He had to be treated as considerable.

She said: 'As I see it, Sybil left you and the children. Desertion. We could reasonably dispute any claim at all, let alone two million.'

'She'll need a bit of cash.'

'But she's not your responsibility now.'

'You can't just step away from that kind of thing.'

'This is what divorce means. It's an act of stepping away.'

Manse didn't get ratty at being given a lesson like this, even though she was a woman and black. In her kind of job she would be used to having her say. They spent their time arguing. In any case, he would admit she was probably right when she said 'an act of stepping away'. Lawyers could be like that – blunt. Manse wondered if he felt scared of stepping away. Did he want to hang on to Sybil somehow? But giving her big money wouldn't help him hang on to her. It would help her stay away from him. He felt confused now.

'I can understand you don't want to seem punitive,' the lawyer said.

'That would be cruel,' Manse said. 'Syb's Syb.'

'Syb's a bit of a slag.'

'Oh, I –'

'We don't reward her for sloping off and ditching you, Matilda and Laurent.'

'She's taken up with some nobody as far as I can make out. He's got no career worth talking about.'

'My notes say he's a vet.'

'Along those lines. Or a roofer. She's used to expenditure. All right, she's living in North Wales where the shops in Rhyl or Prestatyn are not Rome or Paris, but I don't like to think of her having to skimp. If you're stuck in a place like that you probably need to do a lot of purchasing to help your morale. I heard there's a town there that looks like it's made of slate and it's always raining. I expect there'll be a station and trains to London or Manchester where she could find fashion items, travelling First in case of unpleasantness from soccer hooligans and so on. She flits about. Well, obviously. It costs. Plus, there's the skiing and riding and Wimbledon.'

'I'd like to offer them something – a token – to show the sods you're not vindictive, but nothing like what they're asking. This is a real, standard try-on. Of course it is. It's the kind of thing we expect at the start of a negotiation, not much more than a formality, the insolent prats.'

'Ah,' he replied.

'What?'

'You're saying it wouldn't be good for your image or the firm's if you agreed too easily to what they're asking. You'd look soft, a pushover?'

'Fifty grand would be generous beyond,' she said. 'I'll offer them twenty as starters, and see where we go from there.'

'She's the mother of my children,' Manse said.

'Well, yes. That's quite usual for a wife. What's not so usual is she buggers off and abandons them.'

'Have you got children?'

'Have *I*?'

'Well, yes. Have you?'

'This meeting's about you, Mr Shale, not me. We're getting along really well now, aren't we? And so to the will.'

It struck Manse as wrong, this damn breeziness from her. She did not seem interested in whether he could of paid the two million if he had to. It made him feel small. They ask for two million and she's going to offer twenty grand, maybe going to fifty, so as not to seem vindictive, as she called it. Wouldn't it seem like vindictive to reply with a brush-off twenty grand when they'd demanded a hundred times more? He saw now it had been crazy even to think of making a move for her, and even to think of making a move for her and rejecting the idea. This one didn't hardly know he existed. She came from a family tradition going back generations there in the Caribbean or Africa and didn't bother with people like Manse, except as business. He had always recognized he was a flash-in-the-pan. It became so clear when he was up against a lot of history, like hers. He was in off the street from some dump outside London and she'd settle his little matters fast and send him back there. He'd more or less said the two million was OK with him, which meant he had a lot more beside that. But she did not seem to care. She would arrange his life for him like she wanted it and maybe not like *he* wanted it and then it would be, 'Goodbye *Mr* Shale, we've got along really well, haven't we?' In a couple of weeks he'd get a letter saying she couldn't work it down to twenty grand but kept it to forty grand and in a couple of weeks later here comes the bill, terms strictly thirty days, and meaty.

'We have to cater for what happens if you die soon,' she said.

'Well, yes.'

'That is, before the children are old enough to take their shares of the inheritance direct and in full.'

'Well, yes.'

'I know there are physical risks in the haulage and scrap business. Runaway vehicles. Old iron heaps shifting.'

'Well, yes.'

'It's obvious we mustn't have Sybil controlling trust funds meant to guard assets for the children. The divorce helps us here, certainly. She'll no longer have much of a case for administering any such trust. If you remarry or begin an established partnership, we can then do a will that specifically names the new wife or partner as principal trustee. That would finally cut Sybil right out.'

'In her own way, she's quite fond of the children.'

'Which way is that?'

'I don't think she'd scheme to cheat them out of their legacies.'

'Do you want the money you've managed to put by through enterprise and prudence in the haulage and scrap

47

trades, despite competition and hazard, to go to some bed-hopping slapper, and whomever she's shagging at the time, singular or various, instead of remaining safe for Laurent and Matilda until they reach due age?'

'I don't think of Syb as –'

'Are the children to be sole beneficiaries?' she replied. 'I mean, as things stand at present. That is, you, divorced, single, unattached. Do you have other family you might want to see right?'

'Not exactly family.'

'Kith rather than kin?'

'That kind of thing.'

'Women?'

'These are people who –'

'You started relationships for comfort when Sybil pushed off? Did you cohabit?'

'That matters?' he asked.

'It might give extra credibility to any claim they made against your estate. If they had the run of your home it suggests depth. How many?'

'Three in particular, but never at the same time.'

'Each had spells living with you and the children?'

'Very, very limited,' Manse said.

'What duration?'

'Never more than weeks.'

'How many weeks?'

'Four. Perhaps five or six, absolute max.'

'And how far did the cohabiting go?'

'Well, we –'

'I mean, did they carry out domestic tasks about the house – cooking, cleaning, helping with the children: wifely things? If it came to a dispute, these could have a symbolic significance, suggest further depth. Could any of them cite, say, ironing, freezer de-icing, window-cleaning, hosting parties at your place?'

'They were very kind.'

'Have you got names?'

48

'Well, of course.'

'Would you write them down, please?' She pushed a note pad and pencil over the desk to him. He listed the three, Lowri, Patricia and Carmel. She took the pad back and glanced at it. 'At the end of one of these tours of duty, who decided it was over?' Joan Fenton asked.

'This often took place without any sign of distress or anger. I live in an ex-rectory and would hate to have screams and yells in that kind of property.'

'*You* would decide it was over?' she replied.

'I can see the importance of that question, in the circumstances.'

'Did any of them, all of them, ever return for a further few weeks?'

'Never overlapping. They was a real help – I mean, helping keep my spirits up.'

'Etcetera. I'd say you've got to remember each of them for at least a thirtieth of your assets, and possibly a twenty-fifth. Courts would be sympathetic to them. Did it trouble the children – these women alternating in and out?'

'They never got the names wrong or showed they liked one better than the others, which could of obviously been hurtful.'

'Did *you*?'

'What?'

'Like one of them better than the others. Shall we make it, two thirtieths and one twenty-fifth? But that might cause aggro and disputes. Where there are several mistresses per-forming the same services it can be tricky working out which is the *primus inter pares*.'

'I'd rather think of them as friends.'

'An eternal problem where there is a multiplicity of crumpet,' she replied. '*Primus inter pares* – first among equals is an oxymoron, of course, yet like most oxymorons has an accessible meaning.'

'I heard they're well known for it.'

She stood up. 'I suppose that in London you're reasonably safe – lost in the crowd, as it were. But, talking of possible early death, and taking into account your profession and its uncertainties, I hope you normally have a bodyguard, bodyguards, nearby. And a bodyguard, bodyguards, you can trust. Goodbye, Mr Shale. I'll get the trust details worked out. Next time you're in London everything should be ready for signature. Matters have gone very well, I'd say, wouldn't you?'

Shale considered he and the Pre-Raphaelites were very close in a spiritual sense, despite the century and a half gap. At the Denz funeral, Mrs Lake had spoken in quite a decent style of a possible new partner for him, but, obviously, neither of them knew then that on the next afternoon, following the divorce and will discussions, he'd meet Naomi Gage for the first time on this trip. They both came to stand at more or less the same instant in front of an Edward Prentis picture called *The Remembrance*. Shale already had a Prentis on the wall at home, and, eventually, this helped in the conversation with Naomi. But he didn't go forward at a rush talking to her. That would be like trying a pick-up, and he could tell this would turn her off. She did not at all look the type. She gave most of her eye contact to *The Remembrance*. He just stayed there, gazing, the two of them quiet, appreciating. Manse thought the best plan was to let the Edward Prentis do the work.

He could feel an invisible but strong link being made, from the painting to him and from him to her, or possibly the other way, from the painting to her and from her to him. But whichever direction you took, it always started from *The Remembrance*, like that picture had been put there only to draw the two together and offer them a kind of blessing. Yes, he knew this must be rubbish, but the idea did take hold of him for a little while, and brought delight. Although the gallery was quite busy Manse had the notion that the three had become sealed off and private: *The Remembrance*, the woman and himself. Hubert could not of been part of it, even if he'd gone with Manse to the gallery.

Although clearly impossible, Manse would have liked to thank Denzil for causing the visit to London and creating in a roundabout manner the chance for this deep Prentis experience, a kind of unplanned spin-off from his cremation. Manse realized that some refused to class Edward Prentis as a *real* Pre-Raphaelite – not one of the 'Brotherhood', as a group of painters of that period called themselves. But Manse loved his work and he could see at once that Naomi did, too. But, of course, he did not know her name at that stage.

Manse stood in front of the Edward Prentis *Remembrance* painting with Naomi, though, clearly, he wasn't exactly *with* Naomi and did not know her to be Naomi at that time. He had to realize that many people stood close to other people in galleries when looking at pictures, but this did not necessarily bring them together at all, beyond the togetherness of looking at the same pictures. Any linking was with the pictures not with one another. As Shale saw it, the difficulties he met came in two special kinds.

First: how could he start a conversation? Manse would feel ashamed to seem like some slimy git sniffing around galleries for women on their own to chat up. That meant high-quality and famous art would be treated as nothing more than a classy route to a pull, showing rotten disrespect for the Pre-Raphaelites and for Naomi. As Manse saw things, he had come to the gallery for the Pre-Raphaelites, not to prowl for attractive women, but if an attractive woman turned up in front of a Pre-Raphaelite, and the same Pre-Raphaelite that Manse was enjoying, this could be regarded as possibly a pleasant bit of luck. Possibly, yes. The piece of luck could be ruined, though, if he said or did anything that made her think he was just a schemer on the lech trail. *Such glorious use of colour, wouldn't you say? Or, to put it another way, Feel like a fuck?*

Second . . . but Manse found the second problem much more complicated. While they was both admiring the Edward Prentis a family came into the room, parents and two boys, the boys aged about ten and twelve, one crew-cut, the other blond curls. Manse could tell at once these was the kind of offspring who didn't give a monkey's about galleries or the Pre-Raphaelites. He didn't understand why the parents had brought them. They should of left them home with their warder. The two kids started chasing each other and shouting and pretending to fight and did most of it in front of the Edward Prentis. There ought to of been an attendant in the room to tell them to quieten down, but there wasn't and Manse said: 'Now, lads, this isn't the place for games. You're spoiling our view of the picture.'

One boy, the younger one, gave him the finger and the other – crew-cut – said, 'Piss off, ugly mug.'

Manse said: 'That's enough. Get lost.'

The father said in a big, icy voice: 'Hey, you, did I hear you speak to my boys?' He and his wife were on the other side of the room looking at a picture by Sir Edward Burne-Jones, a definite true star of Pre-Raphaelites.

'*Are* they your boys?' Manse said.

'What does that mean?' he said.

'What do you think it means? It means are they your boys?' Manse said.

'He's being rude, Geoff,' his wife said. He was about forty, hefty, wearing a brown leather waistcoat over a red T-shirt. Maybe this was his gallery outfit. Manse could imagine him this morning in Ruislip, or Guildford – that kind of place – thinking to himself, 'What will I put on today for the Pre-Raphaelite exhibition? Ah, of course – the brown leather waistcoat.'

'If they're your boys, and I can believe it, why don't you tell them to act decent?' Manse said.

'Who are you to tell me what I should tell them?' he said.

'I'm me to tell you what you should tell them,' Mansel said.

'The method of his rudeness is to repeat what you've just said, Geoff, and explain your own words to you, as if you're too dim to understand them,' the wife said. 'It's a convoluted insult.' She had a burliness to her not like the women in most of the Pre-Raphaelite paintings.

'Take no notice of him, lads,' he said. 'Carry on as if he never spoke.'

'But I did speak,' Manse replied. This was what he meant by 'complicated', when he considered the situation. Clearly, he needed to go over and scare the shit out of this loudmouth and inform him that if he didn't quell his damn kids there'd be results, and not of the art type. But, along with this urgent idea, Manse did not want the woman he'd been watching the Edward Prentis sort of with to think he was the kind of presence that could scare the shit out of loudmouths by nothing much more than sudden nearness and a handful of sotto words. He would prefer this woman to have him marked in her mind as a lover of high-quality, famous pictures and especially the Pre-Raphaelites. He *was* a lover of high-quality, famous pictures and especially the Pre-Raphaelites, though also the kind of presence that could scare the shit out of loudmouths by nothing much more than sudden nearness and a handful of sotto words. This extra aspect of himself, a sort of bonus aspect, or like the part of an iceberg under water, he would rather stayed unknown to the woman.

But if he did nothing to scare the shit out of this loud-mouth the woman's enjoyment of the Prentis, and his own, would be greatly negatived. Manse believed he had a responsibility to her and to the Edward Prentis and to the world of art generally. He remembered a scene from that American TV gangster show, *The Sopranos*, where one of the toughs thinks a group in a nightclub are getting too boisterous. He puts up with it for a while but then goes and whispers something to one of the men in the group who suddenly looks terrified, and the nuisance behaviour stops at once. A girl watching is fascinated by the delicate show of power and gets to fancy the tough. They're soon off somewhere as a pair and well into passion. But Manse couldn't be sure this woman in front of the Prentis would feel like that. Manse preferred to be rated a Prentis person, a Pre-Raphaelite person, not a Soprano-type person.

Yes, tricky, tricky. Yes, complicated, complicated.

'What a crummy old picture they're looking at, anyway,' the father said.

'Crap,' the younger boy said.

'Feeble,' the mother said. 'Half-baked. Wishy-washy.'

And to Manse now the comments seemed to mean that, unavoidably, he would have to scare the shit out of this loudmouth by sudden nearness and a handful of sotto words. Shale spent a little while carefully selecting the sotto words to be spoken into the loudmouth's ear. They were: 'Get these kids under control, as would be suitable for a room of beautiful and fascinating works, I'm sure you'll agree, cunt, or I'll have your fucking throat out.' Manse could see that the loudmouth heard this pretty well. His face went like that frightened face in *The Sopranos*.

'What did he say, Geoff?' the wife snarled with genuine interest.

'Excuse me, I didn't intend to interrupt your gaze at the Burne-Jones etcetera, but I asked Geoff which of the seven or eight pictures in this room he thought the most Pre-Raphaelitish, if we take "Pre-Raphaelitish" to mean "in the style of the Pre-Raphaelites",' Manse said.

'What?' the wife said. 'Geoff, are you all right?'

'I think Geoff's trying to make up his mind on which to choose,' Manse said. 'It's a bit challenging to have a question like that chucked at you without warning.'

'Boys, we're going,' Geoff said. 'Now.'

'Why?' the older one said. 'Because of ugly mug?'

'Why?' the wife said.

'Now,' Geoff said.

'Has he scared you somehow?' the wife said.

'These aren't my kind of pictures,' Geoff said.

'Geoff seems to me more a Michelangelo man. It's a matter of taste,' Manse replied. When the family had gone, he went and stood next to the woman again, studying the Prentis.

'When it comes to pictures, people's tastes *are* various and unpredictable,' she said.

'My mother used to remark, "There's no accounting for taste." She didn't mean it in a cruel or snobby way. No. Just that people varied. One taste was not *better* than another, but *different*, nothing else. The Pre-Raphaelites don't do the trick for some folk and it is entirely their right to state this and move on to some other art, for instance Michelangelo, as I suggested, or, perhaps, Per Kirkeby or Manet or, indeed, Monet. Or, then, Jackson Pollock. I always think of taste as being truly democratic.'

'But I definitely would not say wishy-washy for *Remembrance*.'

'Nor half-baked. I'd prefer the words "subtle", "refined",' Manse said.

Chapter Eleven

2009

For Harpur, another very notable thing about Iles was that occasionally he would accept advice. At these moments he definitely seemed to realize there might be people around who knew more about a particular area than he did himself. Now and then, Harpur had seen him allow someone else to talk quite a bit. And he'd listen, at least for a while.

At the charity shop siege now he would have to listen to the official negotiator as well as to Andy Rockmain, a police psychologist, who'd been brought in fast. Harpur felt glad to see him. Just before Rockmain turned up, Harpur was beginning to worry about Iles. A lot of lives could be at risk here. So far, the ACC had unquestionably followed settled methods for a hostage crisis, but Harpur feared he might not stick to them. Harpur thought he had already spotted some signs of wavering. He would *expect* some signs of wavering. This didn't mean Iles might order an attack. He'd fear putting lives in peril. But he might decide to do something solo.

God, Harpur loathed those times when Iles ditched the pattern of sane behaviour and might have to be physically neutralized by him, Harpur. That is, if Harpur could do it. Although Iles was comparatively slight, nearly a dandy, he had exceptional power in his limbs and knew head-butting. It had always seemed wrong to Harpur and a collapse of decorum that two officers of high rank should go at each other violently in public, Iles possibly wearing uniform. Bad, bad, for the outfit of an Assistant Chief to get bloodstained in that kind of internal team fracas. Of course, whatever the dispute might be about, he would always top it up with his bitter stand-by rage over the Harpur–Sarah Iles affair, so long ago now, but still raw with Iles. This perennial, wild resentment probably helped put that extra, frantic strength into his arms and legs, and gave the special intensity to all the unnecessary baying, frothing and sobbing.

In the control caravan, towed here for the siege, Rockmain had gone through three recordings of the negotiator's conversation with the gunman and now listened in live to the latest contact, trying to construct some sort of offender profile. Harpur and Iles were also on extensions. Harpur liked how the negotiator worked. His training would have been based on plenty of handed-down experience here and abroad, some of it successful. He was patient, polite, unmenacing, never used the term 'hostages', constantly sought agreement with deferential phrases like 'isn't it?' and 'wouldn't you say?' and often repeated the gunman's words, so giving them an importance boost. He remained reasonable, always ready to chop his own spiel and let the gunman chatter and demand. That's what link-ups were for: to get the suspect talking and keep him talking. Slowly, it might be possible to create a relationship, even a bond, between him and the negotiator. This would have no genuine basis or worth, of course. It was a ploy. The negotiator might be bonding with someone else at a different siege tomorrow. But it often worked.

This slowness could be an asset. It gave the chance to pile up more information about the hostages and the building's layout, as well as the gunman, and to bring in additional personnel and equipment for a possible swat. A mob-handed attack might become inevitable if the negotiations showed no progress signs and the danger to hostages rose. But the objective was to dodge this no-choice finale, if possible. Instead, the siege manager hoped the offender could be persuaded by a negotiator's seeming empathy and sympathy that the most sensible next step was surrender and release of the hostages undamaged.

Logic – the offender's own – should lead him to this decision, not threats and badgering. He must be brought to realize that to give up was a preferable fate to what might happen to him otherwise. And this, of course, *was* logical, impeccably logical. If it came to tactical intervention, he would be priority stun-gunned, possibly gassed, possibly riddled like that deafening, lengthy, fusillade ending of *Bonnie and Clyde*, to stop him riddling others – hostages and/or members of the hit team.

As long as he remained scared, though, logic might not get a look-in. Impulse and despair ruled. The negotiator had to sneak some balance and sense into him by user-friendly, cooked-up, formula mateyness. His brain should tell him then that he was outnumbered and cornered and the ultimate in no-win prats. The amassing of armed officers and assault gear outside ought to be made very obvious, though not blatantly warlike.

Of course, he could still kid himself he had some power: that is, his gun, guns, and bullets and his hold on hostages' lives. But one gun or even two and their bullets wouldn't do much against the sharpshooter mob surrounding him. And, the lives of the hostages could become a weakness, not an advantage.

Ultimately, the siege commander might decide (a) negotiating had bombed; (b) an immediate rescue attempt was now unavoidable; and (c) an intervention attack would be recognized as unavoidable by any board of inquiry and/or court hearing that followed: crucial, this. The siege supremo – Gold, ACC Desmond Iles – had two questions to ask, the second one dependent on the first:

(a) Can negotiations bring the hostages out and disarm the gunman?

(b) If not, when do we go in to do both?

Harpur thought Iles might get the answers wrong, or only right in Iles's individual version of right, which could be wrong.

Rockmain sat crouched forward, headphones on, a pad nearby. He made continuous notes in very black ink with a proper fountain pen. He was not wearing the green cord suit but a mauve cardigan over a black T-shirt, chinos and desert boots. Although he looked more or less negligible, he wasn't altogether that. Probably he had come away in a hurry. The gunman's words, tone, syntax, idioms, pauses, might bring small revelations to Rockmain, and possibly a crowd of small revelations could add up to something worthwhile.

In any case, there were two other very practical purposes of maintaining a telephone link. If it was a landline connection and you had information about the building's interior you might be able to fix his location fairly exactly when he spoke: he'd be near the phone, wouldn't he? Also, to use the instrument would require one of his hands. That meant he did not have two weapons covering his prisoners. This could be relevant when he needed to control anything more than a single hostage. It was very rare for a hostage, hostages, to be hurt or killed while their captor spoke on the telephone to a negotiator.

'I wouldn't be surprised if we had quite a lot of talking to do, and it might make things easier, more natural, if we had each other's names – first names, that is,' the negotiator said into the phone.

'Things are *not* fucking natural, are they? What's natural about this? I'm stuck in a charity shop. You're out there with a carbine contingent.'

'They are only a precaution, believe me.'

'Yes, I believe you. They're only a precaution in case you want to shoot my head off. You'd never mention this, would you, but you don't have to because you know I'll be thinking it non-stop. What else could I be thinking?'

'I appreciate you wouldn't wish to give more than your first name,' the negotiator replied. 'This is not an identification matter, is it? But it would help establish a kind of closeness.'

'I don't want closeness. I want you to fuck off.'

'I'm Oliver, known usually as Ol or Olly.'

'OK, Ol or Olly.'

'Better like that, wouldn't you say?'

'Who for?'

'And *your* name, might one ask?'

'Well, yes, one might. John.'

'Is that right?'

'You mean, "Is that right, John?" don't you? For closeness.'

'OK, John.'

'You were hoping for a name like Beauregard or Hengest, yes? You could feed it into the Criminal Records Office memory and get a manageable shortlist of possibles. There'll be a lot of Johns, though.'

'So, do I get from this that your name's not really John?'

'John will do.'

'Yes, of course.'

'You're doing the sweet reasonableness act, are you, Olly?'

'We're concerned about the people with you.'

'I *want* you to be concerned. It's very wise of you to be concerned. I want you to be so concerned you don't come blasting.'

'I believe there are four. Can you help me on that, d'you think?'

'No.'

'We have a name for one of them, the manageress. This is Mrs Beatrice South, aged fifty-two, living locally at 11 Masterman Avenue.'

'That's a name you have, is it?'

'We believe there are three females, one male, one female possibly in her thirties. The male perhaps forty to fifty. All

Caucasian. Are they well, John? We have nurses and a doctor here. I'm wondering about stress. There's bound to be some stress, isn't there?'

'I didn't hurt her.'

'Who?'

'The one off the street.'

'You took her into the shop.'

'I didn't hurt her.'

'I believe you, John. Is she all right now?'

'Why wouldn't she be all right?'

'Shocked?'

'If someone grabs you and pulls you into a charity shop you'll be a bit shocked, yes. Maybe she thought it was a hard sell – "Get in there and buy something!" And two pigs with guns running towards you and yelling "Stop!" Another shock.'

'You still have your sense of humour, John, haven't you?'

'Most love a joke. My father used to say, "If you can make people smile you can make them your friends."'

'Often, fathers have observed life over some decades and will come out with useful words of advice.'

'What advice did *your* father give *you*, Olly?'

'Where would you have been when your father made that heartening comment to you, John?'

'Did *your* father tell you, "If you're involved in a siege, keep him talking shit, Olly, and, while he's at it, a couple of lads can get in and blow some holes in him of a non-therapeutic nature." I'm assuming your father would have quite a vocabulary, judging by your own.'

'But she's recovered now?' the negotiator said.

'Who?'

'The woman off the street.'

'This shop's full of rubbish.'

'I wondered if you could put Mrs Beatrice South, the manageress, on the line, John. Or any of the others.'

'You wondered that, did you, Olly?'

'It would be simply to establish contact.'

'I can't see this would be helpful.'

'No. Right. Only a suggestion.'

'How many listening to this chat beside you, Olly? You smarm away so well. But who's running things? What's the plan?'

'Obviously, Mrs South's family are worried. I'd like to be able to reassure them.'

'Reassure them then.'

'It's not the same, John, is it?'

'Not the same as what?'

'Not the same as speaking to her.'

'We're all jolly and comfy here.'

'As I said, your sense of humour is remarkable, in the circumstances.'

'Yes, in the circumstances. If you listen you'll hear us all giggling like idiots. This is a game, isn't it, Olly?'

'A game? In what sense would you say it's a game, John?'

'Play-acting.'

'"Play-acting"? I don't think I understand.'

'Yes, you understand. And you're play-acting some more when you say you don't understand.'

'This is complicated! I'm afraid you're leaving me behind.'

'Our palaver, so chummy and tame.'

'"Chummy and tame". Isn't it better like that, John?'

'Better than what?'

'Better than unpleasantness.'

'But the chumminess and tameness, they're phoney, aren't they? And I don't mean just telephoney.'

'There's that astonishing humour and wit again!'

'You're pretending something hasn't happened that has happened, aren't you, Ol? It's a game. It's play-acting.'

'Something that happened? You have in mind the event in Sandicott Terrace, do you, John?'

'Yes, the event. I have it in mind. What else?'

'Now, we have to move on and deal with the results of Sandicott.'

'Tell me about it.'

'In what sense, John?'

'What damage?'

'To those in the car? You don't know what damage?' the negotiator asked.

'How could I know what damage?'

'You don't know because you had to get clear quickly?'

'Because I had to get clear quickly – if this fucking shop and your gang outside amounts to getting clear. What damage?'

'This is what I'm pointing up, John, when I say we have to face the results of Sandicott.'

'What are they?'

'As a matter of fact, I wondered if you'd let some of these people go now, John.'

'As a matter of fact you did, did you, Olly? How many?'

'Well, preferably all.'

'You wondered that, did you, Olly?'

'Or perhaps one or two. This wouldn't alter your position.'

'You mean I'd still be strong through a hostage or hostages?'

'If the woman off the street is in shock it might be good for her to see the doctor.'

'And your people would quiz her or them if I let two go and you'd know everything about inside here – exactly where to start the assault.'

'If you're thinking of letting two go that would obviously be an advance.'

'Ah, you pounced on the "two", thought you spotted an opening. An advance who for? I'm *not* thinking of letting two go. You're doing some guesswork, aren't you, Olly? You calculate like this: he's admitted to two, and he's sure to keep one to bargain with, which confirms at least three.'

'Or perhaps freeing *one*. Any of them. You might be afraid of a trap. But it could be arranged so there's absolutely no danger to you. I guarantee that.'

'You're not in charge there, are you? You're just the talker. The one in charge is on an extension, is he, or she, and getting impatient?'

'There's maximum, continuous agreement and coordination between officers in this kind of situation, John.'

'Which kind?'

'Everyone recognizes that things have to be done gradually and in stages.'

'Which things?'

'Towards a resolution, John.'

'What resolution?'

'Those people free and safe and returned to their families.'

'And me, free and safe and returned to *my* family?'

'Where *is* your family, John, if I may ask?'

'You may.'

'You spoke of your father – affectionately spoke of him, it seemed to me. To know that kind of background would give depth to things.'

'Which things?'

'The situation.'

'How would you describe that, Olly?'

'The situation? Tense but manageable.'

'Manageable by you and yours, you mean?'

'With your cooperation, obviously, John. Your family would wish you to cooperate. I feel sure of that. It's why I asked about them.'

'Oh, I thought it was so you could get an identification.'

'They'd be able to make a more detached judgement on this stand-off.'

'Well, yes, that's because they're not in the shop, isn't it, Olly? It would be difficult for those in the shop to be detached, wouldn't it?'

'We both have to work towards a resolution.'

'Me, free and safe, regardless of Sandicott and the damage?'

'A resolution *is* possible, John. We mustn't allow things to turn out unfavourably, must we?'

'What does unfavourably mean?'

'We must focus on getting a resolution, wouldn't you say?'

'"Unfavourably" means me dead and maybe others, doesn't it, Olly?'

'No situation is unresolvable. I believe that absolutely or I wouldn't have gone in for this kind of work.'

'I know what you'll be wondering, and what your boss will be wondering.'

'What?'

'How can I keep this conversation going with no noise or interruption from the people here. So, are they really OK?'

'Yes, are they really OK?'

'That's what you're bound to ask yourself.'

'Well, actually, I was asking you, John.'

'It's a worry, isn't it, Olly?'

Chapter Twelve

2007

When Geoff had gone from the Pre-Raphaelites with his wife and two sons after those difficult few minutes, Mansel Shale felt things changing between himself and the woman in front of Prentis's *Remembrance*. For instance, they spoke. This would be the most obvious new feature. And the talk came very naturally, not some creepy, greasy-lips, pick-up chatter. It concerned art, which seemed to Manse totally right for a gallery, Pre-Raphaelite or other. And the great fact was, *she* began it. 'When it comes to pictures, people's tastes *are* various and unpredictable,' she'd stated as soon as Manse returned from Geoff. Only a loony would disagree, so a useful start had definitely been made. He noticed the way she put real strength on that *are*, as if to back up Manse's remark to Geoff's wife, although Manse had meant it as piss-taking, of course.

The woman turned her head away from *Remembrance* and towards Manse when she said this, giving it an undoubted personal touch of some value, he thought. And Manse was able to reply at once that his mother used to comment, often in quite a non-snotty fashion, 'There's no accounting for taste.' This, also, would be accepted by most people as very true. Therefore, the atmosphere near the Prentis became really enjoyable. He thought a mention of his mother and one of her remarks helped because it showed he had been brought up in a good, homely style, and that his flair for gutting loud slobs like Geoff via one or two confidential words – 'throat,' for instance – was only one aspect of Manse, though handy. Not everyone had a mother who could come out with advice on general life. She would use these words about people's clothes, or furniture, or moustache, or carpets, or choice of music, and once about Syb after he'd brought her to meet his parents for the first time.

But it wasn't just the conversation that proved there had been a development between the woman and Manse. Previously, he did not think it right to consider himself 'with' her. He was standing not far from her, yes, and he'd imagined a sort of communication linking the Prentis, her and him. *Imagined.* Hoped for. The two of them were not together, though, not in that full sense of 'with'. Now, partly because of Geoff, Manse began to feel he *was* with her, in that full sense. Anyone looking at them would have believed they came to the exhibition as a pair. At exactly the moment she seemed to decide she'd seen enough of the Prentis, Manse decided the same. Surely this could be regarded as a sign of true closeness. They moved to the next picture, a William Holman Hunt. She said: 'I don't hate this one.'

'Hate? No, indeed.'

'Some of Hunt's stuff I detest. How about you? This is OK, just some yokel under a tree. What's your name, by the way? I'm Naomi.'

'Mansel.'

'Don't you loathe that religious rubbish Hunt did sometimes, Mansel – *The Light of the World*?'

'Well, he was one of the original Pre-Raphaelite Brotherhood, Naomi,' Shale replied.

'I know. That doesn't mean he couldn't turn out crap, though, does it? I don't think I've ever known someone called Mansel before.'

'My parents liked to branch out quite a bit. They were famed for it where we lived and even beyond in many directions.'

'My name is in the Bible,' she replied.

'I don't think the name Mansel is. At Sunday school we used to do quite a lot of Bible reading. Although your name is there, and very important in the Book of Ruth, you don't like religious paintings. Strange. The Sunday school teachers loved *The Light of the World*.'

'Well, they would, wouldn't they, Manse? All that hocus-pocus and bogus intensity.' It shook him quite a whack to hear her slaughter a holy painting, where Jesus is holding a lamp and knocking on a door. Manse thought it most likely referred to a text in Revelation, 'Behold I stand at the door and knock' – meaning if you open up you'll see the light and be saved. He had the idea it would take him a while to get used to some London women, such as Naomi and Joan Fenton, the lawyer. They seemed to say whatever they wanted to regardless. 'Did you come to town especially to see the show?' she said.

She seemed to know he wasn't a Londoner. 'Well, no, not exactly.'

'You fitted it into some other programme?' she asked

'That kind of thing.'

'What was it?'

'A funeral.'

'Anyone near to you?'

'In a way near, yes.'

'Which way?'

'A work relationship.'

'But something else going on? Near *and* dear? A woman?'

'No, no, he was called Denzil. A colleague, that's all.'

'Old?'

'Not very.'

'Shall I tell you what I suspect?'

'I'd be interested in that.'

'I get the notion he let you down somehow,' she said.

'I have to say, yes. Regrettable, but yes.'

'It can happen.'

'There was definitely good sides to Denzil as long as you was patient.'

'Many would decide that if someone had seriously let them down they would not go to his funeral. This seems to me a very generous and considerate act on your part. What did he die of?'

'I thought to myself like this, Naomi – Denz had quite a few pressures in the last months of his time with us, and these might of affected his behaviour. I arrived at a plan: let's try to forget his faults and deceptions and give respect to his good and positive talents, which he certainly had.'

'The family would have been very grateful to see you there, I should think. Where in London was it?'

'Some duties cannot be dodged. That's my view.'

'What did he die of?'

'There was several long, heartfelt conversations with some of his relatives afterwards – a brother and a cousin, for example – and the warmth of these one-to-ones proved to me I'd been so right to attend.'

'That's the main thing, your own reaction. Congratulations. Sometimes at funerals the family can be awkward, or worse. What sort of people were they?'

'When we come to Hunt's *The Light of the World*, Naomi, we got to note he gives a message that most in this country can understand straight off, perhaps less so abroad if it's Islam. *The Light of the World* is not like what's known as abstract, where you get a mixture of all sorts in one picture, such as a Trident submarine, cheetahs, percolators, elbows, JCBs, boxing rings. Obviously, that kind of painting can also appeal to many on account of unusualness. One abstract painter went crazy and people said his pictures became even better afterwards. This is a great advantage of abstract – getting Alzheimer's, or something like that, doesn't matter. My belief is there's room for all sorts and William Holman Hunt certainly had a real go in plenty of his works, no messing.'

'And did you have any other London visits to make after the funeral?' she replied.

He didn't want to mention Joan Fenton, though. It would sound big-deal to say he always used a London lawyer. And, in any case, Naomi might start to wonder whether he'd been discussing divorce stuff. Naomi was a clever one. He'd soon spotted that. She got them notions, and they seemed sharp. Questions were a natural for her. She had auburn hair cut very short giving a total view of her face, but this didn't stop her quizzing. Manse wouldn't like Naomi to regard him as somebody divorced who hung about galleries alone, maybe on the pull, and able to terrify any twerp who niggled him. He felt he'd possibly stumbled once or twice in grammar with her, although he'd been trying to concentrate, so talk about his classy lawyer might make Manse seem like a jumped-up prole with loot but not much education, except from Sunday school. Although this was correct he'd rather Naomi didn't realize it, yet. He said: 'I think I'm going to have to try to persuade you to like *The Light of the World*.'

'It will take you for ever.'

'I'll work at it.' He was going to say, 'I wouldn't mind that at all,' but saw this would of been obvious, cheap and flirty, and dropped it.

Chapter Thirteen

2009

Harpur listened to Iles and Andrew Rockmain talk and decided he'd better get into the siege shop alone and at once. He was unarmed but thought surprise would help him neutralize the gunman before he could start firing. Harpur wished he knew the shop interior better: location of doors, stairs and corridors, size of rooms. They'd sent for plans of the building inside and out from city council records, but he would have liked actual familiarity. He'd always found it hard to remember maps and drawings. His elder daughter, Hazel, once described his brain as 'rubbish with visuals, brilliant with verbals,' where 'verbals' meant a suspect's words invented or rearranged by police to prove guilt. Hazel doubted police ethics, not especially Harpur's but Harpur's included. Iles had hinted Harpur should know the shop layout because he bought his suits there. But that was only a joke, just a traditional, insulting Iles jibe at Harpur's clothes.

Rockmain had analysed the gunman's conversation and come up with an elaborate professional estimate of his mind-state. He reckoned that 'John' would crack very soon. Therefore, he recommended continuation of the siege, with more telephone talk, and no intervention – no assault. Harpur interpreted the conversation differently, but could see Iles agreed with Rockmain. This might be one of those occasions when the ACC would accept advice, although in general he loathed Rockmain, found him farcical. The point was that Iles *wanted* above all to be told he should hold back and avoid violence. He hated risking his people. A while ago he sent an undercover detective into a gang, and the officer was rumbled and murdered.* Iles never properly recovered from the mess-up. He would always and obsessively seek the safest method of tackling a crisis. This hesitance and crippling motherliness might be another feature that helped keep him eternally from top command.

He'd argue with Rockmain now because Rockmain was the pathetic Rockmain and Iles the Golden Iles, but Harpur could tell he'd been persuaded – and three-quarters persuaded before Rockmain gave his lecturettes. Harpur had guessed Iles wouldn't want to send in an attack, but suspected the ACC might try something individual. Once Rockmain offered his views, though, even this seemed to Harpur unlikely. And Harpur decided he ought to do something individual himself.

For the last twelve minutes there had been no talk with John. He'd put the receiver down and left it down. In the command caravan with Rockmain, Iles and Harpur, the negotiator sat ready to resume. It was very unusual, against most precedent, for the negotiator to be under the same roof as the operational officers, but Rockmain wanted it like that. He said: 'Well, let's see what we've got, shall we, Desmond?' Rockmain had commander rank in the Metropolitan Police, equivalent to a provincial assistant chief constable. This entitled him, or so he thought, to first-name Iles. Harpur saw a little shiver of resentment, revulsion, go through Iles, but he didn't head-butt Rockmain or spit, not to date.

'What I'd like you to notice is the way John repeatedly takes up the exact words of the negotiator,' Rockmain said. He looked at his notes. 'The negotiator tells him he'd like

* See *Halo Parade*

72

to make things easier and more natural. John's answer? "Things are *not* fucking natural, are they? What's natural about this? I'm stuck in a charity shop. You're out there with a carbine contingent." The negotiator replies: "They are only a precaution, believe me." John says: "Yes, I believe you. They're only a precaution in case you want to shoot my head off." The negotiator mentions that he aims to "establish a kind of closeness". John states: "I don't want closeness. I want you to fuck off."

'Later from the negotiator comes: "We're concerned about the people with you," and all credit to him for avoiding the term "hostages". John ripostes: "I *want* you to be concerned. It's very wise of you to be concerned. I want you to be so concerned you don't come blasting." And then, elsewhere the negotiator says, "I wondered if you could put Mrs So-and-so on the line." John: "You wondered, did you, Olly?" Or, negotiator: "Your sense of humour is remarkable, in the circumstances." John: "Yes, in the circumstances." Negotiator: "You have in mind the event in Sandicott Terrace, do you, John?" John: "Yes, the event, I have it in mind." Negotiator: "As a matter of fact, I wondered if you'd let some of these people go now, John." "As a matter of fact you did, did you, Olly?"

'Now, you're going to say he takes up these words of the negotiator merely in order to reject them, Desmond, mock them, bin them. You'll claim his responses show only that he remains hostile, combative, resistant.' Rockmain chuckled for a few seconds. He was not tall, thin, his neck flimsy, but his chuckle had quite a bit of resonance and boom. This chuckle could have come from someone with a fatter neck, perhaps someone fatter altogether, and happy with his fatness. Although he might be a skinny little prat this chuckle had true amplitude. Harpur wondered whether he'd been on some sort of social communications course which would include chuckling.

Now, Rockmain resumed speaking: 'Well, on the face of it – on the face of it – that is a totally understandable

73

reaction from you, Desmond. I would certainly never call it superficial or simplistic. Never. You are not a professional psychologist but a very successful professional copper, lavishly possessed of the skills required in that calling, but, perhaps, not familiar with the more complex interpretations of human behaviour. Why, I ask, should you be? You, no doubt, have specialist flairs that are sadly lacking in myself – say, how to bash in the front door of a suspect's home at 2 a.m. while yelling "Armed police!" Nobody should undervalue such basic and necessary knacks. There is a place for them. But psychology and what we term "forensic linguistics" – the study of words and syntax – require a slightly different kind of approach and training. I won't say subtler. I won't say more profound.'

'I'm glad you won't say subtler or more profound,' Iles replied.

'The last thing I'd wish to seem is patronizing, Desmond.'

'I'm glad it's the last thing you'd wish to seem,' Iles said. 'What's the first thing you'd wish to seem?'

'I'll concede that on the face of it – on the face of it – John's belligerent way with what the negotiator said appears to mean he's in the very opposite of a surrender mood,' Rockmain replied. 'But let's probe somewhat deeper into the tone and significance of his phrasing, shall we? Let us apply some of that aforementioned forensic linguistics. Yes, I think so. That, after all, is why I'm here, isn't it? Oh, definitely. I get an emergency call to say I might be of use at this siege. I'm asked whether it's convenient for me to attend immediately. My reply? My reply is: "I will *make* it convenient. If I am needed, I'm needed and must – must – go."

'What we have to notice, Desmond, is that his phrasing is often entirely dependent on the negotiator's. Admittedly, he will frequently reverse the sense of it. He'll dispute "natural", for instance, and give a variant meaning to "precaution". But these contradictions are not very relevant.

74

Here's the *real* point, Desmond, Colin – yes, here's the main point: by sticking so doggedly, so slavishly, indeed, to the line proposed by the negotiator he implicitly recognizes who has control. He feels compelled to attempt rebuttals of what the negotiator says, and in doing so accepts that the negotiator establishes the route they both must take. If I may stoop to jargon, he allows, encourages, the negotiator to "set the agenda". I hear a kind of rhythmic inevitability about the negotiator's statements and John's adjusted echo of them. The negotiator puts a word into the air and John takes it, imparts his personal commentary and sends it back. I feel a fugue-like progress, don't you, Desmond, Colin?'

'He agrees with the negotiator by disagreeing?' Iles said. Harpur thought this came over as reasonably sharp and dismissive, but not sharp and dismissive enough – not the full sharpness and dismissiveness Iles was capable of and lived by. His voice sounded more than half won over, as though Rockmain had conferred a revelation on him. The paradox – with agree and disagree equated – seemed to intrigue Iles, enthral him. He wouldn't openly admit this, though. Rockmain had, or had had, a green corduroy suit. Iles couldn't confess to imbibing revelations from someone of that fruity flavour.

Rockmain said: 'John would like to think it is he who has control – through his power over the hostages, a power that constrains us as well as them, so far. But his words show he is not confident of this, show, in fact, the opposite. In due course, and quite soon now, he will most probably relinquish all pretence at control. He will capitulate. We must wait for this frailty to disable him.'

He held up a tiny, skeletal, childlike hand, as if attempting to ward off protest. 'But you'll say, Desmond, "His voice still sounds strong and good." Granted his voice sounds strong and good. There's a showman side to him. He can keep up a pretence, act out a pretence. But not for ever. Or even for very long. Acute stress elements discomfort him.

He has to manage what we believe to be four people. Even though he's armed and they aren't this is a tricky task. If he continues, he'll need to sleep and become off-guard. You'll send in food and drink, but he'll fear this might disguise the start of an onslaught.

'And this brings us to what I'm sure we all recognize as the most significant bit of repetition in the conversations. I refer, of course, to the word "unfavourably". The negotiator says: "A resolution *is* possible, John. We mustn't allow things to turn out unfavourably." This constitutes an expert piece of persuasiveness by the negotiator. The word "resolution" is positive, wholesome, and a clever way of cloaking what it actually means to John: defeat. One can imagine a proud battleship named HMS *Resolution*. And then the "we" –"*we* mustn't allow things to turn out unfavourably" – the "we" suggests they are partners in dodging an unfavourable outcome: mates, buddies, joined together by exemplary good sense. It's as though Olly and John have the same purpose and will plan it jointly. But John isn't having any of it. The fudge factor doesn't work for him now. He answers: "What does unfavourably mean?"

'Dread forces him to see through the carefully vague terms used by the negotiator. "Unfavourably means me dead and maybe others, doesn't it, Olly?" Reality is about to overwhelm John. He feels he must retaliate somehow. He must dominate. He is pushed by this urge into absurdity. He suggests the besiegers might fear the hostages are already dead since there is "no noise or interruption from the people here". But this notion, this tease, this attempt to scare and horrify, drastically weakens his position, doesn't it? Living hostages are the only appreciable weapon he has. If the hostages were dead his own security would be finished. He'd have no bargaining resources left. It recalls that formula we hear now and then from the peace process in Northern Ireland. He would have put his armament "beyond use".

'Such a consummate error in his logic and instincts and tactics tells us he is coming apart, is already a near wreck. I believe, on the evidence of these conversations, that he is intelligent and quick-witted enough to acknowledge this to himself soon, and to seek to end things in some other way than "unfavourably", i.e. by submission and release unhurt of his prisoners. You'll point out, Desmond, Colin, that submission itself is for him an unfavourable outcome and one he has so far resisted.' Rockmain went into another chuckle, though briefer. Then he said: 'Yes, submission will mean matters end unfavourably for him, but not as unfavourably as if he is hugely outgunned and designated a target.'

Rockmain did a fair job at mimicking Iles's voice. '"This is Gold. Shoot him." John might not be aware of the full damage he caused in Sandicott Terrace, but he will know he opened fire and hit the Jaguar. He'll understand that if police kill him now because he won't yield there'll be no public or judicial outcry. Everyone will accept he was an all-round active menace and had to be made safe. He will have opted to be made safe by getting wiped out. He won't opt for it.'

Chapter Fourteen

2007

Obviously, Manse Shale knew he had to be careful about what he said to Naomi and how he said it. When he concentrated at full power he reckoned he got most of his grammar fairly OK. He certainly did not regard grammar as just something fancy. He believed it was sensible to have as much of it as you could by listening to people who already had it and noticing the way they put it all together. You might not get it all at once, but a few very small errors might happen to anyone, known as slips of the tongue. Think of John Prescott, ex-deputy Prime Minister, who'd been to two universities, not just one, and you would of thought they had lectures on how to stop your tongue slipping, by people whose tongues did not slip, showing students it could be done. But John Prescott sounded like he wanted to kick the language to death with a steel-toecapped boot.

Manse could tell Naomi had no trouble with her grammar. She would notice if he really messed up, though she'd probably be too polite to tell him. If she thought he sounded like an ignorant slob, she might decide he was not right for her. So Manse said to himself, 'Watch it, Manse!' That was grammatical! He'd met Naomi only an hour ago, but already felt he'd like to hold on to her. He admired slimness in a woman. It wasn't only that they both loved the Pre-Raphaelites, or, for Naomi, *some* of the Pre-

Raphaelites. Mansel considered this similarity between them just a sign of something that could turn out deep.

Also, obviously, if this did happen, he'd eventually have to tell her what his type of commerce was. In that kind of relationship it would be wrong to keep such a matter confidential. For one thing, she'd need to be warned about the dangers of the game, not just to him but to her, also, and to Manse's children. Some difficult people worked in this trade. They could get impetuous. He had certainly told Syb about his business and advised her to be watchful. The stress might be one of the reasons she cut loose and went to Ivor, this roofer or chef or vet in North Wales. She'd be safer there. How she'd met Ivor he couldn't tell. For now, Manse couldn't tell either whether Naomi did flits, also, but he wouldn't want to give her too much strain this early. She had the sort of face that shouldn't be given strain.

There was a shop next to the gallery where they sold poster-prints of most of the paintings on show. Naomi picked out *Lorenzo and Isabella* by Millais and an Arthur Hughes. Manse didn't feel certain about the best way to deal with this. He thought it would be forcing things ahead too fast if he tried to pay and make a present of them. When it came to women, money could be a difficult topic. He'd hate it to look like he thought he could buy his way into closeness with her. That would be vulgar and flashy.

Also, he had an original Hughes at home, almost certainly genuine: if Naomi ever came to his house and saw the art there she might feel hurt that he'd thought it enough to give her a couple of mass-produced prints. Of course, he hoped she *would* come to his house one day. So, he didn't offer to pay for her posters, and instead let Naomi hand over her own cash.

Naturally, he watched her face and body for anything that revealed she considered him a tightwad – say the sudden screwing up of her lips or an angry limb-twitch. If he saw either, or both, he'd try to make out he hadn't noticed the sale because he was examining some other shop items. Often he'd found that limb-twitches in women could come from a lot of rage and/or disgust. He had a plan ready. Manse might say: 'Oh, you must let me get you those. Please! It's a privilege, in truth!'

Manse often found that if he was trying a line with a woman he regarded as a bit above the usual class he'd produce old-time, long-gone phrases such as 'in truth'. It was like something from an ancient drama about the upper-classes. But maybe it sounded weird and comical to the woman. He had a twenty very handy, to prevent any additional delay in these possible tricky moments. It would be best if he got the money to the shop assistant before Naomi paid. Otherwise, Manse would have to persuade her to take it afterwards. This could be awkward. She'd probably refuse. And, if she didn't, there'd be the matter of change. The posters cost £7.99 each, which meant she'd have to give him back £4.02. He would detest all that carry-on with coins. He'd feel like a shop worker himself. The difficult point was she might not show the anger and contempt at his meanness until after she had paid the assistant. These complications really troubled him.

But, no, Manse spotted nothing to tell him he'd disappointed her, not *before* she paid nor *after*. She acted like someone absolutely used to paying her own way, used to acting independent. Did that hint she had no husband or partner at present? You could tell she was the sort who would have her personal ideas about *The Light of the World*, though many thought it great.

Manse bought a Millais and a D.G. Rossetti poster himself, *Ophelia* and *Beata Beatrix*, using the twenty. He needed to strengthen the idea that he and Naomi had similarities, were a natural pair, but he wouldn't overdo it by buying exactly the same, like naff couples who wore clothes that matched. Obviously, he'd never frame and hang cheapo prints in his residential property. This wasn't the purpose. He wanted Naomi and himself to leave the shop together, each with rolled posters under their arm. In Manse's opinion, this made a kind of bond.

He put the prints under the left arm, keeping his gun hand free. But, as Joan Fenton had said, he was probably safe enough in London, hidden among the crowds. Clearly, it did not matter which arm Naomi carried *her* posters under. Manse didn't think the bond would be weakened suppose she placed them under her right arm. Exact resemblance wasn't vital. If any trouble did come, he'd be able to defend her because *his* posters would not stop him getting fast to his shoulder holster. He considered he had a responsibility for her, even though she didn't know the chief sort of work he earned from and the kind of enemies he might have. Did that Hackney family at the funeral *really* believe Denzil saw himself off, a two-pistol suicide? He hadn't told Joan Fenton about those people.

In fact, it was *because* Naomi didn't know the chief sort of dealing he earned from, and the kind of enemies he might have, that he felt so much responsibility for her. She seemed willing to accept him as he was, and Manse believed she deserved gratitude and protection for this. Manse always thought of himself and his firm as here today, gone tomorrow, or even gone later today: no genuine solidity. He was bound to feel thankful to anyone who seemed to regard him as more than this – as more worthwhile than this. Perhaps it was a type of protection when he spoke to Geoff in that way. He hoped they didn't see the sod now with rolled-up posters under his arm, like theirselves. Plainly, this would weaken the special, even unique, understanding Manse hoped existed between Naomi and him. Geoff would look like he was a part of it, too, although with that fucking leather waistcoat on.

If Naomi ever did come to his home, the one-time St James's rectory, it was sure to be well on in their relationship, involving travel from London and a stop-over. By then, he thought he'd be able to make a kind of joke about not hanging the posters. She'd understand, anyway, when

81

seeing the many originals there, in the rooms and large hallway. He thought he might tell her the situation before she actually came to the property, sort of prepare her for the surprise of finding not posters on his walls but actual paintings. He wouldn't do that now, though, because it would seem arrogant and pushy.

Arrogance and pushiness Manse despised. Lately, he'd come across a word that described spot-on how he felt about arrogance and pushiness. 'Averse.' He was averse to arrogance and pushiness, no question, and to crude boasts of wealth. Besides, she might have more than he did – even though she bought prints – and would find it ridiculous if he started big-mouthing about his boodle and possessions. Her clothes and shoes looked pretty good to Manse. She knew fashion and could afford it. He thought she seemed the sort who would have regular manicures as well as the good grammar. He didn't see any rings.

Manse had no objection to tallness in a woman. He could cope with that. It was summer. She wore a nicely cut, long-sleeved burgundy-coloured silk dress, and half-heel burgundy shoes. Quite a few of the women in Pre-Raphaelite paintings had on burgundy dresses but in flimsier material than silk. Mainly the dresses were blue. The Pre-Raphaelites went for blue.

A small café stood next to the poster shop. They didn't *have* to go in there. They could of left together from the main exit. Or they could of said goodbye to each other in the shop and then gone out separately, the meeting very enjoyable, but over. That wouldn't have been odd. But they sort of turned towards the café together automatically. It wasn't necessary for Manse to say, 'Would you like a cup of tea and a bit of a rest, Naomi, after quite a long afternoon on your feet, though pleasant?' To sit together at one of the pub-style metal and wood tables seemed to occur naturally – unplanned yet like destiny, in Manse's opinion. He believed off-and-on in destiny. Manse considered the way they made for the café another aspect of that pairing.

He thought to just buy tea and toast for both of them didn't mean he was rushing her. He saw it as being civil and, surely, all should try for that in this very troubled world, providing where possible a little relief. They put the rolled posters in their cardboard sleeves on the table.

In front of the Prentis, she had spoken first, so he felt it would be all right, or even compulsory, for him to begin the talk now. He'd worked out in his mind a way of dealing with the matter of his occupation – the main one. Or of *not* dealing with it, at this point. It would be an obvious thing for her to ask what he did. He could say haulage or haulage and scrap and she might believe it, suppose she didn't have much knowledge of what 'haulage and scrap' sometimes meant. What it meant was a front to fool the Revenue and make it easier for Iles to blind-eye Manse's chief career in the various commodities. He decided that the best thing to do was speak very frankly, not about his career, though, but the relationship scene. This might keep the questions away from his business and should also lead Naomi to tell him how she was placed as to personal details.

'Exploring a gallery can be a little exhausting, but I find art does offer a kind of comfort during periods of tension, such as, speaking for myself, the preliminaries to a divorce,' he said. Hit her with it straight out. Manse thought she'd prefer he did it like that. She'd been very up-front about exchanging names. It was how she was.

'Indeed, yes,' she said.

'Have you gone through a divorce, then, Naomi?'

'Not a divorce, just splitting from a partner.'

'Similar, I expect.' He wasn't keen on 'partner'. You couldn't tell the sex. He'd been going to say, 'Similar, I expect, if the relationship had lasted quite a time.' But he cut the last bit because the 'if' made it sound as though the relationship might *not* of lasted quite a time, which could signify she was flighty. He said: 'I don't suppose an artist was thinking like that when he did his painting. He wouldn't be wondering whether his work might help settle

a man's or a woman's nerves owing to broken relationships many a year into the future.'

'Perhaps not, though some had very problematical relationships themselves.'

'Who?'

'The Pre-Raphaelites. Holman Hunt was banging one of
his models, who might have started as a tart. Rossetti
spread himself. A man of great physical beauty, of course.'

These last words worried Manse. She sounded as though
she might have been interested in Rossetti herself if she'd
been around then. Manse never thought of himself as of
great physical beauty, and possibly others didn't, either.
'Maybe it's wrong of us to take their paintings over in that
way – turn them into something not theirs but ours, like a
Prozac prescription from the doc. A kind of stealing.'

'Once it's out there, art belongs to us,' Naomi said. 'It's
made to be looked at. Who are the ones who look? Us.
What we make of it is our business.'

She had things so clear in her mind, and would talk with
real punch and certainty. He loved that. He couldn't
always manage it himself. 'My wife's in North Wales,' he
replied. 'We're separated. We'll be divorced soon. She
never had any interest in galleries. That wasn't what drove
us apart, but she hadn't.'

'Not all do.'

'Instead of saying Pre-*Raph*aelites she'd refer to them as
the Pre-Raph*ae*lites, like "fail". Maybe she was getting at
them. I'm not certain. Or just being clumsy to annoy. Was
your partner interested in galleries?'

'I didn't ask him. He never came with me.'

Manse was delighted to hear that 'him' and 'he'. He
would never object in general to same-sex arrangements,
which there were many of these days, doing no harm. But,
obviously, he would prefer Naomi wanted a man. 'I'm
wondering how it was when you discussed an exhibition.
You'd say, "I think I'll go to a gallery today." And he'd
reply, would he, "Right, till later then, Naomi"? I have the

children. Sybil sees them now and again, of course. There's a definite fondness there, both ways, her to them, them to her. Often she'll buy them presents, not just at Christmas and birthdays. Have you got children?'

'He didn't want them.'

'Did *you*? Is that why you broke up?'

She swallowed most of her tea. 'Who really knows why couples break up – even themselves?'

He considered that very deep. 'True,' Manse said. 'Luckily, my sister will look after the children when I come to London. I can almost always get away for a short while.'

'Is she fixed up with someone else?' Naomi asked.

'Who?'

'Sybil.'

'I think she's got a roofer, or something like that. Most likely he's doing all right. There's a lot of rain in North Wales and big winds off the mountains and the sea, plus plenty of slate. I don't know if he's insured. They go for metal ladders these days, not wood. How about your ex-partner?'

'I don't keep in touch.'

'Is that because you –'

'No, I don't keep in touch.'

'Are you afraid that if there's contact you might want things to restart?'

'When it's finished it's finished.'

In some ways Manse liked this. It was another part of her clear and straight outlook. And it should mean this ex-partner would not come nosing about, as long as he understood that when it was finished it was finished. But her words also reached him as blunt and worrying. They meant that if he lost her she'd be gone for keeps. Yes, he needed to be very careful with Naomi. On the other hand, he had to take some risks going after her or she'd never be his to lose.

Chapter Fifteen

2009

Of course, Harpur knew a solo intervention at the charity shop could be regarded as mad – and would be by Rockmain and, probably, Iles: culpably mad. In fact, if Iles had attempted that kind of thing himself, Harpur would have done all he could to stop him, including any necessary brutality. Most probably, though, Iles would not try it. He'd longed to be assured by Rockmain that risk was not required – and had been assured.

Harpur found Rockmain's jubilant decoding of the phone talk off track and dangerously optimistic. But, Rockmain was the trained and experienced psychologist. The Home Office routinely sent for him to do his mind readings at this kind of crisis. That must mean his record showed he generally got things right. Hadn't he described how the Home Office came to beg his intervention, and how he'd agreed with gush and conscientiousness? Who was Harpur to disagree with him – and, incidentally, with Iles? Harpur did ask himself the question, and asked it often. He got harsh and deflating answers. This didn't stop him listing in his head the points where he thought Rockmain had things haywire this time.

1. 'I want you to fuck off,' John had replied to the negotiator's call for 'closeness' between them. 'I don't want closeness. I want you to fuck off.' Rockmain believed the way John picked up and stuck to the negotiator's words

revealed a crucial weakness. The word was 'closeness' here; elsewhere, 'natural', 'precaution', 'circumstances', 'as a matter of fact', and so on. In Rockmain's guru view, this copy-cat dependence proved John realized he did not control things and must always let the negotiator direct their discussion, and, ultimately, John's actions. He was boxed in by the negotiator's words, as much as by the siege force backing him. Rockmain thought John knew it and knew, also, that his next step had to be out of the building with his hands up, followed by the unharmed hostages.

To Harpur, though, these chat extracts said John wanted to take the negotiator on and defeat him – defeat him in the most flagrant and humiliating style by fixing on his own words and shredding their sense. He turned them into a joke. The negotiator says the armed police outside are 'only a precaution, believe me.' John seems to agree. 'Yes, I believe you.' But what he believes is enormously different from what the negotiator wants him to believe. 'Yes, I believe you. They're only a precaution in case you want to shoot my head off.'

And, on the matter of closeness, John's reply meant something like this. 'Closeness? Not exactly: I want your distance, your absence.' John was saying: 'Stuff closeness. If you're after closeness you'll have to come in and get me. And there'll be big collateral damage to those in here with me when you do. We're what you could call *very* close.' Obviously, he knew the huge, surrounding battalion was not going to fuck off until they'd got him, one way or the other. He could watch it grow and savour its fixedness. He was meant to watch it grow and savour its fixedness. He couldn't hope. But he might choose to go out blazing away.

2. 'Unfavourably.' This Rockmain regarded as the most significant word of the lot. 'A resolution is possible, John. We mustn't allow things to turn out unfavourably,' says the negotiator. And John replies: 'What does unfavourably mean? Unfavourably means me dead, and maybe others, doesn't it, Olly?' Rockmain seemed to think this response

showed John was ready to see reality. He couldn't be put off by soft, vague words like 'unfavourably'. But it also might have indicated he had become more formidable, more combative, more of a menace. Then, though, in Rockmain's opinion, he abruptly ceased to be formidable at all. He hinted that the hostages might be already dead. Rockmain decided this was a 'tease' and a stupid, panicky one, because the hostages, alive, provided his only real strength. Rockmain deduced John was 'coming apart, is already a near wreck'. He seemed intelligent enough to recognize this and would soon cave in. He did not want things to end 'unfavourably', in the hard and bloody sense of that diplomatic word.

Harpur agreed with part of this analysis – the part saying that John could see exactly and realistically how things were, and wouldn't be lulled by the lingo of fudge. His 'tease', as Rockmain called it, was, yes, a retaliation against the bleakness of his prospects clearly, unflinchingly faced. Perhaps the 'tease' *was* foolish and unconvincing. There had been no sound of shots to suggest any hostage had been killed. Rockmain forecast that John would see the absurdity of his resistance and capitulate. Harpur feared John saw the absurdity of his resistance and might be pushed into the actions of crazed despair, an attempt to turn the absurdity into doomed valour – going down with the ship, falling on his sword, swallowing the cyanide, and other brave and noble terms.

3. 'A fugue-like progress,' Rockmain said. Harpur had an idea what a fugue was: a starting melody in a piece of music would be picked up later in the work and get interwoven with a new melody. Perhaps this could reasonably be applied to the John–negotiator exchanges. Yes, perhaps. It was the word 'progress' that Harpur couldn't swallow, though.

4. Rockmain thought John must realize the police needn't worry much about an inquiry followed by blame if they shot him. Everyone would recognize he was a

threat and had to be 'made safe'. Rockmain believed John wouldn't choose to be made safe by getting wiped out. Harpur couldn't see how Rockmain convinced himself of this. The logic seemed to stop, to be replaced by wishfulness, and the dodgy assumption that John must see things as Rockmain saw them.

But would an experienced, star psychologist make that kind of vast, egocentric and elementary error? Harpur dropped into confusion. He could understand, though, how Rockmain convinced Iles. Obsessed by a past disaster, the ACC had yearned to be told the siege would work out peacefully. And this Rockmain conveniently and cleverly told him, with gobbledegook knobs on.

Chapter Sixteen

Manse did what he'd promised himself earlier, and just before Naomi's first visit to his home he mentioned the Pre-Raphaelite originals he had on the walls there. He tried to say it in a matter-of-fact, very, very unblaring way – in fact, he considered he gave it a total absence of blare. Conversational was the tone Manse aimed for. He had thought quite a bit about the actual words.

Early on he'd considered something like, 'As chance would have it, I been able to bring together quite a few actual Pre-Raphaelite paintings, the result of a fortunate mateyness with an art dealer called Jack Lamb who by a wonderful slab of luck, Naomi, happens to be local. They hang in various rooms of the house and in the stairwell. The children as well as myself are extremely fond of them.'

He thought that by stating the pictures had come to him only via a couple of happy flukes, he wouldn't seem big-headed and boastful to her. Big-headedness and boastfulness Manse truly despised. These remarks would make it sound like anyone could of built up this collection – as long as they loved the Pre-Raphaelites, obviously, and knew Jack. Then, if Manse brought the children in, it would give a sort of pleasant, family touch, and 'extremely fond of' might be what somebody would say about an old labrador or cat or battered but very much loved sitting-room couch, nothing high-falutin or swank-based. He felt pretty certain he'd come across that opening statement, 'As chance would have it', spoken by a woman at the golf club in just the chatty way he was after, or a character in some TV play about classy people, poised and very handy with phrases.

Of course, by the time Naomi came to Shale's house she and he were pretty well established with each other – what many would refer to as 'an item', though Manse considered this quite a vulgar term, like comparing two people to something on a shopping list. The main purpose of the visit was not to show her the art but to meet Laurent and Matilda. This he regarded as an important move. When the children heard she had come all that distance from London in the train, they would understand it must be a serious carry-on, not a slight and temporary job.

Manse knew they'd behave OK when introduced to this new face. They always did with new faces. He told them he'd met Naomi in a gallery containing top grade Pre-Raphaelite works. He thought this helped the children realize that the relationship had true quality, and with an art side. Manse was sure it did. It had grown in a gradual but very sure manner. Laurent and Matilda knew the term 'Pre-Raphaelite' because Manse had often told them most of the paintings in the house came from that group. He also told them not to talk about the collection outside because you didn't want some villain breaking in when the house was empty and taking the fucking lot in a van.

He drove the Jaguar down to the station to meet Naomi. The children was at school. The train journey gave Manse another of them cash problems, like with the poster-prints. Should he ask if he could pay for her ticket, first class, naturally? And again he decided no. He knew her much better now, didn't he, and had a very strong idea she would be insulted if he offered. It could make her seem like freight he'd ordered being sent by rail. But she *wanted* to come to his home, and paying for her own ticket would prove this. That would most probably be as she considered it.

While he waited outside the station he tried once more to prepare his words about the art on the walls at home. He'd come to think that his first effort wouldn't do. He could see a bad flaw in the comments about chance and luck, and he knew Naomi would spot it, also. In Mansel's opinion she had quite a head on her. Possibly he would not of been attracted to her if not, despite her lovely looks and cleverness with fashion. The thing was, Manse had grown to realize that chance and luck wouldn't be no use on their own. There needed to be money, and very good money, to buy the pictures from Jack Lamb. So, it would be stupid to pretend anyone might of got a collection of Pre-Raphaelites together as long as they bumped into him locally. Bumping into him wasn't the main thing at all, nor the localness. Having enough moolah for that grasping, crooked bastard, Lamb, was.

Manse altered his art statement. In the car on their way to his house he said, 'I forget whether I ever mentioned to you, Naomi, that, over the years, I been able to lay my hands on several original Pre-Raphaelite pix and I know you'll be interested to see whether I've hung them in the best light and so on.' He thought she'd decide he had only been able to afford the pictures in instalments, not a Mr Big splashing the loot around willy-nilly, but a Mr Little-by-little. In fact, because of the sodding prices Lamb wanted, it hadn't been little-by-little but big-by-bloody-big. This way of describing things kept some of the luck idea in them words, 'been able to lay my hands on', which sounded like he saw a chance and grabbed it. That was as far as the luck part of it went, though. He wouldn't overdo it.

He made sure he let Naomi seem the true expert on art, not himself, by saying he wanted her advice on how to hang the works in his property. Calling them by that slangy term 'pix' should prove he wasn't stuck up about the pictures. He hoped she would not remember he'd bought a couple of posters himself on that first day together after the gallery, the Millais *Ophelia* and D.G. Rossetti's *Beata*

Beatrix. It had been just a move to make himself seem the same as her, really, so they could both leave the building carrying the prints rolled up in their cardboard containers. Obviously, he could not hang them in his home. They would of looked extremely production line against the genuine originals. That is, if they *was* genuine. You could never be completely certain when you was dealing with that sod, Jack Lamb. Manse had given the posters, still in the container, to a charity shop in the North Bewick district. The shop might get a tenner for them and send it to Africa to help beat the drought.

Naomi's own property in London was nowhere near as big as Manse's ex-St James's rectory, but OK just the same, in Manse's view. They'd gone there by taxi after that first visit to the gallery and shop and café. She had a flat in Ealing, which he regarded as generally speaking a very decent district for London. You could see people here walking to the shops without getting knife-mugged, at least in daylight. Naomi and Manse had certainly not made love in the flat on that opening visit. He would of regarded that as bad-mannered and rabbity, even though he guessed she might not of minded, and even expected it.

Manse had to consider what kind of life and trouble he could be drawing her into. That helped slow him. Although for most of the time he felt he wanted her long-term, moments came when he wondered whether that would be fair to Naomi. This was another reason not to hurry her. She seemed a gallery person. Also, she had a job as a consultant, she said, on a London 'celebrity sheet'. He didn't really grasp what that meant, but he thought she wouldn't know much re the kind of filthy domain wars that could go on in streets, public parks and music festivals.

On a second trip to London to see her several weeks later matters changed. By then she'd had the posters she bought framed and they hung in her sitting room. Manse thought they looked reasonably all right, as far as prints could. It would be wrong and unkind for him to go on and on in his mind about them being naff. Clearly, he would never say to her that they was only copies. She had chosen white frames which suited the pictures damn well, helping to bring out their colours, especially blue, in the way frames should. Because of the happy and exciting time they had together on that second visit to her flat, the posters in the sitting room didn't really matter, anyway.

That repeat visit could be regarded as the true start of things between them, he thought. Her trip now to his home could be seen as carrying matters quite a long way forward. He felt sure Naomi would like his home, the one-time rectory. The clergyman and his family who used to live in Manse's house had been moved to a smaller place. The church found running this property too expensive. He thought there might be a bit of what might be called a parable about modern Britain in that. The church could not afford the seven-bedroom house – lighting, heating, repairs, cleaning. A substances lord such as Manse, could. In some ways this saddened him. Many would regard the situation as a sign of bad decline. However, he had to admit he enjoyed owning the residence. Denzil Lake used to have a flat on the top floor, empty now. Manse hoped it might be really helpful for the children when they was older and maybe applying for jobs to have 'St James's Old Rectory' as the address on their letters.

Usually, Manse felt he wouldn't want them to follow him in the kind of career he had, although it did mean he could live in a large place and keep them in that pretty good private school, Bracken Collegiate, where the uniform was blue edged with black, nothing gaudy. Gaudiness he hated. Because of the good earnings from his business Shale hoped he could buy a splendid education for Laurent and Matilda, even including university, and so turn them away from the business that paid for the splendid education. He realized a lot of people would regard this as strange, one end of the idea pissing on the other. But you could sometimes run into such a mix-up in modern life, known as the twenty-first millennium. If they went to university he wouldn't want them climbing spires or jumping into rivers like some students did as pranks. These students longed to be daredevils and get noticed by the media, but daredevils could hurt theirselves owing to the height of spires with poor footholds or rat disease in rivers.

The thing about Laurent and Matilda when Shale brought somebody quite unknown to meet them such as Naomi now was they didn't ask the same questions as they asked the one before or the one before that. The questions was really completely right for this person. Manse thought it proved the value of Bracken Collegiate. The school did not have actual lessons in politeness, but by what could be called the atmosphere there it seemed to give them a bright habit of interest in other people, or a good show of that.

When they was all sitting in Manse's 'den room' after the children came home from school Laurent seemed fascinated to hear she came from London. He remarked that in the past the river Thames, dividing London into north and south, would sometimes freeze so solid that banquets could take place on it. He wondered if Naomi thought that, owing to climate change, this might happen again. Matilda pointed out how some now believed London to be the fashion centre of the world, displacing Paris. Did Naomi, a Londoner herself, think this correct? Naomi replied she couldn't be certain on either of them points.

Then Laurent asked her whether she liked living in the capital with all its many undoubted facilities but some drawbacks such as overcrowding on the tube because of many foreign visitors wishing to see Buckingham Palace, the Houses of Parliament, Madame Tussaud's and so on, especially Americans and Japanese.

Matilda wanted to know whether Naomi enjoyed express travel by train, which, because of motorization and even electrification, had improved a great deal since the first railways of the nineteenth century, when an important politician was killed by a locomotive at the opening ceremony of a new service between Liverpool and Manchester.

'William Huskisson, 1830,' Naomi said.

Manse felt a real thrill listening to them. It seemed grand that Naomi not only fucked so brilliant, with true sweetness, eyes rolled right back and sincere, very thankful gasps, but also had terrific knowledge over considerable areas, yet didn't pretend she could answer every query they chucked at her in their welcoming style.

Chapter Seventeen

2009

Harpur thought he saw Iles begin to change. In any case, it was not a natural state for the ACC to agree with Andrew Rockmain on siege tactics. It was not a natural state for the ACC to agree with Rockmain on very much at all. Normally, Iles regarded him as one step up from grossest shysterdom, though, if the ACC felt generous for a moment, one and a half steps. He'd accepted Rockmain's analysis because this brought comfort. Now, the comfort seemed to fade.

Iles had never been a great one for comfort. On the whole, he preferred rage. Comfort could fuck up and water down rage. Naturally, Harpur had become a tireless expert on Iles's mood swings. He needed to be, in self-defence. 'I see myself as protean, Col,' Iles had said not long ago.

'This is a word with considerable promise, sir.'

'Meaning, capable of endless variety.'

'That's you to a T, sir. Or, because of the endless variety, you to a W or a J.'

'Protean from Proteus, a sea god in classical times, who could alter his shape as he wished.'

'Classical gods were so brilliant at that. One of my kids told me a god turned himself into a swan for a while – the whole thing, feathers, webbed feet, big wings, beak,' Harpur had said. 'Other gods wouldn't have recognized him – might have thrown him crusts.' Although Iles's

97

shape stayed more or less constant, he could alter his mind and disposition as he wished, and at flabbergasting pace.

Harpur wondered now whether the ACC would order an immediate attack on the shop. Harpur's own plan to try something solo might have to be speeded or shelved. They lacked an absolutely clear identification of the target, crucial in big team action, and this fretted Harpur. They knew from the officers who chased him on foot that he was middle height, slightly built, and probably between twenty-five and thirty-two years old with plentiful fair hair.

But there might be at least one other man in the shop. They had no description of *him*. Sergeant Pardoe *thought* he had glimpsed another male. Suppose this figure came close to the description of the wanted man – he could get shot by mistake in the rush and mêlée of an assault. The priority would be a quick kill to prevent 'John' turning on the hostages. But police could hit a hostage or hostages in error.

They had a couple of visitors in the command caravan. Harpur could see these men influenced Iles, especially the second. He influenced all of them, including Rockmain, but Iles above all. A sergeant had rung Harpur from the police cordon: 'We've a Mr Gary James Dodd here, sir, age thirty-seven. He thinks he might know the woman forced into the shop from the street: his live-in girlfriend. He heard about the siege from somebody listening to local radio. At first he didn't see a connection with her. She doesn't usually shop in this area. She'd normally go to the Esplanade Tesco. But then he tuned into the radio station himself. He realized the description of the clothes is right, and her estimated age. So, just to check, he tried to get her on her mobile but it's voice-mail only. He fears her phone's been taken from her. He believes the woman could be Veronica Susan Cleaver, age thirty-two.'

The sergeant brought him to the command caravan. Dodd wore a decent dark suit and blue and silver tie. He must have come direct from his office. He was tall, very thin, his face sharp, pushy.

Harpur said: 'We believe she and the others are all right, Mr Dodd. We have good contact with the man holding them.'

'Good? How can there be *good* contact with someone who drags a woman in off the street and threatens her with a gun?' Dodd said. Yes, the voice managerial, as well as his face. Harpur forgave. This lad was in shock.

'Tell us about Veronica,' Rockmain said.

'Who's in charge here?' Dodd replied.

'I am,' Iles said. 'Mr Rockmain is an adviser. Don't be put off by his clothes and the skinniness of his neck.'

'I can't understand the tactics,' Dodd said.

'Which aspects?' Iles said.

'This is someone half mad or worse, isn't it?' Dodd said. 'He's already killed two harmless people. Now he's got four more, and you do nothing.'

'Tell us about Veronica,' Rockmain replied.

'I'm sure it's she,' Dodd said.

'Always I thrill to neat grammar,' Iles said.

'We accept that it's Veronica. But tell us about her,' Rockmain said.

'We have to try to assess how people might behave in this kind of situation, Mr Dodd,' Iles said, 'the hostages and the gunman. Mr Rockmain is our designated Psychology wallah. He got a straight B for it at O level.'

'Veronica's not a well person,' Dodd said.

'In which respect?' Rockmain said.

'Clinical depression,' Dodd said.

'Under treatment?' Rockmain said.

'She has been,' Dodd said.

'Medication?' Rockmain said.

'Yes,' Dodd said.

'Monoamine adjustment?' Rockmain said.

'Successful, apparently,' Dodd said.

'Psychotherapy?' Rockmain said.

'For a while, yes,' Dodd said.

'Now?' Rockmain said.

'She seemed to be coming out of it,' Dodd said.

'Hospitalized at any time?' Rockmain said.

'She was,' Dodd said.

'How long?' Rockmain said.

'A couple of months,' Dodd said.

'Locked ward? Psychotic features?' Rockmain said.

Dodd said: 'Something like this, it could – If she breaks down again, panics, becomes a nuisance, becomes what he considers a nuisance and a danger . . .'

'We have to establish definite identity,' Harpur said. Always that.

'It's Veronica,' Dodd said. 'She should have been home by now. She didn't much like going out at all.'

'Symptomatic,' Rockmain replied.

'The loss of the phone – no communication with me or friends – will terrify her,' Dodd said. 'Everything that's happened will terrify her. She'll feel she's away from all support.'

'I don't like it,' Iles said.

There was the previous visitor, too. A couple of officers had been sent to find the husband of Mrs Beatrice South, manageress of the shop, and bring him back. Rockmain had said in a fine, comradely tone: 'Mr South, we are indebted to you for joining us. We have some general assessments of your wife's personality, but you will be able to tell us so much more. We understand she is of a strong and calm nature and is likely to cope well with the special circumstances she now finds herself in. Obviously, this is a considerable plus. She will be an example to the other people held with her.'

'Well, yes, Bea is usually pretty steady, but something like this – I don't know. She's never been in such a situation before,' South said. He would be touching sixty, stout, bald, round-faced, in jogging trousers and a navy sweater, plimsolls.

'We're grateful for her presence,' Rockmain replied. 'We call it calmness, but perhaps we should go beyond that – it is courage.'

'But you don't know that she *is* calm in there, do you?' South said.

'I've confidence in her,' Rockmain said.

'You make it sound like she's holding this situation together,' South said. 'But, really, it's you, the police who should be taking control, isn't it?' He spoke more softly than Dodd, was more deferential, but the message amounted to the same.

'We're working towards that,' Rockmain said, 'believe me. Perhaps you could give us some instances where your wife's calmness under pressure was apparent.'

'In our holiday chalet when the lights went, Bea was the one who looked for the trip switch and put things right.'

'Deciding it was the trip switch, then locating it, this is evidence of what we'd call a sequential thinker,' Rockmain replied. 'Excellent. In popular language – unflappability.'

'She and the others are imprisoned by a fucking unpredictable killer,' South replied.

'Unflappability,' Rockmain said. 'Such a gift!'

'Do you keep stand-by candles and matches in the chalet in case lights failure is nothing to do with the trip switch?' Iles said.

'I want her out of this shop,' South replied.

'I understand that,' Iles had said. And a little while after South left, Gary James Dodd arrived, to argue the same case, but with extra power, though no swearing.

Chapter Eighteen

2007

Naomi had been to the rectory now and met the children, but Mansel Shale still frequently played over in his head all the exciting and also tricky bits of that key second trip he made to London to see her a while back. Although he considered too much secrecy very bad between people fond of each other, Manse obviously didn't feel it convenient to tell Naomi he'd visited his solicitor, Joan Fenton, again to check over the Lowri, Patricia and Carmel legacies, and other details. Everything seemed tidy, and he signed the will, before going on to the restaurant meeting with Naomi.

Joan's secretary signed as witness. She was white and looked quite a warm piece as she stooped over the desk with a pink fountain pen in her fingers. Manse didn't see no rings on that hand nor the other. He thought it probably quite all right for Joan Fenton to have a white girl expected to jump when called by intercom – 'Come in, would you, Angelica?' – because Joan definitely knew law and its many wrinkles, most likely through a college and training, and therefore deserved the big job regardless of being black. Manse considered it quite interesting that Joan had a short and ordinary first name, but Angelica's was unusual. Joan didn't need any of that fancy help, owing to her prime qualifications, most probably after expensive courses which she passed with many a distinction. And again he thought he could feel centuries of family strength in Joan, most probably concerned with voodoo and the cure for snake-bite in them earlier days, but now updated into magnificent worship of the law, and a constant professional wish to fuck up attorneys on the other side.

Manse had realized even when he started out from home that this second get-together with Naomi would be very important, even maybe what could be referred to as life-changing. Nothing must muck it up. He could do with some life-changing. He would admit he had things pretty comfortable, but Manse saw himself as someone needing to be more than just comfortable. He wanted to feel devoted to a truly worthwhile home-sharer, and to have that devotion returned. Manse hadn't taken Hubert V.L. Camborne with him as bodyguard on the second trip, considering it unnecessary. This would not be like going into Hackney and having all them friends and relatives of the late Denz around him, and possibly problematical on account of the two pistols popping simultaneous in a throat direction. In any case, Shale didn't want Hubert to know too much. You could never tell how much these people talked, and who to.

Manse had discussed with Joan Fenton other points in the will, also, and heard about the divorce negotiations, meaning money. Ongoing: that was how them dealings had to be described. Manse decided it might be best not to mention the solicitor at all to Naomi. He could say he'd gone to a business conference, which in some ways it was: if he didn't have a business there wouldn't be no funds to leave in a will, would there?

As during the earlier time with Naomi, he believed it could sound like showing off to say he preferred a London lawyer to a local one. *Well, hark at him!* Manse despised flashiness. And if he told her he'd been to see the solicitor, Naomi would naturally expect him to explain something about it. She'd never ask, being too polite. But she'd wonder. He couldn't see no need to put such unhelpful questions into her mind at that stage. Later on, if matters went OK, there could be alterations. Well, of course. If they went *truly* OK, long-term OK, Naomi would get her own generous section in Manse's will, as Joan Fenton had suggested, no question – the only proper thing. Naomi would be taking on some peril by a full link-up with Manse and all the endless territorial shit, so she undoubtedly deserved a will spot, supposing she was the one left, which must be likely, but not certain.

Although they had gone to Naomi's flat in Ealing during what he thought of as the Pre-Raphaelite and Geoff occasion, he certainly did not know whether she would ask him there again. They had talked several times on the phone, of course, to make arrangements for this visit in a social sense, but nothing definite about Ealing was said, and he still took care not to behave like pressuring her. All right, she had seemed ready for it that first time, but you could never be totally sure with a woman, unless it actually happened, bringing equal enjoyment for each, this being vital and the real test of willingness. Obviously, coming should be hung on to and hung on to until he could tell from the rhythm and breathing and the tightening nails grip in the cheeks of his behind that the finish would be harmonious for both, like a good platform duet at a sing-along. He booked himself a single hotel room at his usual Park Lane place for the night, in case he needed a bed. He had an account at the hotel, so they wouldn't give a monkey's if he failed to show, because of Ealing. The charge would be on the bill at the end of the month, unused bed or not.

Manse wondered whether he ought to tell her he'd booked the room, so she wouldn't feel he came to London this time actually *expecting* to be tucked up with her at the flat, sort of partnerly, and banging her like totally entitled. That could seem so boastful and rude, even an insult, if he was reading her appetite wrong. Shale would hate Naomi to think he regarded most women as slappers. Although a number definitely went that way, this did not signify the lot did, for God's sake. Royalty used to give a wholesome example and the Queen especially, even when young. On the other hand, Manse mustn't let Naomi feel he didn't fancy her, or that he had trouble getting it up owing to some defect, temporary or for keeps, a condition that could hit any man even in this twenty-first century with its stiffy pills. Would she decide he was strange, cold and, so to speak, half cock if she heard about the hotel? On the whole, he felt he better leave this room unmentioned, unless it grew very plain she would not be inviting him, perhaps because she was afraid that asking him back twice really gave a fuck-me-do-I'm-gagging-for-it-Mansel message.

Of course, he realized that if it had been Ralph W. Ember in a situation with Naomi, instead of himself, Ralphy would not bother much about treating her with honest care and patience. This stupid, arrogant business associate of Manse in main trade back home thought he looked like the young Charlton Heston when he was Ben Hurring and El Cidding etcetera. And so he believed every woman of every age, education, race, religion and kink craved to satisfy him now, Now, NOW, NOW! – no need to waste time on chat, smarm and a show of genuine, simple respect for the female gender pre knickers-off.

Ember most probably thought that most he met didn't even *wear* knickers, in case they missed their chance with him while getting them down. Ralph Ember behaved non-stop like he had an iron duty to stuff any woman he considered OK, because she'd be longing for him so bad, the way troops wounded in no man's land during the Great War longed for stretcher bearers. Manse felt true disgust at Ember's attitude, and knew he couldn't share it, didn't wish to share it. In fact, this attitude reminded Manse of certain animals, which shouldn't be blamed, because nature made them like that, so the breed would continue. For them it was fuck and get fucked or die out, such as the dinosaurs. But human beings ought to go more gradual at first. Manse believed in delicacy.

105

When the secretary had left, Joan Fenton said she thought she could conclude the settlement soon with Sybil at £38,320. The will didn't vary the payments to Carmel, Patricia and Lowri: kept them all on a thirtieth share, as suggested earlier. Joan had decided it might start what she called costly 'envy actions' if there were differences. Manse agreed with this. He couldn't of picked one as deserving extra, anyway. They'd all been very positive and cheery, but never rowdy or careless with breakables, real pluses at the rectory, and clean. Manse would hate to think of these three bitter and squabbling because the will paragraphs dealing with them was skew-whiff. If one or more pre-deceased, their cut would go back into the general pot, not to the girl or girls still alive. It would seem wrong for one or two of them to profit on their own from a previous death.

'Should there be something kindly in the will for Syb?' Manse said. 'Not big, but, like a gesture?'

'What type of gesture?'

'Sort of to say that not all our time together was bad. You know, "Let bygones" and such.'

'*You*'ll be a bygone by then. That's enough bygones. The only gesture we give that high-energy, peripatetic slag is the finger,' Joan Fenton replied. 'She smashed the marriage. But the £38,320 is, in fact, a gesture, and more than a gesture. She'll have absolutely no cause to dispute the will. She buggers off to North Wales with a vet but still gets a sweet little package of notes. I might get it to £38,275.'

This seemed to be all Joan Fenton thought of: disputes, and how to win them or dodge them. For her, it seemed to Manse, life – and death – was just an eternal war, all to do with enemies and people trying it on, and grab-alls, if they *could* grab-all, or grab a nice chunk, anyway. Maybe this was how lawyers had to be, especially at the top in London. If you hired one, you let them run things.

Manse didn't mind her glasses at all. In any case, they were not structural like big ears or a snout nose, and could come off easy enough in a passion merge. She had a longish face, but nothing bony, nothing pointed, and lovely smooth skin of her special category. He could imagine this face under him, no glasses, still longish and unbony, not pointy, but also lit up by delight as unhurried intimacy took place in some excellent surroundings, such as a room with bare stone walls where tapestries hung showing knights, flags, minstrels and rivers, that sort of scene. There might be a low table in the room where decanters stood grouped containing very dark red Madeira and Marsala wines.

'What are the prospects, as you see them, Mansel?' she said.

'In which area?'

'Marital. Business.' She said it like this was very obvious. 'For my guidance. We need a strategy. Take business first. Do you see haulage and scrap proceeding in profitable style, notwithstanding occasional reverses? You have a good, steady continuing customer base, do you? Are you buoyant in that respect?'

'Our market is stable. I like to think of the people we deal with as friends rather than customers.'

'Though they *are* customers, and plentiful? Growing in number? There'll always be twice as many nostrils as people, won't there? This is a happy statistic. You weather the steep ups and downs in wholesale prices all right?'

'I believe we can reasonably claim to offer a fine service,' Shale replied.

'Suppliers reliable? They've got the fix in OK back in their own countries?'

'I'm very particular about good personal relationships. It's commerce, yes, but this does not mean the human touch must be absent, I hope. Remember the Cadbury family and their thoughtfulness towards the masses, as well as the money-making choc factories. But then the company was sold and things changed.'

'And no trouble from the authorities here?' she said.

'The authorities?'

'Yes, you know, Manse, the authorities. They sometimes tell us of great coups they've brought off at airports or on the coast, the street value millions, billions, people banged up.'

'Coups?'

'Interceptions.'

'Interceptions of what?'

'Yes, that's it, interceptions,' she said.

'Why would the company have trouble from the authorities? Oh, Health and Safety, d'you mean? Some mock – call it "Elf and Safety". But I consider they have a worthwhile task. Absolutely. People's well-being. We're always very careful. Many notices around the walls: "Hard hats must be worn at all times." That kind of thing.'

'Brilliant,' she replied. 'And as to marital?'

'I'm still at the stage of getting used to the break from Sybil. I don't know whether *you've* ever gone through divorce, Joan – I mean personally, not just handling cases.'

'Carmel, Patricia and Lowri are, or have been, of wonderful assistance in this, I imagine,' she replied.

'Unparalleled.'

'Except by one another. And the possibility of something more established soon? I don't necessarily mean with any of those, rather a different type of acquaintanceship – potentially more lengthy. It's not my wish to pry, but we need to have in mind the smart readjustments that might be required then. This is the essence of good legal practice – anticipation.'

'You're talking pipe dreams, I'm afraid.'

'They can be quite comforting. Does anybody special figure in them?'

'And the way the children are taken care of in the will seems to me intelligent and completely watertight,' Manse replied.

'This vet with Sybil.'

'Yes, a vet. Or under-manager in a fruit machine arcade. Something like that.'

'Might he be awkward?'

'In what manner?'

'They can be devious. I've had vets in some damned snotty cases. They're used to helping cows give birth, so they fancy themselves as life-creators, and expect to be paid as such. They want to be called "veterinary surgeons" at all times, not merely "vets". Will he persuade her to contest your will?'

'Well, they won't know about it.'

'I mean when . . . I mean if the will is activated. A will becomes a public document then. But perhaps Syb wouldn't need persuading. She sounds like a ton of rancorous bother in her own fucking egomaniac right.'

'Activated? Activated how?'

'Yes,' she said. 'That's in the nature of wills eventually, or sometimes sooner than eventually. What we need to provide for, also, Mansel, is a situation where you do, ultimately, meet someone suitable – suitable in the sense of remarriage or, at least, quasi permanent or genuinely permanent shacking up in the rectory, not just weeks or months, but established on a continuous basis, known to and respected by neighbours, a familiar sight bringing out recycling waste bags, mail delivered there with her name on it preceded most probably by "Ms". And, thus, another person's financial state becomes relevant and the disposition of *her* assets by last testament likewise relevant. I would hope that in those circs you'd recommend Crossman, Fenton and Stuckey handle both wills, hers and yours. We have to make their separate provisions complementary, as far as we can, for the sake of Matilda and Laurent. Separate yet integrated.'

Manse always grew edgy and suspicious if someone said 'thus'. It seemed to mean you had to let their argument win because the logic of it was so obvious and perfect. He himself would never use 'thus'. He did not

109

accept things could ever be as clear as 'thus' seemed to make them.

'Any woman you take into the family at this stage in your life, and, most probably hers, is almost sure to have a previous connection, or connections, and this or these might influence her money status and property status,' Joan Fenton said. 'I can't see you choosing for the long haul some bimbo, all tit, bum, labia-piercing and lip-gloss, who'd have little or no mazuma or real estate behind her. That would hardly be the Mansel Shale I've come to know and understand. The Mansel Shale I've come to know and understand has discrimination, depth, seriousness, horizons.

'Oh, obviously, we've discussed Carmel, Patricia and Lowri. And, as to labia-piercing, I noticed how you inventoried Angelica and the way she bottom-presented when bent over the desk, jerking off that fleshy-looking fountain pen – a regular performance from her if there's a bloke under eighty-five in the room. Your trouser-stirring relief mechanisms are absolutely forgivable during this interim spell with no steady companion post Sybil, indeed routine and to be expected. But we have to cater for something much more substantial, durable, meaningful, haven't we? Man cannot live by dong alone.'

'I don't know whether he's a farmyard vet or just someone with an office in the town where people bring their treasured cats,' Shale replied. 'There might not be much money in that. This could be somewhere like Bangor even. People in these places won't go in for big outlay on pets.'

'I suppose she sees Laurent and Matilda sometimes. They visit her new household, do they? Have they ever said this is a dump, poor-looking, in need of subsidy? Have you been there yourself?'

'We use a service station for the children hand-over. I'm thinking that if the vet game is tottering sometime in the future a boost from the will might be so useful for Syb.'

'If the vet game is tottering, too sodding bad. She shouldn't have picked him instead of you and the haulage and scrap as it were, should she? Anyway, Mansel, she could well go before you if she's living in Bangor. Or, suppose next year, the year after, she hears you're thinking of getting remarried. She might come back and try to mess things up. They can be like that.'

'Who?'

'Flit-about women. Divorce aftermaths will sometimes feature very uncharming, destructive behaviour.'

'Joan, have you yourself ever –?'

'You need to be alert for it. They can ruin the church service or the reception, screaming and cursing, pulling faces, flinging solids, that kind of bitch-in-the-manger carry-on. And, talking of wills and when they come into their own, are you still moving around without protection? Casual can lead to casualty, Mansel. I hear there are constant turf troubles in the haulage and scrap industry, sometimes leading to violence. Minders are chargeable against tax, you know, and you do pay tax on the haulage and scrap income, don't you? The employment title for bodyguards recognized by the Revenue is "Licensed Ambient Security Advisers", LASAs. Prod your accountant.'

Chapter Nineteen

2009

In the siege command vehicle, Iles said: 'Do you know what I see when I look at you, Harpur?'

'This is quite a tricky one, sir.'

'In which respect?'

'Oh, yes, a tricky one, sir. It would mean I have to become you on a temporary basis in order to look at me, as I appear to you. But we have to ask, can this be valid because I wouldn't be fully me on account of having to become you so that I can look at me as you might, which could be different from the way I'd look at myself, if I wasn't trying to be you temporarily.'

'What I have a lot of, Col, is instincts,' Iles replied.

'Many have spoken to me of this. They'll say something along the lines of, "That Mr Iles – such instincts." Quite often, they mean it well.'

'It's something I was born with, Harpur. Some babies get a club foot, I got instinct. My mother used to cry out now and then after an observation I'd made as a child of six or seven about forthcoming nutrition problems abroad, or the possibility of washing-day rain, "Desmond, your instincts approach the magical!" Apparently, I would just smile slightly and give a small nod. This would signify that, owing to exceptionally advanced self-knowledge, I was aware of my instincts but did not wish to grow vain about them. Typical.'

'Guess what I wish, sir.'

'Tell me, Col.'

'I wish I could have been there when she cried out like that, and to watch your response – the smile and the nod. This is a real family tableau of considerable distinction. What about your father, sir? Did he endorse what his wife said? Fathers can be damned envious of their sons and offer only sour comments. What did he feel about your instincts? On the whole, I think mothers are a plus. They unquestionably have a true role in life. Think of Judy Garland and her daughter, Liza Minnelli.'

Iles said: 'My instincts range remarkably, and can be opinion-forming.'

'Many would agree that as an Assistant Chief and, at present, Gold, you're entitled to have quite a few points of view.'

'*How* many would agree this?'

'Oh, yes, many.'

'What about the others?'

'There's room for various shades of opinion in a democracy.'

'Bollocks,' Iles said. 'All right, listen: I'll tell you what I see when I look at you, Col. The instincts I've mentioned tell me you're someone who believes he ought to saunter solo into this siege-episode charity shop and put everything right by his unaided, undaunted, unsupported, egomaniac, witless intervention, while the rest of us wait here like dismal, fait néant twats, i.e. do-nothing twats.'

'Few would regard *you*, in an individual sense, as a fait néant twat, sir. I'm almost sure of that.'

'Which few?'

'Extremely few.'

'Would they regard me as both parts of it or only one?'

'Sir?'

'A fait néant *and* a twat, or *or* a twat.'

'It might be worth asking around on this. People can be very sympathetic.'

'If you try one of your fucking famed single-handed acts of gung-ho gallantry here, Harpur, you could cause destruction to God knows how many lives, including your own,' Iles said. 'You wouldn't want to leave your two daughters, Hazel, Jill, orphaned in that creepy dump of a place, 126 Arthur Street. How will they feel having to explain to their school chums that their dad was arsehole enough to get shot in a bloody charity shop? Not the Battle of Stalingrad, is it? Don't humiliate them, Col. This is a place with racks of clothes at least as shagged-out and quaint as the stuff you wear, and old videos of films like *Terminator 2* and *The Secret Adventures of Tom Thumb*. Then again, that undergraduate, Denise, who comforts you most nights in term time at least, would feel the loss for anything up to forty-eight hours if you got killed.'

Andrew Rockmain said, semi-snarled: 'Obviously, there are to be no single-handed operations here. None.' He was sitting at one of the three screen monitors in the caravan, looking flimsy but authoritative. Iles had helped design the command caravan. Anchored metal-framed office chairs stood in front of the screens. Communications equipment occupied part of one wall, with another fixed office chair near for the negotiator. Some siege experts specified that the negotiator should be housed entirely separately, so as not to be affected by, or to affect, the operational work. But Rockmain wanted the main participants together. He obviously thought he spanned both functions, the negotiations and the crisis management, and required them all to be within reach of his advice and influence.

A safe contained four Walther handguns. The combination changed weekly and was given only to Gold. The caravan had a sink unit, Calor gas stove, first aid cabinet, and a fold-away, leather-covered couch for either between-watch sleeping, or laying out someone injured. A control panel could switch one or both of the roof-mounted search-lights to automatic sweep or home-in focus.

114

Iles and Harpur were on their feet, watching the charity shop through the big side window of the caravan. Gary James Dodd had remained in the command vehicle with them and sat on a padded wall-bench not far from Rockmain. Dodd picked up one of Rockmain's words: 'So some operations are banned. OK. But are there going to be *any* operations at all? What's this damned inane talk between yourselves and with him in the shop?'

'Are you one of that few?' Iles said

'Which few?' Dodd said.

'The few who do regard me as a fait néant twat,' Iles said.

'This *is* an operation,' Rockmain said. 'The waiting, the patience, the daft babble – they are integral. The talk fills the time, you see.'

'And are you calling little Andy Rockmain a fait néant twat as well, Mr Dodd?' Iles said.

'Let me speak to him,' Dodd replied. 'To John, as you call him, inside the shop.'

Rockmain turned away from his screen and towards Dodd. He said: 'It's possible. I've known something like that happen in other sieges.'

'Mr Rockmain is quite a one for sieges,' Iles said.

'My partner is in there with someone armed and unstable,' Dodd said. 'Please, let's do something.'

'But we don't know as fact that she *is* in there, do we?' Rockmain said. 'We've no definite identification. You've given me an analysis of her mental condition, but it's only relevant if the woman pulled in from the street is, indeed, Veronica Susan Cleaver. Why would she be in the, as it were, "wrong" part of the city for her shopping today?'

'If I talked to him I might be able to confirm it's Veronica. Perhaps he'll even let her speak to me,' Dodd said.

'Yes, I've known something like that happen, too, in sieges,' Rockmain said. 'But it's usually much later on, when the hostage-taker is weakening and needs something he believes will boost his chances. He calculates that a loving, sorrowful conversation will dramatize the plight of the people being held and lead to concessions by the siege master. It's like the way Middle Eastern kidnappers get pictures and statements from their prisoners on to television. The sentiment card. Pressure.'

'We've no contact at present,' the negotiator said.

'And such a conversation gives the hostage taking part in it a context, as it were, fleshes out her or him,' Rockmain said. 'She or he becomes more than a hostage. He or she acquires a background – social, familial, sexual. It is there, enacted before the hostage-taker. It may help reach his human feelings.'

Iles said: 'You mean that until this phone chat he imagined the people he's holding had had no personal lives but hung about solitary, waiting for the chance to start a hostage career, like tadpoles destined to be frogs?'

'Mr Iles can be relaxed whatever the situation, and no matter how many lives are at risk,' Rockmain said with a fine chuckle. 'It's what the Italians call *sprezzatura*, I believe, and the French *sang-froid*. He'd do brilliantly in Interpol. Such a waste to have him cooped up here, yet at the same time a boon to all present, naturally.'

'Can't we renew contact?' Dodd said.

'He doesn't reply. We have to wait for him to call us,' the negotiator said.

'Tell me how you'd run it, Mr Dodd,' Rockmain said.

'Run it?'

'The conversation. With him first, if he wants it, then possibly with her.'

'Well, it's obvious, isn't it?' Dodd said.

'I'm asking you to tell me how you'd run it, so it isn't obvious, is it, or I wouldn't ask you,' Rockmain replied. He said it softly, gently, the voice of conciliation, although the message was, 'Watch your fucking step with me, Doddy.' Harpur thought Rockmain achieved a brand of miniature dignity. He might not be playing this situation right, but he behaved as if he was and as if he knew as a total certainty he was. This would be what had got him up to Commander in the Met, despite his quaintness.

'I'd tell him I believe one of the hostages might be my girlfriend, my partner,' Dodd said, 'and that I cared for her very dearly.'

'No. We don't use the word "hostage",' Rockmain replied. 'It can be an antagonizing word, you see, Mr Dodd. It presumes a crisis.'

'But it *is* a crisis,' Dodd said.

'We do not confirm that categorization to him. In crises, people can react impulsively, ungovernably, destructively,' Rockmain said.

'That's what I fear,' Dodd said.

'It's what you fear but not what you let him know you fear,' Rockmain replied. 'If you let him know you fear it he will be forced to recognize he is in a totally duff position and that you and the rest of us are afraid this realization will push him to . . . to act out of despair.'

'To shoot the hostages and possibly himself, you mean?' Dodd said.

'To act out of despair,' Rockmain said. 'You probably know, Mr Dodd, that despair is considered by Christian thinkers to be the unforgivable sin. That's because it denies the power of God to save. We are not God, though Mr Iles is Gold, but we do not want John in there to feel we regard him only as a target in our eventual assault. So, when we refer to the hostages, when the negotiator refers to the hostages, we use a blander, less definitive phrase, such as "the people with you", or "the members of the public involuntarily involved in this stand-off".'

Dodd said, 'Right, so I'd ask whether one of the people with him was –'

'That's the way,' Rockmain said, with a lovely smile of congratulation. 'Possibly, he will not know the names of the hostages. Their names are, in a sense, irrelevant. A hostage is a hostage is a hostage.'

117

'Or, The people with you, The people with you, The people with you,' Iles said. 'Alternatively, The members of the public involuntarily involved in this stand-off, The members of the public involuntarily involved in this stand-off, The members of the public involuntarily involved in this stand-off.'

'But perhaps he'll ask the people with him,' Dodd said, 'ask if the woman is one of them.'

'He might,' Rockmain said. 'We have to be ready, in fact, for six contingencies. One, he refuses to talk to you. Two, he refuses to ask the hostage for her name. Three, he asks, or purports to ask, but says nobody of that name is there. Four, he says, "Yes, there is someone of that name." Five, he refuses to let her speak. Six, he allows her to speak. Shall we take them in order? One, he refuses to talk to you.'

'But why should he refuse?'

'What's in it for him? He thinks only about retaining his power. To block your requests is power. To agree to One or Two he might feel is compliant, a step towards weakness.'

'So what do I do?' Dodd said. 'Entreat? Plead?'

'Not either of these. We don't want to endorse or increase his sense of sovereignty. That could prolong things – make him less tractable, at least for a while.'

'So what do I do?' Dodd said.

'Repeat the request.'

'And if he still refuses?' Dodd asked.

'Abandon it,' Rockmain said.

'But, my God, I – we – are left in ignorance,' Dodd said.

'We are left as we were before you asked,' Rockmain said.

'In ignorance,' Dodd said.

'Not in ignorance,' Rockmain said. 'We have learned he is still defiant and a call on his compassion is not the way to look for progress.'

'Which *is* the way?' Dodd said.

Harpur's mobile phone sounded and he went outside the command caravan to deal with the call, and not interrupt Rockmain's delicate briefing of Dodd. The Control Room put through Adrian Morrison Overdale, aged forty, of 7B Cortilda Square, chartered surveyor. 'He thinks he might know the woman abducted off the street,' the Control Room inspector said.

'We already have a possible name for her,' Harpur said, 'Veronica Susan Cleaver.'

'Yes, that's right. It's the name Overdale gives us. It sounds as though he's in some sort of relationship with her. Do we know her background? He's very emotional, sir.'

'Cortilda Square is just around the corner from the charity shop, isn't it?' Harpur replied.

'It's one reason he thinks the woman might be her,' the inspector said. 'Plus the description, of course. He was waiting for her at his flat. I'll transfer him to you now.'

Harpur said: 'Mr Overdale? I gather you might have some information for us.'

'This is terrible, terrible,' Overdale said.

'You believe you know one of the hostages?'

'Oh, hell, it's Veronica, isn't it, Veronica Cleaver? But, if it's not, please, please tell me, tell me if it's not. I'm so worried for her. Is it, is it, Veronica?'

'You think this woman, held with others in the charity shop, was coming to see you in Cortilda Square and is Veronica Susan Cleaver?' Harpur replied.

'Terrible, terrible.'

Chapter Twenty

2007

What really astonished Manse was that it seemed so natural after his restaurant lunch with Naomi for them to go back to Ealing together. All the worries he'd had about how things would turn out looked so unnecessary now in her bed, so stupidly fearful. It was a king-size, which probably meant she'd bought it with her partner way back, so as to get plenty of space, but also intimacy when required, but Manse did not mind this. No bleeding point in minding it: the past was only the past and you could not hope to govern it, or wipe it out, or chip inconvenient bits off of it. What had happened had happened. Even if it happened a lot, Manse wouldn't get in a sweat about that now. He didn't expect this to be the first time she'd found out about sex. She had been entitled to pre-Manse love. Well, think of him and Syb. You had to be reasonable about these things, and he would really try.

Manse realized as they drank their coffees and brandies at the end of the meal that she regarded this as only the start of their day, perhaps leading into tomorrow and other days and nights. He saw she knew about relationships and could tell just which point they had reached. She would be certain they should go forward now, or the present thin link might come apart. It was thin because so new and recent, not because of poor feelings. Manse agreed there must be progress. He recognized a true understanding between them, something precious to him.

She had told him she knew the restaurant from when she half owned that magazine – what she called a weekly London 'celebrity sheet' – and some top staff used to eat here and entertain people who might figure in the paper, as well as advertising and press relations executives. Naomi said they'd probably see some colleagues here today. It bucked Manse up a lot to think she wouldn't mind being spotted there with him. He felt glad he had put on his custom-made Tirrel and Clay single-breasted, light grey whistle. People in this sort of eatery would spot at once if a suit came from the reach-me-down rail in Marks and Spencer. Naomi did wave to a couple of women at one of the tables, thirties, wearing pricey business gear, in what seemed like big office talk together. Naomi said that as a matter of fact she'd sold her share of the magazine not long ago but stayed as a consultant.

At her flat later on, she had begun to undress herself but then seemed to sense he wanted to do that for her and took a few quick, happy steps towards him, rebuttoning the ones she'd started with. If you'd met someone in a gallery where, it didn't really need to be said, everyone kept their clothes on and examined the art, it would show a true change of things if, in another location, you could strip that person to her skin and get no fight back, the opposite. Manse didn't mess up on this. He knew about zips and clips and buttons. Even though he felt big excitement and got hit by some small shakes he could still be deft. Then, *she* took *his* clothes off and when he lifted his arms pulled the singlet up over his head in one strong, easy tug, like his body had been greased. This was maturity, he thought. This was high desire.

The singlet had not been cheap and flimsy and fitted him real snug, but Naomi didn't let this trouble her at all. As well as her general skill with relationships, she clearly knew singlets. Again, this showed something about the past and the man or men she'd been close enough to to pull off their singlets in these kinds of private, run-up conditions. She did not try to hide that flair, and Manse admired her honesty. He decided he would never nag about her knack with singlets and ask about the stories behind it.

In bed she lay on her back and bent her arms into sideways Vs on each side of her head like wings, a sort of surrender position. But that did not mean it was a mock rape. No, he believed she wanted to say to him, 'You deserve me, Manse, you deserve it, Manse, and I deserve you, Manse, I deserve it, Manse.' He felt a brilliant harmony existed. Shale knew if dicks could sing his would of now. The whole day, from the beginning of the lunch, had been like this – the harmony – and he hoped all days from now on would be like it. Even though she'd been dressed then, he had guessed in those first few minutes at the Pre-Raphaelite gallery that it would be great and meaningful to bang her, and he'd been so right. He was not always right about women in this aspect, besides which, some of them, although he thought it would be meaningful and great to bang them, didn't let him anywhere near, and might even give him a foul earful if he kept on scheming for it, so there'd be no possibility.

Naomi seemed wonderfully different from these. She would put her arms up like that at the beginning, but, then, when things was really getting some pace going, she'd bring them down to hold him across his back, pulling him hard to her, flattening out for these excellent minutes her perky breasts under his weight. He could tell she didn't resent this. Soon, they would plump up again, to proper tit shape, the nipples bonny, uncrushed and nibbleable. Sometimes he would put his own hands in hers when she had these up alongside her head. This seemed to complete the join of her and him, like fusing. Their fingers meshed in such a perfect style that Manse knew – yes, *knew* – things would be long-term fine between them. Fingers were more than fingers once it came to something like this. Fingers could speak a bond. He craved bonds with her.

What he didn't want was for this lovely closeness to be only money calling to money – her money from selling her share in the celebrity paper, his money from the firms. He knew that some relationships *were* mainly money calling to money, and he would not deny money did matter. But not the main thing. To Manse that would seem sick and doomed, like them Hollywood weddings, or the upper classes.

When she shifted her hands to grip him across the back, he'd get his own hands down to lock around her waist, helping to maximize his depth into her. She had her eyes open and smiled all the while. He preferred this to when a woman went blank-faced, eyes closed, concentrating on her personal come or multi-comes, although Manse recognized women certainly had their needs, which should not be sneezed at. But he considered there ought to be happy communication at all levels, face and lower.

He thought: so this is how a celebrity sheet consultant looks when she delightedly opens her legs in Ealing for someone met at a Pre-Raphaelite gallery. And, to be unbiased, he imagined *she* might be thinking, so this is how a haulage and scrap merchant looks when he's giving it, in a very considerate and genuine way, to someone whose kisses probably taste of a great lunch with wine and brandy she's just swallowed. Because of the celebrity sheet, Naomi most likely had plenty of words Shale would never use, though he might know their meaning. He had noticed the word 'diligent' lately somewhere and liked it, the quiet, very unbrassy sound. He'd looked up 'diligent' and found, as he'd thought, it meant 'thorough' and 'persevering'. He hoped Naomi would consider him diligent when at it, as well as considerate and genuine and, of course, passionate.

Manse believed it was these kinds of possible discoveries about the other person in a sex situation that made the first fuck with anyone so important – sort of sacred. It answered certain interesting questions. Later fucks might answer extra questions but the first one was bound to be the most definite eye-opener, as you might call it, even if some preferred to have their eyes shut for this eye-opener. Naomi's eyes were green and her pupils would roll back during the strong shove-up movements of middle and late-stage love-making leaving only the whites. The green section disappeared. She might of been having a fit or even croaking from the joy of it, and this scared him early on.

But no. It was like the pupils had done a climb into Naomi's head to check her brain would be OK subsequent, because, at present, she was getting fucked brainless, and very nice, too, though he'd admit she had to think there'd be ordinary life afterwards, when she might need her brain as consultant on a celebrity sheet, deciding who should go on page one and the size of the picture, plus spelling the names right, many being foreign.

If some time ahead he revisited Joan Fenton to get Naomi put into the will, it would prove he did not need any longer to have horny thoughts about Joan herself, nor the juicy, arse-proud, pink-penned secretary, Angelica. Although Naomi's arse was older, there had been no great drift of the cheeks towards north-south lozenge-shape, and no galloping spread east and west. Her behind was still very neat in tightish jeans, like she had been wearing that first day in the gallery, and which had started Manse thinking. And naked today it continued to look prime, in his opinion. No question, jeans that hugged a good bum caught beautiful its ripe, jolly spirit. But these days jeans was also cut to put a fierce focus on the crotch, and sometimes this took most attention, like a destination sign on the motorway. Shale regarded this as extremely unfair to the good female arse. He had often considered writing a protest letter to one of the fashion magazines about it, such as *Vogue*, using a false name.

Naomi hadn't worn jeans to the restaurant but a long, striped skirt in blue and white with a zip on the side, and

124

a four-buttoned white silk blouse. This blouse remained completely unstained by food during the meal, despite everything. The place was not starchy or formal or anything like that – more a cheery media flavour – but jeans would not of been right, he agreed with her on this. As far as Manse could make out, the celebrity sheet reported which eminent folk was in London this or next week, and what they would be doing. 'Acres of lovely puffery surrounded by ads,' she said. He didn't know for sure what this meant, but thought it might be a joke and had a smile. Although she had sold her share of the business she still worked two days for it now and then in that consultancy role. The firm kept an account at the restaurant and she and Manse were eating on it, she said. 'No attempts to pay, please.' She had decided to do nothing much for a year, 'just look around'. He hoped she'd been looking around when she saw Manse in the gallery and considered him all right, especially after the Geoff matter.

Manse had loved the restaurant. It seemed so . . . well, so *positive* – the atmosphere and the furniture and the layout – yes, so positive, that even if he had been thinking of telling her about the earlier conference with Joan Fenton he would of changed his mind and stayed shtum on that topic. He decided such a discussion would be all wrong here: too weighty and historical and complicated. Besides, legal talk might remind Manse of them moments when he imagined the shared joy of having it off with Joan Fenton, her glasses put aside. It was not the type of flashback he'd want while taking a meal in this very worthwhile restaurant with another woman altogether, who did not wear glasses, namely Naomi. That would be quite untoward, in his opinion.

Manse prized decorum. He wanted as much of it as could be reasonably got. As a matter of fact, he felt pleased that he had never mentioned Naomi to Joan Fenton, despite some prying. They were very much from two different compartments. He would hate to have Naomi tainted by his dreams of making it with the lawyer – not because the lawyer was black – that would be racist and totally bad – but because she was not Naomi. This restaurant and Naomi seated opposite him struck Manse as exactly the sort of setting he'd been made for. The Tirrel and Clay suit he had on seemed totally correct for a visit to the solicitor and then for this type of restaurant. A double-breasted would of been too uptight. Manse meant to guard the delightful charm of the luncheon. This hadn't been because, if the meal went OK, he might get another invitation to Ealing. The lunch itself seemed an occasion worth taking the very best care of.

Although Manse liked restaurants, and especially this one in Dean Street, he didn't care much about food or wine. But he *was* keen on menus, printed or handwritten, in the better sort of places, where they put a country or region near the names of some of the items, such as 'Highlands of Scotland salmon', 'Royal Berkshire beef', or 'Welsh coast cockles'. This helped give special scope to a list of dishes, he thought. Just to say 'salmon', or 'beef', or 'cockles' struck Manse as rather crude, a belly thing and that was all. But when you had the geography, you could imagine a brave and handsome Scottish salmon doing its terrific time-and-again leaps up them specially made stone steps in a river, determined to get itself or its offspring to the kitchen here eventually. You could listen to the Berkshire cattle having a low, and spot the Welsh cockles lying under a golden surface of sand, washed time and again by tides until dug out and collected one day for boiling up.

Naomi had seemed to get at her food very well indeed and, of course, Manse made himself match her. He would hate to look picky and unhearty. Manse reckoned that if you was being fed as a treat you had a true duty to clear the fucking lot. She could chat on no trouble, even when eating awkward mixtures such as goat's cheese salad as prepared in Turin and then 'West Country liver, bacon and onions'. He didn't know why, but he had an idea the piece of West Country would be Shepton Mallet. Most probably, she was used to not letting lunch get in the way of conversation. It must be one of them skills of a consultant.

Manse and Naomi talked about many subjects, not just art. He thought that would be too narrow and boring. If she had asked him about the haulage and scrap trade he would of told her, and some of it completely true, but she didn't. It wasn't the kind of area for this sort of restaurant, with its celebrities and executives. Although Manse knew he definitely would not rate as a celebrity himself, he *was* an executive of the haulage and scrap firm and the other bigger commercial enterprise. However, he'd admit these would not be the proper *kind* of executive posts for such a restaurant. Tone. Manse had always been very particular about the right tone for a place and for people. It didn't seem to worry Naomi whether he was an executive or not.

They had one more brandy. And then she'd said: 'Shall we go now, Manse?' He could tell at once that this was not a question but a blessed let's-do-it signal. She put her initials on the bill, no big deal flourish, just a quick jot of the two letters, N.G. He thought some folk in the restaurant who knew her job might wonder if he *was* a celebrity giving an interview during the meal, but one they couldn't quite recognize. TV actors had to wear wigs or sunglasses or, in old-type plays, plastic warrior helmets that hid most of their face, and perhaps they'd look quite different having lunch here in a Tirrel and Clay single-breasted.

Chapter Twenty-One

The negotiator's phone rang as Harpur came back into the command caravan after talking to Adrian Morrison Overdale. 'Hello, John, how are things with you now, then?' the negotiator said. Harpur thought the greeting, regreeting, fizzed with emptiness and formula. Naturally it did. It came from the manual – *Besieging for Dummies*, or something like. And, just as naturally, this boy, this boy 'John' in there could recognize smooth-textured bullshit. Very likely these calls would contain nothing but. In fact, perhaps ultimately there'd be so much he would get disorientated by it, half smothered by it, gently and mercilessly chinwagged into collapse and surrender by it. But, maybe he recognized this hazard and left the phone dead for spells while he got his breath back.

Now he spoke, though. 'Things are fine, Olly. As they were. But thanks so much for asking.' The phone was on to Conference, so everyone could hear him.

'"Fine. As they were." Good,' the negotiator said.

'How come you repeat everything?'

'You ask, why do I repeat everything?'

'Why do you repeat it when I ask why do you repeat it? That's not a conversation, it's an echo. Is it to give you time to think, or to lull, or annoy, or what?'

'To show clearly, "Message received and understood," John, and that the message is respected, word by

128

acknowledged word. To show we're pleased things are fine and as they were. I'm glad you called. We're going to have to talk food and drink soon. Can we make some arrangements for bringing you, and those with you, food and drink?'

'We're all right.'

'Are you *all* all right, John?'

'Yes, we're all all right.'

'We're happy you're all all right, John.'

'I can feel the glow of your happiness from here.'

'You're satirical, but I assure you, John, what I say is true. We want you to be all right, and those with you.'

'Especially those with me.'

'There's someone particular who'd like to speak to you,' the negotiator replied.

'Police? I mean, higher police than you?'

'No. Not police. But special, John.'

'Not a priest, or some other sort of holy Joe?'

'No, not a priest or some other sort of holy Joe. That's not our area.'

'What *is* your area?'

'What we have here is someone who thinks he might know one of the people with you. That is, the lady who was not already in the shop, but walking by at the time of your arrival there.'

'The one I grabbed?'

'The one who was walking by at the time of your arrival there.'

'Why didn't you repeat "the one I grabbed", like you repeat everything else? Are you scared of "grabbed"?'

'The one you grabbed, then. Our visitor thinks he might know the one you grabbed. Have you got a name for the one you grabbed?'

'I haven't got a name for any of them. Why should I?'

'Why should you? Yes.'

'"Yes." Always you agree with me, don't you, Olly? "Repeat what he says, agree with what he says." This is

129

how you were taught on the negotiator course, is it? What's the objective? Keep me sweet and harmless – until you decide not to, and come storming, a battalion of you?'

'"Come storming"? That's the last thing we want, believe me, John.'

'I do believe you, Olly. It's last, and very dicey all round, but it's on the list, isn't it?'

'I would have thought you'd know the names, at least the first names, in case you wanted to give different instructions to one or other of the people in there with you.'

'You'd have thought that, would you?'

'That's what I would have thought.'

'They all get the same instructions. It's "Do what I tell you or . . ."'

'Will you ask whether one of the people with you is called Veronica Susan Cleaver, aged thirty-two? Veronica Susan Cleaver, thirty-two.'

'This would be the one I grabbed, would it?'

'Yes, the one you grabbed.'

'Is she special, then?'

'"Is she special?" I expect all the people in there with you are special to someone, John.'

'Touching, Olly.'

'It's true, though. All the people in there with you must be special to someone, or special to more than one, John.'

'Well, I certainly fucking hope so.'

'You "hope so"?'

'I *fucking* hope so.'

'I don't follow.'

'Hostages wouldn't be much use if nobody cared about them, would they, Olly? If nobody cared about them they wouldn't count in any deals, would they, because who'd bother whether they were alive or dead? But maybe you think you don't have to do deals with me. I'm stuck here, surrounded, outgunned.'

'Ah! They "wouldn't be much use if nobody cared about them." I suppose you're right, John. "They wouldn't count

130

in any deals, would they, because who'd bother whether they were alive or dead?" I haven't thought of it like that before.'

'What do you mean, "Ah" – like a revelation? Of course you've thought of it like that before. It's why you and your boys and girls are out there with their guns and dogs. It's because you care about the hostages. You don't want dead hostages on your ground, do you? Not nice for your boss-man's career. You're too delicate even to call them hostages, aren't you, Olly?'

'It's only a matter of terminology.'

'It's a matter of trying to knock me. It's a matter of not admitting I've got bargaining chips.'

'I find it hard to think of people as bargaining chips, John.'

'Oops, so sorry. Think of them as aces then.'

'"Aces." There are four aces in a pack. Have you got four people in the shop with you?'

'Oh, Olly, you're so quick.'

'Have you got four people in the shop with you?'

'Oh, Olly, you're so quick.'

'And then something else you said, John,' the negotiator replied. 'You said, "Maybe you think you don't have to do deals with me." This, surely, is not true. Why else do we want to keep this telephone line open? Why do we regret it when you cut that contact?'

'You aim to wear me down.'

'Veronica Susan Cleaver, aged thirty-two,' the negotiator said. 'Could you ask, please, John, whether that is the woman you grabbed?'

'I'll have to think about this.'

'We realize you'll have to think about it.'

'I'd need to work out what's behind it, wouldn't I, Olly?'

'"Need to work out what's behind it." In which sense, John? "What's behind it" in which sense?'

'Yes, work out what's behind it,' he replied.

131

'As I said, John, we have someone here who thinks he might know her. It's to put his mind at rest.'

'I don't have to worry about his mind. I've got my own stuff to worry about.'

'We realize that, John, but −'

'How will it put his mind at rest if it *is* her?'

'If it isn't.'

'But if it is?'

'So you see why we'd like you to ask her,' the negotiator said.

'I'd have to think about this − as to what's behind it.'

Rockmain sat close to the negotiator, gazing through a one-way window at the charity shop. Harpur thought it was as if Rockmain believed he could control the talk between the shop and the van by his nearness to this end of it, and by massive, thrumming, bulldozing willpower radiating from him, despite his measly body: he seemed clenched in concentration, shoulders bent forward, bony, childlike. He didn't speak, but occasionally, as he listened to the negotiator and John, looked down from the window and made a note on his pad. He knew how experts were expected to conduct themselves on an operation. Although not Gold, he needed to show he wasn't clinker, either.

Dodd had a seat not far from him. There'd been that moment of impatience with the pointless chatter in the van, and Harpur thought he still seemed in a frantic rage, though managing to hold back for now. He'd gasp occasionally at some of John's statements and replies. Dodd obviously didn't spot the music and slick patterns in the talk. He'd hear from John only evasion and dangerous nerviness. And from the negotiator he'd hear idiotic and dangerous tolerance, feeble and dangerous dither.

Iles, like Harpur, was standing. The ACC also watched the shop, through another of the one-way windows. He'd be listening as well, of course. He didn't make notes. He didn't need to make notes. After one hearing Iles would be able to quote verbatim the whole chat, including pauses and coughs. He despised this talent, regarded it as possible evidence of a bad lack. What was that astounding memory but a kind of serfdom? Did it make him a prisoner to what others said? Could he only follow, only parrot, not originate?

Occasionally, when clobbered by one of his loud, long, sobbing moods of self-pity, the Assistant Chief might put these questions to Harpur, and he would consider, and take quite a heavy-going time with his answer, giving proper attention to the many fine points. Then he'd always reply along the lines of, 'You can come up with some very deep discussion topics, sir, very deep. Nobody would deny that. Nuances – you're a dab hand at nuances.'

Rockmain found a fresh sheet of paper in his pad and swiftly wrote something. With no sound he tore this page free and passed it to the negotiator. As it moved between the two, Harpur, looking down, could see that the message seemed to be in capital letters. It began 'ASK HIM WHETHER HE'S AFRAID TO DISCOVER –' but Harpur didn't have time to get whatever came afterwards because the negotiator took the note and his head and body obscured it. The negotiator said: 'I wondered, John, whether you are afraid to discover the names of the people with you because this would sort of humanize them too much, make them objects of possible pity, weaken your control over them.'

'As a matter of fact, Olly, I already know they're human. Oh, yes. That shock you? What else would they be?'

The negotiator glanced at Rockmain. It looked as though the upper-case prompt from him didn't go beyond that one question. The negotiator seemed confused, at a loss about how to deal with come-backs. His uneasiness perhaps explained why some hostage situation experts demanded that the negotiator should be strictly and totally isolated from all the rest of the siege party. 'What I meant, John, ' he said, 'was –'

133

'You're trying to soften me, aren't you, Olly? Or someone with you there is trying to soften me. You're saying that, really, under it all, I'm no cold brute, and it's unnatural for me to be putting the hostages through it like this. You want to plant a sentimental seed in my head, so that, in a while, I'll turn nice and cooperative, ready for self-sacrifice – in the cause of humanity.'

Rockmain mouthed: 'Fuck, fuck, the smartarse fuck.' Harpur took that to be an admission John read the psychotactics right. Iles leaned over and tapped Rockmain on the arm. When Rockmain turned towards him Iles pantomimed a lavatorial scene, holding his nose with one hand and pulling an imaginary flush chain with the other: his thoughts on Rockmain's intervention.

This bit of infantile play-acting must have infuriated Dodd again. He'd obviously decided the siege leadership was flippant and undirected, no leadership at all, just like kids fooling and competing. He stood and moved very fast to the negotiator who seemed still half muddled and off-guard after the reply from John. Dodd grabbed at the telephone receiver. He surprised the negotiator, but not quite enough, not quite enough to take the receiver from him. The negotiator held on. There was a struggle. Dodd, though, had the maddened strength to pull the phone, still in the negotiator's hand, close to his lips for a few moments. He yelled: 'John, you bastard, you've got my lover in there and I want her out. You hear me? You've no right. I want her out. She's sick and I want her out. I'm coming for her now, you rotten, murdering thug.'

'What? What?' John screamed through the amplified phone line. 'Coming here? Are you looking for a bullet, you twat?'

But Dodd let go of the receiver and stepped to the door of the van, pulled it open and rushed out. Although Rockmain howled a protest, Dodd began running up the road towards the shop. He had no coordination. His legs looked about to buckle. His arms windmilled. When he had covered a few yards Iles left the van and charged after him. Rockmain stood up, and with a kind of lunge, made a useless attempt to stop Iles. The ACC broke Rockmain's limp grip as if it wasn't there. Iles still refereed rugby games and probably played himself when younger. He had strength and some speed. Outside, he very quickly gained on Dodd and brought him down heavily on to the tarmac, though not with a classic rugby tackle. He didn't go for the wobbly legs. Instead, Iles flung himself on to Dodd's back, arms around his neck and waist, encompassing him, the way a JCB's grab claws might descend on an outcrop rock. Also, Harpur was reminded of TV safari programmes – a leopard or cheetah leaping on to its prey, enveloping it, halting it, forcing it to totter, then helplessly drop, under the extra weight. In the same way, Iles floored Dodd.

It wasn't only a matter of stopping him, though. The ACC's body lying on top of his would shield Dodd if John panicked and started shooting. As Harpur knew, Iles could be more than a memory man. Iles had declared himself Gold, and Gold brought *noblesse oblige* responsibilities towards his team and hangers-on, Dodd being one of the hangers-on.

Chapter Twenty-Two

Manse felt really glad Naomi was not staying at his house when Egremont Lake, Denzil's brother, called there. This was an ex-rectory, for God's sake – well, yes, for God's sake until the church sold up – but he just rolled in from Hackney wearing a foul, pricey, two-vent sports jacket, no phone call or anything like that to ask if it would be convenient or suitable. He reckoned because he was who he was he would be welcomed all over, even at an ex-rectory. 'Protocol' was another word Manse had come across not long ago and greatly liked on account of all them o's strung out so tidy in a line, though separated, and sweetly cooperating with one another in the changing 'o' sounds, but, obviously, that sod Egremont didn't give a twopenny fuck for protocol.

It happened like this: Manse heard the sound of a vehicle and when he looked from his den window saw a silver Bentley convertible pulling up on the drive. Manse had the idea that in the old days rectors wrote their reports to the bishop, and sermons and testimonials and that kind of thing in this den, as Manse called it – really, a study. He'd bet no fucking rector ever looked out of the window here and saw someone such as Egremont, with that jaw as big as a sideboard, arrive on the property in, admittedly, first class lace-up black shoes, seen when he walked to the front door, or strutted, more like.

He would know Manse's address. Denzil used to have a flat at the top of the house, and was still living there at the time he passed away so unexpected by some, because of them pistols going off simultaneous towards his personal throat. Denz had always been very thorough. He was known for it, respected for it. If you mentioned Denz's name among commerce people anywhere in Britain, including Cotswold villages, and even abroad, on the French Riviera, for instance, someone would remark, 'So thorough, Denzil,' or the same in the language of the other country. Manse thought it might of been tricky explaining to Naomi who Egremont Lake was, especially in that jacket. It could of meant telling her, also, about Egremont's late brother. A while ago, it had seemed wise for Denz, as Manse's driver and bodyguard then, to be handy, accommodated on the premises. He had changed into a traitorous sod, the traitorous sod. But when he first took the flat, Manse had trusted him totally more or less, regardless of what he looked like.

Although Naomi had spent quite a few spells at the rectory in the last couple of weeks, she'd said she had to pop back to London yesterday for some work matter with the celebrity sheet, and Manse didn't see no reason not to believe this was the true reason. Consultants had to be there to be consulted now and then. It looked like Egremont drove from London hisself, or at least the last part of it. A heavy had the passenger seat. The man stayed in the car. But Egremont left the Bentley and came over to ring the front door bell, arms swinging, head up, a bit of a smile on, staring around at the house and gardens. Anyone watching him would think he had a complete right to visit, the brassy-necked bastard. That's how people from London could be – full of theirselves, no idea of decorum or protocol. You'd think the strength needed to move his jaw for the smile, even a small smile, would exhaust him, like weight-lifting or mouth-breathing in a cross-Channel swim, but, no, he seemed nimble.

The jacket was basically earth brown, though with yellow, red, green and mauve flecks in it. Most likely someone in London had told him squires in the counties wore this kind of sick gear with a flap at the back to go over the saddle when cantering across acres, known as hacking. Perhaps he wanted to merge, although not on horseback. Maybe squires *did* go out dressed like that in defiance, not caring a fish's tit in a squirely way what ordinary people thought about the rotten mess of colours. It was a change from that nearly-OK dark suit at the funeral. The heavy did have one of them on, though – 'Regalia', as some called it, because Reggie Kray used to dress very formal like that. Obviously, Manse couldn't tell yet whether Egremont owned the Bentley or had hired it for status show. Shale could of had a Bentley or more than one, but who wanted to seem flash, like some football star?

Manse didn't have nobody in the house with him for protection. Although he had taken Hubert V.L. Camborne on the funeral trip to London, that was what would be termed a one-off, a Hackney must, like a doctor putting a mask on at certain points. Manse did without a constant bodyguard these days. When someone as close to you as Denz had turned out false you worried if the next one might be the same. Would he talk about you to someone else, did he scheme with someone else? Manse did think of ringing Hubert now and telling him to get over here armed, maybe with a few others, but then he decided this would look nervy and feeble – not just to Egremont, but to Hubert. And Hubert might put the gossip around among staff. Something like, 'Shale was shitting hisself because he had a caller from the smoke. I had to help the poor prick get back to normal.' This would not be good for leadership. And, perhaps the word wouldn't stay inside the firm but reach that smug ponce, Ralph Ember, who'd get a long, superior chortle from it, although he was known as Panicking Ralph, or Ralphy, because in rough situations he'd go yellow. Plus, sending for help was the wrong kind of behaviour in an ex-rectory: no dignity. This property had stood here for more than a hundred years, so solid and calm, which included right through the bombing in the Second War. Whoever lived here now ought to behave with some of that same quiet toughness and bravery.

So, Manse did not make a call but went to open the door and greet Egremont Lake head-on, no chickening. Manse almost totally believed it was impossible for the Lakes to of dug out anything new and awkward about the way Denz went. Manse would still argue that Denzil could of done himself with the twin shots, despite what some troublemakers said, truly the result of his famed thoroughness. Although Manse kept weapons in a wall-safe behind one of the Pre-Raphaelites, he certainly had nothing on him at present. In his view, it would of been deeply vulgar and out-of-proportion to wear a harness and pistol in his purchased-outright-for-cash home, with its churchy past. Some vicars and even rectors felt up altar boys and went further, yes, but Manse had never heard anything like that about the history of this property and room. It wasn't the kind of thing you could ask an estate agent.

'Mansel!' Egremont Lake said, with very pleasant warmth and plenty of good cheer. 'I'd bet a grand or ten that you'd prefer to have substantive talks in this very fine, old, three-storey hutch about overall prospects, instead of at the after-funeral do in London with a crowd all round, and some, like my creepy cousin, Lionel-Garth Field, trying to eavesdrop, then, afterwards, cornering you for an unwelcome and comically presumptuous ear-bending. Inevitably – though perhaps a little slowly, for which I do apologize – yes, inevitably I came to see it as a prime duty to travel here and discuss matters on your home ground, as it were, and to have an educational trip around the relevant business territory with you as guide and supreme mentor, so that I know what we're talking about when we're talking about it, seeking a brilliant forward sales plan acceptable to both. I'm very keen to *see* the streets and pubs

139

and clubs we'll be utilizing. I believe in familiarity. I believe in actual early contact with new locations. Denzil used to speak of the Valencia Esplanade area as a major dealing site, but that's about as far as my geographical data goes, I fear.'

'It's a true surprise seeing you, Egremont, on, as you so rightly term it, my home ground,' Shale replied in what he considered quite a mild tone.

'You attract such a pilgrimage. You merit such a pilgrimage.'

'Thank you, Egremont.'

'You have so much taking place in your life yet you can find time to backburner these items and hobnob with someone like yours truly.'

Well, maybe. Manse did have a lot taking place in his life, or possibly about to, anyway. Such as, when he heard the Bentley, Manse had been wondering in his den-study whether it was nearly time for Naomi and him to get engaged. In fact, he'd examined this topic quite a lot these last weeks. Most likely they didn't have to wait until the divorce was all wrapped up. Sitting in the den and wondering about vicars and even rectors with altar boys, Manse wanted to get to something normal. He knew many didn't go in for engagements and that kind of thing now, just took a property together and became what was known as 'partners'. Manse regarded this as unimpressive and slack, and he thought Naomi might, too.

He knew Percy Ardoyne, the jeweller in Nash Street, very well from the time when Perce had a big habit – big though more or less manageable. He was clean they said, lately, but he and Manse still kept a kind of acquaintance-ship going, and Manse had seen some very possible rings on display in his shop window. Naturally, Manse didn't care about cost, but he thought Percy would act favourable towards someone who had looked after him, and looked after him personal, in them so fondly remembered snort and soar-away days. Perce would hope to keep things good between them in case sometime he wanted to go back to it, and to know for definite what he bought was quality, not some cheating half-filler mix that could flay your inside-nose quicker than the genuine and, also, give only a drabbish, half-cock buzz.

Manse preferred a simple, single-diamond ring, although Joan Fenton's double hadn't seemed over-showy. He hated anything too fussy, too blingy. It clashed with his deep down taste. His mother often used to say, 'Go to the heart of things, Mansel. Forget the fripperies.' He believed he had been born with that kind of outlook, anyway, and his mother's words just beefed it up. He thought Naomi would agree on this, too. But he'd definitely ask her about the kind of ring she'd like, and maybe even take her to Percy's to choose. You had to recognize that women could have their own thoughts about jewellery. Because she bought production-line Pre-Raphaelite poster-prints it might be wrong to think she'd always go for tat. And, in fact, he thought them poster-prints framed looked all right on the wall in Ealing. If she wanted a ring that was more multiple and fripperied than Manse might of picked, he would go along and not in any way reveal disappointment. She was the one whose finger it would be on, after all, and some regarded bling as fine – sort of breezy and in-your-face and full of fun, what they called 'life enhancing'. He could make sure he told people she had picked it herself, but he'd grin in a forgiving, loving way when explaining it, like 'You know what women are for flaunting, even Naomi.'

Egremont Lake said: 'D'you know, Mansel, I look at this grand and previously sacerdotal villa and recall that here, at the top, my brother lived and served your companies. It's a massive, thought-provoking notion.'

'Indeed, yes.'

'I feel his presence even as we speak.'

'Denzil carried with him what is known as an ambience,' Manse said. 'Maybe you've come across the term. Some have it, some don't. Perhaps, yes, Denzil's endures, as high grade ambiences sometimes will. Remember Elvis. Remember Mother Teresa. It's a privilege to enjoy some part of such a legacy, although in posthumous circumstances, as, of course, is a condition of legacies.'

'Many's the mention Denz made of you and the rectory, never other than positive, believe me.'

'I've let the flat stay empty as a kind of tribute – a modest tribute, Egremont, yet, yes, a tribute just the same. Although in due course I expect I'll find some use for those rooms, at present to convert them to a rumpus and TV nook for Matilda, Laurent and their boisterous friends would seem disrespectful to the dear and cherished memory of Denzil. His individual chest of drawers containing garments is still there as well as much of his crockery, shampoos and travel brochures. I feel the time has not yet come for a complete clear-out and severance.'

'This is in harmony with the impression of you I'd already formed in conversation after the funeral, Mansel. Sensitive.'

Manse would not dispute that term for his character. He believed in being considerate and extremely unbulldozing towards quite a few people. For instance, although Naomi already wore rings on the right hand, one an opal, one a violet amethyst, Manse did not mind much, and never referred to them or asked where the fuck they came from. They, also, like the Ealing bed, was the past. When she got them rings she could not of had no idea she would be meeting Manse in a Pre-Raphaelite gallery, and leading on.

If she wanted to tell him about the rings he'd listen, of course. To ask could not be right or charming – or sensitive, to use Egremont's word. Besides, she might of been given them by her mother and father or bought them herself only for a fashion purpose, which would most likely be necessary when often meeting celebrities certain to be togged right up, which Naomi would have to match. If there was a wedding eventually, Manse believed it would

142

be a lovely and notable occasion, though he'd have to watch out in case Syb heard of it and drove from North Wales to bugger everything up by any of a large choice of methods, or a combination.*

Although she didn't want to live with Manse and the children herself, he thought she'd grow evil if she found he'd fixed to marry someone else. Syb didn't seem to think much of marriage when it meant married to him, Manse, but he had an idea she'd grow ratty if he got the divorce and then married Naomi. Syb had been all right about women such as Patricia, Lowri and Carmel spending time with him in the rectory on a here-today-gone-the-week-after-next basis, but a wedding would most likely give her a real hormonal niggle. It might seriously hurt Syb to know Manse was happy in a settled way. He did not want to upset her, but now and then he had to give hisself priority. In a strong and crazily violent way, Syb could be rather weak.

Manse said, 'You see, Egremont, a certain period set apart for thought about Denzil as a man, colleague and friend seemed to me only decent in the circumstances.'

'Not all in your kind of position would be so considerate, Mansel.'

'It is only one human being's quiet tribute towards another.'

'Are you going to keep me out here on the fucking doorstep in this crummy porch stinking of cat's piss then?' Egremont replied.

'Yes, I think I am.'

'You've already fixed something with Lionel-Garth, have you, you two-timing, two-pistols, murderous turd?'

'How *is* Lionel-Garth, and your family in general, Egremont?'

'You've hatched a deal with him, have you?'

'What sort of deal?'

* See *Hotbed*

'Running the territory for you.'

'*I* run the territory,' Manse said.

'He's got in first, the sod, has he?'

'If I need a chauffeur I'll let you know,' Manse said. 'Denzil used the fire-escape to get to his flat. He didn't need to come into the actual house. I felt it was better like that, he being how he was. If you like, I'll take you up the escape for an in memoriam, brotherly look at the layout of his place, and after that you and your thug chaperone can shove off back to London. I wouldn't like you to think your journey was a complete waste.'

'You've got that fucking Hubert from the funeral and his armament up there, waiting, have you, you sly bastard? And maybe others. You've been expecting this call? Why? How? Where does your intelligence come from?'

'My mother has quite a brain. Often she gives almost workable advice on life.'

'I saw you watching my arrival through that window there. You looked full of hate and contempt.'

'Rectors would probably use the window to check whether they should open the door to a caller from the congregation or pretend to be out. I'd guess some church members could be very boring when discussing their souls.'

'You phoned up to Hubert and the rest in the flat to get ready did you? "Safety catches off, lads. I'll lull him with sweet doorstep chat, then bring him for you."'

'Some see it as a bad sign that the church should have to sell this house to a trade figurehead and move their rectors into something smaller, meaner, single garage only,' Mansel said. 'They sense decline and the creep of materialism.'

'I came here in good faith.'

'As I say, there's not so much of that about these days.'

'You owe us,' Egremont replied.

'Who?'

'You.'

'I owe who?'

'Us.'

'Who?'

'The family.'

'Owe what?'

'You know what.'

'I'll be glad to go up there with you to show Denzil's pre-death accommodation. This could be a sort of keepsake experience.'

'Deliver me to an ambush, separated from my trooper? Do you think I'm bloody mad?'

'Well, you did buy that fucking jacket,' Manse said.

Chapter Twenty-Three

2009

Harpur hadn't realized it at once, of course, but Gary James Dodd's wild, fond, probably deluded, gallop towards the charity shop, and then the talented squashing and straddling of him from behind by Iles, set things moving fast towards the end of the siege, and towards the messy disaster that came with it. Parts of this sequence, Harpur saw and heard for himself. The rest of it he had to put together later from statements of survivors in the shop, some of it garbled and contradictory because people were so scared and confused, their memory of events a jumble.

He felt a kind of sympathy for Rockmain, whose careful work was smashed. He had built a classic, subtle, balanced procedure for conduct of the operation, sticking to all tried and successful British and US siege advice. This crumbled totally, though, once Dodd began his run, and Iles began his. Appalled, Rockmain had yelled, 'No, no,' at Dodd, and then tried to stop Iles following. Rockmain was seated near the negotiator but stood quickly and bellowed the ban when Dodd suddenly pushed the van door open. Rockmain had a surprisingly deep and commanding voice for someone so weak-looking, as if he was mainly voice and not much else, but Dodd ignored it. He was powered by love. He obviously believed he must try to save Veronica Susan Cleaver, his cherished partner. So, this stupid, lumbering, dud sprint, most likely altogether undeserved by her in any case, supposing it *was* Veronica Susan Cleaver bundled in from the pavement, Veronica Susan Cleaver, who'd apparently been intending to spend secret time with Adrian Morrison Overdale, chartered surveyor, who lived in nearby Cortilda Square. She seemed to be a very lovable woman. Both men worried about her.

Once Dodd had gone, Rockmain seemed to sense Iles intended pursuit. Maybe from the moment he joined the siege, Rockmain feared a collapse of patience in Iles. Harpur had feared the same. Come to that, perhaps Rockmain had expected a failure of patience in Harpur himself, also. Harpur had certainly thought about a solo invasion of the shop, and Rockmain's trained psychological asdic might have picked up the signs, so he'd be all-round alert. But now it was Iles – Iles very blatantly about to dog and, if possible, halt Dodd. Near to hysterics, Rockmain took a miniature step or two and grabbed at the Assistant Chief's left arm.

One of the things about Iles was he never got uppity and princely because someone manhandled him, no matter with what violence. For instance, often at funerals of murder victims Harpur had to quell him. Iles would abruptly take over the service and give his own well-meant sermon, blaming the Home Secretary or the Meteorological Office or the Pope or the Prime Minister or the Archbishops of Canterbury and Westminster, or the European Union, or Masons or the Trinity, for letting the country and/or the world get into the sort of condition leading to this particular death. These outbursts sometimes got reported in the local media and on the whole were not helpful. Harpur might have to use quite a slice of force to shut the jabbering sod up, and occasionally drag him down steps from the pulpit so the priest or minister could resume control, as was patently their right. Most probably, they had not been instructed in training how to handle this kind of interruption. When Harpur took hold of him, Iles would fight back, yes, and fight back with all his filthy, cultivated skills and

147

astonishing strength, careless of the setting, but he would not pull rank about it, though he'd be in his magnificent blue ACC uniform. He took the scrapping as entirely in the normal run of things. Iles considered that few funerals were complete without an episode of this kind fairly soon after the coffin arrived. Iles rabidly envied all the attention given to the corpse. He hated sharing any spotlight. Also, Iles regarded funerals as ceremonies where emotions should run, and the Assistant Chief had emotions. In its inconvenient way, Harpur found this endearing, but applied the brutalities if timely, all the same.

Now, when Rockmain gripped the ACC's uniformed arm, attempting to detain him in a sort of parody arrest, Iles escaped from this hold at once, naturally, but didn't then pick up Rockmain and chuck him against the wall of the caravan, or kick his feet away and knee and gouge him on the floor. Iles seemed to recognize, as Harpur did, that Rockmain might be entitled to salvage the approved siege pattern he'd created, if he could – in fact, was duty-bound to try. His little soul lived and took its shape and health from those ruses. Although he detested Rockmain, Iles would see he had professional obligations and, to a degree, the ACC respected these. Now and then the Assistant Chief could become amazingly proportionate.

All he did today was take a handful of Rockmain's shirt near the throat, lift him for only a moment in the air – without any hint of butting, although the two faces came damn close – and then slam him back into his seat near the negotiator, like throwing down an empty rucksack. It was swift. Iles did not speak or whoop or laugh. He knew he should not waste breath. He still had the time and pace to catch Dodd well before he reached the shop.

Harpur thought Dodd's forehead had been shoved forward in a jerking movement and slammed hard against the highway surface when he collapsed with Iles on his back. Dodd was thin, with a long neck as skinny as Rockmain's, which would be liable to such uncontrollable

148

flexing. Although the ACC was not burly, his weight would make that a bad blow for Dodd under him. Harpur saw no movement from Dodd on the ground. He didn't struggle to throw Iles off, or attempt to wriggle free. Dodd must be concussed. Iles remained on top of him, also motionless, but as a shield. Without turning his head back towards the caravan, the ACC shouted, as if into the tarmac, or a roadside rain drain, or Dodd's ear, 'I am Gold. I, Iles, remain Gold. I await our man's recovery. All of you, stay where you are. I repeat, stay sheltered. I repeat, it is Gold who speaks. I, Iles, am Gold.' The outside audio detector picked up his announcement and broadcast it booming in the caravan. Harpur thought the words had a fine, solemn, Old Testament rhythm, as if the letter l should be dropped out of Gold. There was a chaos of noise. John continued to hurl questions over the Conference telephone: 'What's happening, you sods?' 'Who are these people?' 'Are you attacking?' 'Is this the start?' 'Who are they? Who are they?' 'Do you want fucking war? War is what you'll fucking get, and so will these in here with me.' 'Who's the talky-talky one in the big-brass uniform? Is he mad?'

'I'll go and help the ACC bring Dodd in,' Harpur said. 'He'll have to be carried.'

'That will be defiance of Gold,' Rockmain said.

'Yes, technically. I often defy Mr Iles. He expects it. He despises obedience. He'll say things like, "Take a peep at the Atlantic. Not much obedience there I think." He has his own way of looking at things. It's not quite lateral thinking. Quadrilateral – he sees all sides, one or two of them more or less sane. I'm Gold for the moment,' Harpur said.

'You can't be Gold while he's still Gold,' Rockmain said. 'There can be only one Gold.'

'It's impossible for him to be Gold,' Harpur said. 'How can he see things overall when he's like that on Dodd?'

'He explicitly did not hand over Gold status,' Rockmain said. 'Very explicitly.'

Harpur could part sympathize with Rockmain's objections. Harpur himself loved the clarion nature of that cry, 'I am Gold' – the certainty, the unquestionable authority and worth, the absence of maybes and but-on-the-other-hands. Rockmain's attitude to Gold, the title, proved its absoluteness. Harpur had, for a moment, queried that absoluteness. Iles seemed incapable of being Gold, spread-eagled over Dodd. For Rockmain, though, Gold was Gold, spreadeagled over Dodd or not.

Yes, Harpur sometimes wished everything could have the bare, declarative strength and power of 'I am Gold.' So much of life was secrets, half-truths, quarter-truths, non-truths. 'I am Gold' said what it had to say and said it short, plain and straight, able to enthral even a high-falutin, passably reputable (Cambridge starred First, apparently), arrogant, jargonizing , psychologist cop like Rockmain.

And then Harpur thought, yea, yea, yea. Could you run a police force without secrets, half-truths, quarter-truths, non-truths? Could you run a life without secrets, half-truths, quarter-truths, non-truths? Adultery generally required some secrets, half-truths, quarter-truths, non-truths, didn't it? Hadn't you, C. Harpur, specialized in secrets, half-truths, quarter-truths, non-truths, when you were cuddling up and so on with Sarah Iles, the ACC's wife?* 'I am dross' could have been your cry then.

The negotiator said: 'Rest easy, John. I note your question: "What's happening?" You asked what's happening, didn't you?'

'Yes, what's happening?'

'I thought you'd ask what's happening, John.'

'Well, of fucking course I'd ask what's happening if something is happening, namely, two men running this way, then hitting the ground.'

'It is only an incident, John.'

'I can see it's an incident.'

* See *Come Clean*

'I certainly understand that this kind of incident would puzzle you, John. It's only a single, minor incident. It doesn't affect the general situation.'

'What kind of single, minor incident that doesn't affect the general situation is it? Is one of them lover-boy?'

'You're bound to ask what kind of one-off incident it is.'

'And what sort of general situation is it?'

'The situation in general.'

'What I think is, a decoy – something to make me look that way when the trouble's coming from elsewhere.'

'It's natural for you to think it's a decoy, John.'

'*Is* it a fucking decoy?'

'"Is it a decoy?" I can see what you're getting at, John – the implications.'

'You can see what I'm getting at. I say, "Is it a decoy?" And you say you can see what I'm getting at such as, "Is it a decoy?" Fucking brilliant.'

'This is another of those questions.'

'Which?'

'Questions I'd expect,' the negotiator said.

'But you're not going to say, "Yes, it's a decoy, John," are you, because then it wouldn't be a decoy any longer, would it?'

'You ask would it still be a decoy if I said, "Yes, it's a decoy, John," because it's vital with a decoy that people don't know it's a decoy, otherwise it's no decoy. The essence of a decoy is that the person or people it's intended to deceive don't realize it's a deception, a decoy. I appreciate your point.'

Harpur said: 'If John flips and starts firing at Dodd and the ACC we'll have to go in – the full assault team.'

'Yes,' Rockmain said.

'I'd have to order it,' Harpur said.

'Iles could order it from where he is,' Rockmain said.

'He might not be able to, if John has been firing at them,' Harpur said.

'It's a long way for a handgun shot.'

151

'They might get hit, all the same.'

'In that case, if Iles were hit and . . . yes, you'd be Gold,' Rockmain said.

'It might be too late for Dodd and the ACC then,' Harpur said. 'I'd be Gold but only because Gold was dead or crippled. I've got to go and get them.'

'Gold has ordered against that,' Rockmain said.

'I'll go,' Harpur said.

'That fucking Dodd,' Rockmain replied. 'An idiot.'

'Maybe more than he knows,' Harpur said.

'What? How?' Rockmain said.

'John?' the negotiator said. 'John, are you there?' He couldn't keep urgency, anxiety, out of his voice. That was not typical. He had played calm and repetitive, as the negotiator manuals recommended. John didn't answer. There'd been earlier spells when he refused to reply: the line would stay dead because he'd leave the receiver down. It seemed different now, though. The connection remained open, but John didn't talk.

Over the amplified system they heard sounds Harpur couldn't place at first. He'd been about to leave the van and crouch-run to Dodd and the ACC, ready if necessary to clobber Iles, suppose he offered Gold trouble, and he almost certainly would. But Harpur waited and listened: a couple of thuds, a woman's brief scream, grunting – male – furniture splintering, a man's shout, though no words. Harpur read anger or panic in these shouts. The noise varied in volume, as if the phone at the shop end might be hanging loose on its wire and spinning, so its pick-up field continually changed, a fading, an increase, then the same sequence again. Harpur decided some kind of physical battle had started.

Rockmain said: 'Have they gone for him in there?'

'They might need help,' Harpur said.

'Yes,' Rockmain said. 'A new phase.'

The main shop window on to the street shattered with a great, very brief, jangling din. The negotiator said: 'John,

John, what's happening? We note the window. Have you noticed the window? A breakage.' Through the caravan's open door, Harpur saw Iles suddenly unhook himself from Dodd and stand. He would have heard the glass break and cascade, and he'd probably agree with Rockmain: a new phase. Dodd remained prone on the ground and still. Iles stood with a leg on each side of him like the victor on an ancient, hand-to-hand battlefield, and yelled, 'I'm Gold. I, Iles, am Gold.' He waved an arm, urging immediate onslaught. 'All go, go, go,' he called. Harpur thought the ACC in his pale blue, insignia'd uniform looked glorious, whatever the outcome, and the outcome might be terrible. But this was the kind of moment Iles fitted into so sweetly. Evening sun gave a rich, steely shine to his cropped grey hair. He had no cap on. He'd left it in the van.

The road was empty, of course, cleared but for these two. Iles, fixed there, staring about, his body tense over the other body, had suddenly claimed this piece of land as his realm. Of course, in a sense it had always been his realm, his and Harpur's, part of their manor. They knew all these streets and the buildings and some of the people living or working in them. But it was as if the needs of the siege had grabbed this area of ground away from them. Here was Iles taking it back. The solitariness, except for Dodd, made him epic. Circumstances – the Dodd circumstances – had pushed Iles into a prickly situation, and he emerged from it now aglow with obvious, towering leadership, resolve and dignity. The nuisance at his feet, stubbornly blotto at present, could earlier have fucked up just about everything. Iles had neutralized him and, perhaps, through personal magic, had even converted Dodd's deep lunacy into a gain.

Perhaps, perhaps. As Harpur saw things, and as Rockmain seemed to see things, also, the hostages had possibly turned on John, surprised him, while he was distracted, trying to work out what Dodd and Iles and their short, frantic scamper from the van signified. There'd been

153

that rambling chat about decoys, John's agonized nerves showing throughout. He hadn't known which direction an invasion might come from. Had the hostages been able to cash in on his confusion and try to overpower him?

Something somehow or somebody somehow had burst the window. Who had the gun or guns? There'd been no shooting. Not yet. Iles's finger, pointed stiffly at the target building, seemed to say, 'Here lies our challenge, our future, and I, Iles, can deal with it, you lucky sods. Yes, it is I who speak: I, Iles, Gold.' Occasionally Harpur remembered lines of poetry he had learned at school and now he recalled the beginning of a verse about some old hero and his followers sighting a coastline and safety after a perilous, long sea voyage. It went, '"Courage!" he said, and pointed toward the land.' And it was as if Iles might part echo this: 'Courage!' he'd say and point toward the shop.

Harpur thrilled watching him, and when, now, he thought back to that long affair he had enjoyed with Iles's wife, Sarah, it seemed a terrible treachery against such a lustrous, fluctuating colleague. Harpur knew he hadn't felt anything in the least like that at the time, though. Most probably, an itchy conscience couldn't be a natural feature of affairs while they were actually under way or there wouldn't be any affairs. Occasionally, of course, or more than occasionally, Iles would still scream accusations and mad, agonized, brilliantly consonantal abuse at Harpur about it, but this evening the ACC displayed a kind of massive, unwavering nobility. Harpur felt policing was privileged to have him. Farce sometimes touched Iles, but so did a kind of special Ilesian grandeur. He made the job theatrical in very, very nearly the best sense. 'First aiders here,' he called. 'Doddy's into a total doze.' Then Iles ran unarmed towards the shop. Harpur, unarmed, followed.

Chapter Twenty-Four

2008

And then, of course, so obvious, Egremont Lake's cousin, Lionel-Garth Field, arrived on Shale's ground for a conversation, a turn-and-turn-about visitor procession. Them two, Egremont and Lionel-Garth, didn't do much conversation together, that was clear. Or no conversation about nothing serious, such as getting into Manse's firm here at a majestic level, owing to family connections through Denz. This would not be the haulage and scrap firm they had in mind. No, the main one. Well, really, as far as takings and undisclosed profits went, Manse had to admit, the *only* one.

When Egremont came he thought Lionel-Garth might of already had talks with Manse here. Wrong. Now, when Lionel-Garth came he thought Egremont might of already had talks with Manse. Right. If the first one was wrong, or right, the second one had to be right, didn't it, because the first one meant Egremont must of come here and had talks with Manse? But the fact that Lionel-Garth came anyway meant he felt unsure there'd been talks with Egremont and, if there had been, guessed they must of gone nowhere. Right, again. If he thought for definite there'd been talks and they'd got *some*where, Lionel-Garth would not be here now, because he'd know he was too late. Egremont would be, like, in – 'in' meaning into an executive post in Manse's firm.

But the question that then had to be dealt with was, why had Lionel-Garth left it so late? Although he would get no further than Egremont did, Shale considered it damn casual, almost an insult, to of waited so long. Months. Didn't he consider Manse's operation worth some urgency? People in London could be like that, the arrogant twerps. They thought everything worthwhile had to be there, in London, except, maybe, that rave at Glastonbury or Cowes for boating. They regarded other areas as what they called 'the sticks', full of what they called 'swede-bashers', signifying, village idiots. Maybe Lionel-Garth took his time because he rated Manse a swede-basher, and could not believe any firm in the sticks could really produce – not in the style and amount London could produce.

Shale considered that Lionel-Garth's slowness in following up the chat in Hackney after the funeral showed he decided in a cool way he could take it or leave it, as far as Manse's firm went. He wasn't certain he wanted a spot in the business or not. It was like, when he'd attended to all the *important* stuff he had in Hackney and around, he might, *might*, spare a small part of his red-hot brain to think about that commodities operation down in . . . where was it? Run by . . . what was his name? . . . the one Lionel-Garth's other cousin used to be in trade with at the time of death. This Lionel-Garth had some fucking neck. Well, necks could get wrung.

At least he didn't come hunting Manse at the rectory, in that disgusting style of Egremont. This might mean Lionel-Garth had some idea how to behave proper, even if it *was* out here, not London but the deepest bush! Instead, he hung about near Bracken Collegiate school where Laurent and Matilda went, usually driven there and back by Shale in the Jaguar. Lionel-Garth knew of the school and had mentioned after the funeral that he wouldn't mind his children going there if he moved the family when he joined Manse's outfit. So bleeding gracious. Lionel-Garth must of done some research about what time they would arrive and who would be driving. Manse didn't like that. Lionel-Garth knew about digging, did he, as well as a bit of accountancy?

In one way, Shale thought it might be just as bad using the school for a meeting spot like this, as calling on him at home. Lionel-Garth had arrived in a big green Vauxhall now parked near the gates and flashed his lights like a bloody secret agent job when he saw the Jaguar. Laurent and Matilda was still in the car and noticed the signal. 'Some mate or admirer, dad?' Laurent said.

'The school doesn't like cars or men hanging about outside,' Matilda said. 'People waiting near schools could be sort of dubious and of a tendency. Sometimes, the school calls the police to check.'

Well, yes, Lionel-Garth was dubious and of a tendency, and double dubious and of a tendency, but not in the way she meant.

'He's waving. He seems really friendly,' Laurent said. 'Why doesn't he come to the house if he wants to see you?'

Because he knows better than to come to the fucking house. He got no entitlement. Shale didn't say it, though. He never swore in front of the children. You didn't send them to a refined, big-fee-grab school like Bracken Collegiate and then undo everything by cursing like some fucking uneducated yob where they could fucking hear. 'I hardly know this guy,' Shale said. 'Don't ever take a lift from him.'

'You sound like the school, dad,' Matilda said. She and Laurent left the car and walked in through the gates. They joined quite a little crowd of pupils also moving towards the school, but Lionel-Garth would of had a clear sight of which was Mansel's children. He didn't like this, either. Yes, research might be another of Lionel-Garth's specialities. Shale began to think that, because of the artfulness Lionel-Garth showed, he might be more difficult to deal with than Egremont, meaning more difficult to squash and get rid of. His slowness coming here could be a ploy, not a sign he didn't care. Maybe he wanted to get Manse off-balance through wondering about Lionel-Garth's absence, then, wham, he's suddenly here, flashing his lights like 'So glad you could make it, Mansel.' Also, he'd had time to survey Manse's ground and business.

The thing with Egremont was, he had seemed to consider an arrangement with Manse would all be very easy and natural, like fixed by Fate and the blasting of Denz. So, it really knocked him when he realized Manse would not be letting him into the house because letting him into the house might mean Shale fancied some sort of partnership with this grand Hackney marquis, which Manse absolutely did not and wouldn't never. Clearly, Manse had not deliberately arranged things so the porch smelled of cocked-tail toms, but in his opinion that had been a very useful extra in destroying Egremont with his bling Bentley a bit more. It gave the message – 'Kindly, piss off, Egremont.'

And Egremont was really a mess after that. He went to the jabber level, the retreat level. But there would be no chance of getting Lionel-Garth into that handy, downgrading, cat's pee environment because he did not come to the rectory. Obviously, he didn't not come to the rectory on account of the porch stink, but owing to working in a subtler style than Egremont's. It seemed plain to Shale that Egremont had not told Lionel-Garth he'd been to see Manse, and, therefore, Lionel-Garth probably would not know about the unhelpful porch, even though he did research.

What Manse Shale still couldn't tell about Egremont and Lionel-Garth was how they regarded the snuffing of Denz. He hadn't known, either, what the whole lot of family and friends believed on that quite ticklish issue when he went to the funeral. So, he had taken Hubert and armament with him. Sometimes Shale thought Denzil's family wondered whether he really did do himself in, and wondered, also, if Denz truly held the kind of boardroom billet with Mansel

158

that they thought he did, or pretended they thought he did. It was like they was saying to Manse, 'Right, I know Denz was seen off by someone else, or maybe more than one, naming no fucking names, chum, but, anyway, not by hisself, and I know you stuck him in a dogsbody job, but I' – that 'I' could be Egremont or it could be Lionel-Garth – 'I can swallow all that, as long as there's something nice and continuing for me and definitely not dogsbody status in your present personal set-up out there in Dumpsville, UK,' 'me' also meaning Egremont or Lionel-Garth.

It seemed a sickening way for members of a family to think, but that's how some of them might be, through living in London. No, Shale realized it was mad to say that – too simple, childish. People didn't lose all their good feelings because they lived in London. Or not all people. He knew there were London districts with trees in the streets and well-looked-after properties, where the residents might be fairly OK and not really bombastic at all. He wondered where Joan Fenton lived, the lawyer. She could probably become like quite a normal person when not in her office. He wondered if there were times when she might be in her house alone.

Anyway, perhaps this family – the Lakes – regarded vengeance as daft and anti-business. London might be bad but it wasn't Sicily. They didn't do vendettas. If there'd been a death, and there had been, get something from it. That could be their philosophy. In the high cause of trade they would also scheme against each other, such as Egremont and Lionel-Garth. That might be the truly important thing for them, not the removal through internal small-arms gunfire of a brother or cousin who had been in a baggage guy's berth, truly a failure. They might even believe Denz to be such a disaster he was bound to want to do the big quit, or bound to get given the big quit by others, just one of the inflexible laws of the game.

They thought selfish, this Hackney gang. They thought win, win, win. They did not think, Denz, Denz, Denz,

159

because Denzil had been a glaring flop. These Denz relatives planned to hatch a bargain, but a bargain nobody spoke about, just a bargain understood by both sides: lots of silence regarding the terms. The bargain said, without any bugger saying it, 'We play nice and ignorant about our dear brother/cousin, Denzil, famed for his commercial flair, though now dead, *if* you carve out a good slice of your operation for us.' No, not 'us'. For *me*, being Egremont or Lionel-Garth. Each of these sods wanted to win, win, win, even against the other. Each of them could say, but wouldn't, 'Sorry, Denzil, but I got to think about what comes next, not what come lately so rough to you in your pitiful flunkey career, RIP.'

Although Lionel-Garth didn't have the kind of brassiness Egremont used when he came to Shale's individual, unmortaged property like that, and then complained of cats, Lionel-Garth had plenty of cheek hisself. For a start, he believed Manse would recognize him through two windscreens in an unusual spot although they had only met once a while ago. And then he obviously decided he was the one who better organize things now, outside the school, although a stranger here. Once the children had disappeared into the forecourt, Lionel-Garth drove to alongside the Jaguar, stopped for a moment, and pointed a finger down the road. It meant, 'Follow me,' a dumb-show order. Anyone could of seen Lionel-Garth expected Shale to obey. Well, Shale did.

The thing was, of course, he didn't want this blubberface, Lionel-Garth, making a pest of hisself around the town, maybe turning up again at the school, or even coming to Mansel's home. Crush him now. The Vauxhall led to Glaythorn Fields, a big park, with plenty of places for cars at one end under the trees. Yes, Lionel-Garth had done some earlier reconnaissance. He liked knowledge, this character. He'd have to be watched. He wasn't so casual or indifferent after all.

160

Manse would admit Lionel-Garth had the decency to get out of his own car and come on foot to the Jaguar, not expecting it to happen the other way around. Manse remembered Egremont's statement about people wishing to make a pilgrimage to him, Manse. Some aspects Egremont had right. Lionel-Garth opened the passenger door then leaned in and shook hands in a strong, thoughtful way, like someone signalling, 'I'm the lad you can trust.' This was how Manse's father had told him a handshake should be, hearty, strong, unhurried, sincere, even if it wasn't, or especially if it wasn't. Lionel-Garth got into the Jaguar and closed the door. But how to get the bugger out and soon? When he bent to come into the car Manse could see how far that mousy hair had gone back. He wore a denim jacket, jeans and what could be the same crimson and cream training shoes he had on at the funeral. Maybe he had bad feet and this was the only comfortable pair he'd found.

Shale considered balding people should not pick denim. It looked like a brave, comical, never-give-up, pathetic fight against fact. Time could not be stopped by garments. Lionel-Garth said: 'I thought I could achieve two objectives at once – see the school and make contact with you again, Mansel.'

'It's a good old building, Bracken Collegiate,' Shale said with terrific neutrality, in his opinion. 'They've looked after it well during the century plus. And they added extensions that fit in, although more modern, such as the language laboratory.' Parents had been asked to give a special donation on top of fees for that, instalments by direct debit for any who couldn't cough a lump. But, naturally, Manse put the whole lot down at once. He would hate gossip to get around that he had to do it bit by bit. Did he want Laurent and Matilda to look like pauper kids? He didn't object to the cost of the extension. He thought Britain was becoming a shit-hole and would be more of a shit-hole by the time Matilda and Laurent grew up, so they ought to have languages in case they wanted to shove off to somewhere else foreign and be able to ask where the bank with all their transferred funds was. Of course, they wouldn't need another language if they went to America, but that was becoming as big a shit-hole as Britain, according to what Shale heard, the jails full of con-men, mostly white. These days he sang 'Land of Hope and Glory' to hisself less and less. Was everything going into decline – the Church, this country, other countries, quality of the substances even when unmixed?

'I don't know whether my cousin, Egremont, has been along to see you, Mansel,' Lionel-Garth said.

'In which respect?'

'He's blood, on my mother's side, and I wouldn't say a word against Egremont, believe me.'

'Family bonds are *so* precious.'

'Yes. I see you with your children today. It's obviously a fine relationship. You're the one who normally drives them, I know. Heart-warming to observe. Denz would mention these arrangements.'

The mouthy prat. When Syb was still living with Manse at the rectory she would do the trip now and then. Obviously, if he had gone away bulk-buying, or seeing the London lawyer, or tracking some bastard who'd been skimming off the top, or creating a workable alibi in Preston or Tarragona, Syb would *have* to do it, except in vacations. But he knew she regarded this driving as a drag. He couldn't *not* know because she'd often told him it was a drag, usually in exactly the same words, 'I'll do it because I have to do it, Mansel, but it's a drag. Why can't sodding Denzil or someone else from the firm take them? Am I a fucking chauffeur?' Syb didn't worship education, the way Mansel did, on account of her previously going through quite an education herself, and she often said: 'What the hell did it get me?' Shale had sometimes wanted to reply: 'Well, I found that very attractive in you, among so many attractions, Syb.' But he knew she would come out with something cruel and coarse to that, so he never did say it.

Syb had to be played careful, but even that didn't work and she went. Several times she'd come back. Now, no. In any case, he'd started the divorce. That lawyer, Joan Fenton, would speak harsh about Sybil. He didn't think it was necessary. He would love to give Joan Fenton one, and while it was actually happening murmur in a very soothing, intimate voice to her, 'Please try to be tolerant to all womankind, Syb included.' Of course, Joan Fenton might not be able to reply or even understand what he said if he'd brought her to her ecstasy point, he had to realize this. So, he'd come to this topic early on in the bang.

Lionel-Garth said: 'The point about Egremont – in some ways it's a good point, I wouldn't dispute that – but the point about Egremont is in any business set-up he has to be the only one who really counts. I expect you know the type. A combination of Mussolini, Napoleon and Walt Disney. To be frank, Manse, which I'm sure you would prefer me to be, he doesn't know the meaning of the term "partnership" or even "colleague". He *must* dominate. For him, delegation and cooperation are not just dirty words, they are words that don't exist.

'As I've mentioned, this is in some ways a plus. It gives him great drive, terrific impulsive brio, and determination, a son at Charterhouse. But it can be uncomfortable for those working with him, for those working with him even at boardroom level. They will have the *appearance* of power but, in fact, no real power or influence at all. A firm like yours, Mansel, built personally by you – I can't imagine you'd want to bring in someone of the nature I've just outlined.' Lionel-Garth still talked fast with gasps, but Shale got most of it OK.

'The school is oversubscribed at present,' he replied. 'A quite considerable waiting list, despite expansion. This is always going to be the case, I should think, with schools that are generally recognized as good. Drugs are no problem there. I've told our people very, very blunt, to stay away from Bracken Collegiate, pupils and staff. This is an

163

absolute ban. I don't like them around schools, anyway, but definitely not Bracken Collegiate. A word like "collegiate" shows that the people who started this school believed it should have dignity, considerate behaviour and no trace of skunk or even grass. Parents will want to get their children into such places, especially when the local comprehensives are all tumult, teacher-teenager-shags, and knives. Even Left of Left MPs send their kids private. Oh, they're a bit ashamed, but they say in a big, creepy gush, "I can't impose my politics on my children and their schooling." But, of course, by passing Acts in Parliament they do impose their politics on other people's children and *their* schooling – the ones who can't afford private. And, from what they earn in pay and juicy expenses when imposing their politics on other people's children and their schooling, these MPs *can* afford to send their own kids private and not to the roughhouse schooling they've cooked up for other people's children.'

'You certainly do your share of the driving on these school trips,' Lionel-Garth said. 'Something over ninety per cent, I believe.'

'Nothing much to it.'

'Of course, your wife's away, isn't she? North Wales direction? The marriage over? But she's skipped off previously, hasn't she, and returned?'

'Driving them to school and back gives us time for useful talks together,' Shale replied. 'In the house, they're busy with their friends and TV games and hobbies and homework.' Naomi was at the rectory today and for several days, but Shale didn't think it would be right to ask her to drive the children to school because some teachers there would naturally have seen Sybil occasionally bring the children, and they knew her to be Manse's wife, Mrs Shale. Syb could be downright fucking memorable.

Manse had decided it would look a bit off if another woman brought them, and not a Mrs Shale, not yet. It was the kind of school where people would make remarks, what was referred to as 'judgemental'. In the past, as Syb mentioned, he hardly ever let Denz do the school run, either. Denz had not looked right for Bracken Collegiate, even as only a driver. He lacked something. Manse had thought Denz's face a bit short of what could be termed cohesion, and that was a good while before the Astra pistols damage. Also, his mouth had become slanted downwards to the left through gabbing over his shoulder, when Denz was chauffeur and Shale in the back of the Jaguar. Although the Jaguar had a glass partition that could be pulled across to isolate the driver from rear passengers, Shale hardly ever closed it. He would regard that as cold and high-handed, even though Denzil generally talked such shit.

'This is as good a place as any for our discussion, Mansel,' Lionel-Garth said.

'Excuse me, which discussion?'

'Policy.'

'Policy regarding what?'

'And you wouldn't want that kind of weighty chit-chat in your nest when the new lady is perhaps there, yet unavoidably excluded from such confidential talks,' Lionel-Garth replied. 'Divisiveness – the bane of home life, don't you agree? A closed door and only the indecipherable murmur of male voices audible. Unpleasant for her. And possibly you'd prefer she didn't do the school trip yet. It could look odd. These changeovers need a little time, don't they?'

He turned in the passenger seat to give Shale a truly matey smile. Manse didn't mind some fleshiness to a face as long as it was in them parts of the cheeks back towards the ears. That could give a strong, ungaunt touch, like the head would be great under one of them old style Prussian helmets in documentaries. On the whole he didn't like gauntness. It often made a person look ratty, sick and arrogant.

Ralph Ember, his business associate, probably regarded himself as gaunt, but in a handsome, impressive style. He

165

believed he looked like the young Charlton Heston, who definitely had a certain gauntness. Always, Ralphy pretended to be surprised when anyone spoke to him of the resemblance. But, really, you could see he enjoyed such remarks, especially from women, especially from young or youngish attractive women. This gave him such a great start. It excited these admirers to think they might be on the way to getting banged by El Cid. One of the reasons Shale loved the Pre-Raphaelites was you hardly ever got people in them pictures with bulky chops, yet they was not gaunt either. Manse really hated fatness in the cheeks near to the nose on each side. This was Lionel-Garth. It made Manse think, any more increase and the rolls would push up and shut both his eyes. When Shale met somebody with this kind of nose-area face fat he would want to get a blade and slice a good divot out of each lump to help.

Manse offered Lionel-Garth a smile just as truly matey in return. 'The thing is,' he said, 'you should of had a consult with cousin Egremont before coming all this way. He could of told you it's not on – what you call policy is not on. I got a policy, yes, because nobody can run a business without, but – I'll speak blunt – but this policy don't include you or Egremont. Why the fuck should it? *I'm* the policy. You're London. That's what you know. Stick to it, is my advice. There's nothing for you here, nothing for either of you. I've told Egremont that. Ask him about the cat's piss. Now, I'm afraid I must get on my way, if you don't mind.' Manse believed in politeness where at all possible. And he didn't want no violence getting Lionel-Garth out of the Jaguar.

'She's got her own problems, of course,' Lionel-Garth replied. He was gazing out through the windscreen towards the fine, very green greenery of the park, like far away in his thoughts.

'Who?'

'Naomi Gage.'

That really shook Shale. He had the sudden idea this was the chief topic Lionel-Garth wanted to talk about. He could do the same sort of oozy polite chat as Egremont, but now there seemed something else. 'You know Naomi?'

'In researching you and your firm, Manse, this was a name bound to come up, wouldn't you agree?'

'Why was it? She's not in the firm.'

'But *you*'re in the firm. No quibbling about that!' He had a small laugh, meaning what he said was obvious and didn't really need saying. 'You *are* the firm, thus far. Your, as it were, extramural life will unavoidably come into the reckoning, won't it? Your wife, children, Naomi.'

'Which reckoning? Who's doing a reckoning?'

'For someone of your status, Manse, there can be no sealed-off private life, can there? It is one of the penalties of success, and of fame.'

'Have you had a fucking tail on me?' Shale said.

'I think you'd expect me to do some background inquiries before taking what by any criterion must be regarded as a considerable change in my circumstances if I move out of London and come here. The new school for my children would only be part of that upheaval.'

'I don't expect you to think about any change, considerable or measly – not in this direction. Weren't you listening when I just told you that? You and/or Egremont, just stay away, right? You get it?'

'What is it army people say?' Lionel-Garth replied.

'Which army people? You mean about the poor equipment in Afghanistan? That's disgraceful, I agree.'

'Soldiers are taught, "Time spent on reconnaissance is never wasted." I'd certainly go along with that.' But he did a pause, like regretful. 'Perhaps, though, I shouldn't have referred to the army. An army unit's reconnaissance is directed against an enemy, isn't it? I'd regret it if that were the case here, Mansel. No, no indeed, the reconnaissance I have in mind is for the benefit of both of us. Oh, yes, certainly. Naomi might have her problems. Which of us is free from *all* problems, for heaven's sake? By recognizing and being aware of her problems we are on the way to resolving them, I feel, and I suspect you'll fully concur.'

'What problems?'

'Naomi Gage would clearly be one object of my pre-research. It would have been a slight on you and her to neglect it.'

'*One* object?'

'And perhaps the principal one. But, then, this unusual business arrangement you seem to have with Ralph W. Ember – the two of you allowed by the Iles cop to run your trade alongside each other as long as this keeps battles and bloodshed off the streets. Unique? I think Iles must read that very heavy journal, *The Economist*. It's been arguing for years that drugs should be legalized. The editors think gangster power would be smashed if the substances were easily available. I'd say Iles does his own take on that theory. He lets you and Ember run the trade as if it was legal, but only if you guarantee not to war with each other.'

'Naomi – what problems?' Shale said.

'That Ember, though!' Lionel-Garth replied. '"Panicking Ralph", as some call him. And the club he owns – the Monty? My God, what a hole! More police toleration. And somehow you two have divided up the city and can function almost like a partnership, but no partnership, just operating the same kind of trade in your separate areas, no frontier or turf troubles. Definitely unique, I'd say. Whether it can continue is questionable, though. I'd need to look at the details with some thoroughness.'

'Naomi – what problems?' Shale replied.

'Your priority! I can certainly understand that. A lovely woman, and willing to make allowances.'

'Allowances?'

'She despises snobbery and pretentiousness in any form. Well, I don't need to tell you, do I, Mansel? She'll no doubt treat you as she would any of her smart pals in London, regardless. I'd bet she wouldn't mind being seen with you in really quite chi-chi restaurants and so on up there. You wear decent suits and shoes, don't spill the soup over yourself, and she'll be content with that. She'd detest any sort of discrimination. It's to her credit.'

'Have you had some fucking tail on me?'

'Yes, a splendid woman. But reverting to Ember and the pact, or pacts, rather – one between you and Ralph and then the other one between the two of you and Assistant Chief (Operations) Desmond Iles. I do wonder about this,' Lionel-Garth replied. 'For one thing, there's a new Chief Constable over Iles, isn't there? A titled Sir, too. Iles used to be able to terrorize the predecessor into accepting his policy of do nowt about you and Ralphy. That might not be the same with this new Chief. What if he starts zero-tolerating? It's the mode in many areas. Some top officers admire the results in New York. And then there's Iles's right-hand man, Harpur. He doesn't really agree with Iles's non-interference regime, does he? All right, he hasn't got Iles's rank, but Harpur's word counts, as I understand it. We'd need to be alert, adaptable in case of fundamental realignments.'

'Naomi – what problems?' Shale said.

'Anyone can see how it might happen.'

'How what might?'

'Quite. I'm sure your eyes are open to that. You're no sucker, Manse, that's plain. The ways of the world? You know them.'

'In which respect?' Shale said.

'It's probably a comfort for Naomi to be able to get out to an obscure town like this for a while,' Lionel Garth said. 'The provinces. That rectory is an oasis. In the old days, religious houses could act as sanctuaries, couldn't they? People fled to them when pursued and took refuge. Perhaps she sees something of that quality in your current home, no longer a religious house, it's true, but with a comforting godly history behind it. The pressure is lowered. But, obviously, this is only temporary. People of that kidney won't rest.'

'Which kidney? Which people?' Shale thought it bad for this kind of dark, hint-hint conversation to take place among trees and leaves. It seemed damned inappropriate. He considered Glaythorn Fields as a place to relax and enjoy the openness, and totally genuine Nature, though within a built-up city. This was a plus to what was known as the environment.

'I might be able to help you fight them off, would be proud to, in fact,' Lionel-Garth said.

'Which?'

'Oh, yes, I'd have their measure,' Lionel-Gath said.

'Whose?'

'A very fine park this,' Lionel-Garth replied, gazing.

'Brilliant.' Manse certainly did not like *all* aspects of Nature, though. Even before that stuff re global warning, he used to look at the sea and wonder whether the bastard would one day break out from where it was supposed to be and get up over the cliffs and promenades, swamping everything, houses, discos, snooker halls, factories, TV masts, the lot. Them tsunamis might be only the start of it. He hated the way waves came in and banged down on beaches like they wanted to conquer this bit of land and then all other bits. Manse carried an organ donor card, but what use would that be to anyone if the sea got every-where? Nature had real, worrying power. But he thought the Glaythorn Fields fairly OK, not at all savage. Sybil and Manse used to come here and walk years ago, when she seemed more content – loud and bolshy even back then when younger, yet also loving towards him and the children, unrancid, full of vim, and able to name the breed of all dogs being walked by their owners, including Samoyeds. The Fields was not a spot for rotten news, or half-news, like this stuff from Lionel-Garth now. Manse thought of decline again. He saw that everywhere.

Lionel-Garth said: 'How it often is with these celebrity papers, isn't it, Mansel? Typical. Sadly typical.'

'How what is?'

'They look harmless enough, even trivial, and *are* trivial in some respects. Just a fringe part of the London scene. So, where's the danger? But most probably I don't have to ask. You'll see it. Or perhaps she's spoken of it.'

'What fucking danger?'

'There's frequently – almost routinely – a naughty link between the celebrity folk, the show-biz crew, plus, say, soccer people and media people, yes, a link between them on the one side and the more sinister areas, isn't there? Overlap.'

'Which more sinister areas?'

'Oh, yes, some of these sinister areas are very shady indeed. Hard, unscrupulous.'

'Criminal?'

'Many an example. Those kinds of links may look harmless, and frequently *are* harmless between the celebrity side and the lawless side. Although they might be risky, louche, worldly, raunchy, thrilling and stoked of course by A1 substances, it's nothing worse. Fun, of a sort. Not everyone approves or would seek it out, yet ultimately harmless – except, possibly, to those taking part. Matters can go beyond that, however, can't they, Manse? We've all heard of times when situations have turned nasty because of sex and jealousies, or alleged disrespect, or unpaid snort accounts, or money generally – all the customary ingredients. Yes, money in the main. The sums some of the people are concerned with can be huge, can't they? Big box-office takings involved, sponsorship deals for sports stars, product endorsements and so on. Sinatra and the Mafia involvement is the most glaring case, isn't it, Manse? And think how this developed – Sinatra, at the request of that arch crook Joseph Kenndy, getting the Mafia to help with the election to President of that clean-limbed, idealistic contender, Joseph's son, J.F.K. This was very big deal, yes, but there are many other instances, not quite as striking and financially massive, but to do with significant loot all the same. Now, nobody can run a celebrity paper and not

171

have significant contact with these rather free-wheeling TV, film, football, press, advertising and PR people, and therefore, in some instances, with the extremely dicey underside of London, and perhaps the underside of New York, LA, Moscow, Colombia. It's easy – perhaps inescapable – for someone influential in the publicity field like Naomi to get pulled into this kind of shady social group. It can bring perils, Mansel.'

'I don't believe Naomi is touched by anything like that. Where does all this come from – your information, if it *is* information? More like rumour and fucking London prattle.'

'Mansel, Mansel. I can appreciate that you don't want to believe she could have bad trouble.'

Shale hated it when someone used his name twice. It nearly always meant something super-shitty was on the way.

Lionel-Garth said: 'Naomi would have regular, welcome access to all sorts of glam people needing publicity, including some known to have a habit and the earnings to fund it, and who have friends who have a habit and the earnings to fund it, and who lay on very well-funded parties for those with a habit. Suppliers of stuff are bound to see someone like Naomi as a very useful facilitator in reaching such loaded potential customers. Very useful facilitators qualify for very considerable commission.

'But they may also qualify for very considerable enmity from the commodity suppliers she is *not* associated with, because, as they see it, she's helping the opposition, boosting their competitors. This is not always a gentlemanly trade, Mansel. Well, you've had years running a firm, so I'm not breaking any news to you. I admit I didn't know this London commercial setting until my routine curiosity about you and your operations here brought in Naomi, and then, naturally I did a little inquiring among the celebrity press as well. I know Naomi has sold her share in the paper, but her connection remains, doesn't it, through her consultancy?'

'Are you telling me she's a mega-pusher?'

'Probably not, Mansel. She puts people in touch with people. As I say, a facilitator, perhaps. An intermediary. That may be all. Puts the *right* people in contact with the *right* people. This is a major, rare skill and deserves and gets major rewards, as I understand things.'

'It's all fucking imagination and guess. You got no evidence.'

'I'll concede Naomi is very wary,' Lionel-Garth said. 'Not naive. Determined, capable, but discreet. I'm sure she wouldn't get brash and ostentatious with any wealth that might have come from off-colour sources. For instance, Manse, I understand you've got quite a collection of Pre-Raph originals in your property, including an Arthur Hughes and a Prentis. More than one Prentis? I forget. Denz mentioned how you really loved your paintings of this school.

'Although a safe with the armament and ammo in lies behind one of them, that doesn't taint or take away any of the beauty, does it? Indeed not. The guns stay absolutely hidden, and the fact they are hidden by a lovely work of art in no sense diminishes the loveliness of that work of art. Now, for you, Mansel Shale, businessman, owning such pictures is absolutely OK, above board, even commendable. You've decided this is how you will invest profits from a successful enterprise, or series of enterprises if we bring in the haulage and scrap yard, and why not? Yes, why not? Who can question or object to your devotion to art and the wish to bring together in your home wonderful, original examples of this art? Many entirely respectable commercial figureheads have done the same. I'd mention the advertising tycoon, Saatchi of Saatchi and Saatchi, naturally. But someone like Naomi Gage could most probably never risk flaunting her riches in that way. Why? Because her funds may have been piled up by what we'll refer to as very roundabout methods. I gather she, like you, is fond of the Pre-Raphs. This might have helped bring you together. Grand. A fine basis for a relationship. '

'Have you got some sodding spy called Geoffrey, who takes his wife and swine-kids along on jobs for cover?'

'But the difference for Naomi is, she'd never shell out for the actual paintings, despite admiring them so much, and despite being able to afford them, most likely,' Lionel-Garth said. 'People might start wondering *how* she could afford these works, and I don't mean just the authorities wondering – not only the police, that is. No, folk more hazardous than that, members of those sinister areas we spoke of could show an interest. They'd get curious about which of their rivals, competitors, enemies she was in cahoots with – very profitable cahoots. This could be perilous for your lady. There'd be folk who wanted her out of the way, so as to damage their rivals, their enemies. Again, some members of that sinister world who know something of art, and know also where and how to sell stolen, high-value paintings, would perhaps visit her flat and turn rough if she tried to stop them lifting the target items. Naomi Gage might buy Pre-Raph *prints* or *posters* to brighten her place at Ealing, but never, never, never original works, and possibly not even good forgeries, in case career robbers got a dud tip from, say, a window cleaner doing some observation, leading to a break-in just the same, and that potential violence.'

'Someone gumshoed me to my lawyer and then that gallery? You had a stooge, stooges, behind me from the after-funeral do? God, but this is so dirty and totally disrespectful to the memory of Denzil – using the occasion that way.' Manse experienced very true rage.

'I know you're bound to feel like that about Denz – someone who had been so close to you, and whom you prized. I'm sorry. But, Mansel, I had to think of the practicalities. I needed information about someone I might soon be working with at an important though provincial level as colleague. It may seem distasteful to you momentarily, but I think you will come to recognize that this kind of preparatory move was essential to the interests of yourself as well as me. I'll admit I wasn't familiar with the London celebrity–villain interplay – not its scale – but I'm able to talk to acquaintances there who can fill me in with the details. Well, they already have on the basics. Some owe me a service. Repayment's a matter of honour in our community. As an outsider, this is the kind of material you would never be able to access for yourself, I'm afraid. The London nexus is a very tight and exclusive one. It will look after its own, and only its own. Luckily, so far that includes me and a few of my mates.

'Because you are brave and honourable, Mansel, you will want to protect Naomi Gage, who has brought new joy and order into your life and home. Sybil is gone, almost certainly for keeps this time. She and her present partner have had quite extensive work done on the North Wales house, including installation of a jacuzzi and construction of an octagonal conservatory. This would suggest long-term, settled thinking, don't you agree? And then, on your side, I take it the trips to the lawyer have much to do with a permanent break. Divorce. Crossman, Fenton and Stuckey are known as a very efficient firm in that kind of work, and especially Joan Fenton.

'I'm sure you were never able to find full contentment with Patricia, Lowri and Carmel. These were excellent rotating friends, nobody fair-minded would gainsay it. But Naomi – Naomi Gage – something of a different proposition I feel. You want this connection properly, lastingly established. Oh, yes. It will be a privilege to help you ensure her safety, Mansel. Without wishing to romanticize or overstate, I feel the irresistible pull of Destiny here. I expect, with your influence hereabouts, Mansel, you'll be able to have a word with the school about admitting, without the usual delay, children of one of your vouched-for colleagues.'

This talk – the talk about Destiny – really angered Manse. It was the kind of talk you might get from someone like Lionel-Garth, smarmy, on the make, without decent feelings about his dead cousin, Denzil. All right, Denzil had been a two-timing sod, no question, but he hadn't been two-timing Lionel-Garth, only Manse. Surely there ought to be an amount of decency, even affection, towards somebody linked to Lionel-Garth by blood, and he had spoken of that blood hisself. Lionel-Garth was saying, wasn't he, that this pull or push by Destiny meant he had to move in on Manse's operation and on things between Manse and Naomi. Like he didn't have no option. Fate had stuck the responsibility on him and he could not resist. Well, Lionel-Garth better tell Destiny and Fate to fuck off. Manse would tell Lionel-Garth to fuck off also.

And then that unforgivable stuff about helping his kids queue-jump into Bracken Collegiate. Manse loathed any dodging of fairness and equality, unless it was really necessary. Well, it wouldn't be necessary for Lionel-Garth's children. It wouldn't be necessary for two reasons. One, they would not be coming here, anyway. And, two, even if they was coming here, Manse would not do anything so shifty as pulling wires for them at the school. 'No, I don't think I'll be needing you in any capacity, thanks, Lionel-Garth,' he said. 'Your car awaits. *My* car has to get going to somewhere else, with just me in it.'

Chapter Twenty-Five

2009

Harpur, running towards the charity shop behind Iles, heard what had to be a shot. It came from inside the building. Iles must have heard it, too, and seemed to up his speed. Although other sounds could sometimes mimic shooting, Harpur felt sure it was a pistol. Iles obviously thought the same. In this current siege, the gentle, well-tried gospel of wait-and-talk had nosedived. For once, at least, attrition didn't work. Harpur's instincts had done a better prophecy job. He'd suspected Iles would make a dash, and had considered making a dash himself. And now, here they both were, strung out like a hue and cry on the road, making a dash. Suddenly, dashes were the thing, because it looked as if 'John' in the shop had opted out of Rockmain's forecast and fired.

But fired where? At Iles? At Harpur? Both were possible, though he had seen no weapon pointed this way. That might be because of distance. But he had heard no bullet whine past, and noticed no kick-up of road surface. Iles, obviously, had not been hit. Neither had Harpur. So, maybe John had shot a hostage. Oh, God. They'd tried something against him, had they, and he defended himself? Or he might have cracked and gone gun nuts. There could be more shots soon. Harpur tried to accelerate.

He saw another possibility, of course. Iles – Gold – bestriding Dodd, had called for the all-out attack to start.

Harpur hadn't seen any police responding to that yet. But the cordon surrounded the shop. Had some armed officers broken in at the back of the building? Could be, though Harpur thought this unlikely. Firearms police would normally use more than one bullet. They were taught not to rush into shooting but, if they did shoot, to make sure the target couldn't retaliate, which normally meant a big barrage wipe-out. See Stockwell underground station.

Although Iles ran faster he had not lost any style. The ACC would probably not have run at all if he'd thought he had to ditch style. His head was back, grey yet steady and potent. His legs and arms were neatly coordinated. His feet seemed only to skim the ground, progress looked so flowing and easy. This was nothing like the crazed, panicky floundering of Dodd. Iles's sprint had dignity. It had brilliant doggedness. It had wide and deep symbolism: watching the Assistant Chief's unfaltering pace and determination, Harpur could half believe law and order might have a chance after all, not just here, but throughout the world, including Manchester's Moss Side, Detroit and Johannesburg.

The ACC loved his own legs. Harpur had often noticed him admiring them at quiet moments, and even at less quiet moments. They were not especially long but straight and slim and he had his trousers – uniform and civilian – cut to emphasize this. His legs went beyond the ornamental, though. As well as grace they had power. His running now proved it. Harpur could only just about keep up. The ACC obviously hadn't done himself any damage in stopping Dodd with that high leap and enveloping, flattening descent.

The shop's door on to the street was shut, though possibly not locked. But Iles didn't try it. He stepped in through the big gap made by the missing window, neatly avoiding tall spears of glass that remained jutting up ballswards from the lower frame. Harpur could guess at his thoughts. Iles would see this method of entry as the only right one. Direct and immediate, it took account of the altered state of things. It was practical. It put him into the heart of the situation while he might still have been fiddling with the door. A saviour had arrived. That's how he'd regard it. But a saviour who'd be an easy target stepping through that space. If you were Gold you had to get to where Gold could claim or reclaim mastery of a crisis, though, even if you were gunless.

Harpur flogged himself to go faster. If you were Gold's Silver aide you had to get with him. As Harpur reached the ex-window area he heard Iles from behind a rack of very second-hand dresses say: 'Oh, God, what a muck-up. But I don't blame that fucking Rockmain entirely. He was trying his little best.' It looked as if a wheeled rack of clothes had been pushed against the window during some sort of fight.

Chapter Twenty-Six

2008

'No, I don't think I'll be needing you in any capacity, thanks, Lionel-Garth. Your car awaits. *My* car has to get going to somewhere else, with just me in it.'

Shale had expected Lionel-Garth to ignore such aggro-filled words, or argue or even turn rough. Instead, though, he said with quite a show of what could be true sadness, if you could believe it: 'Well, Mansel, I'm sorry I've been unable to convince you of my potential worth to your operation. Of course, I can understand your attitude. You'd hardly wish to admit there could be anything untoward about your new and much valued lady, Naomi. In some respects, this is an admirable reaction, a wonderfully loyal and loving reaction which you believe is completely deserved by her. After suffering so much distress via the wandering Syb, you are naturally very sensitive to any suggestion that her likely replacement might also have . . . well, might also have disturbing aspects. But I'm terribly afraid, Mansel, that this attitude could leave you seriously exposed. Yes, seriously.'

'How?'

'Please accept, Mansel, that I wish you only well.'

'Right.'

'It pains me that, in order to help you, I have to deliver what are troubling facts about someone who is so whole-heartedly esteemed by you.'

'Right.'

'Mansel, I feel a considerable debt to you for the way you took care of my cousin, Denzil. You gave him accommodation at the top of your own fine property and provided him with a distinguished career in a company created and developed by you through extraordinary personal endeavour.'

'I believe it's part of being human that we should try to help those around us,' Shale replied immediately. And he did think this answer was correct, up to quite a point. Up to a point: obviously, Manse did not want to help someone like Lionel-Garth or his cousin, Egremont, nor any of the other pirates from fucking London who decided they'd like a slice of this ground, or more than a slice – the lot. This kind of try-on invasion was happening all the time and had to be smashed.

Lionel-Garth said: 'The fact that despite the grand treatment you gave Denzil he may have killed himself in what has to be described as an exceptional, even gaudy, fashion is in no way attributable to you. Very much contrariwise, surely. As I see it, that death displayed massive ingratitude. Admittedly, we can't know the inner state of Denzil's mind at the time – his secret problems and failings – but we can still ask whether this self-destruction was a proper response to the infinitely considerate reception given him by you and your firm. Note the double guns in the mouth, as though he wanted to be totally sure he saw himself off and didn't have to put up with any more of your kindnesses, Mansel, so freely given. It's bound to be damn hurtful. Anyone can see that. People who ask, could he have pulled both triggers at exactly the same moment and, if not, how did the second trigger get pulled when the first bullet would have killed him? – questions of that sort are no more than base mischief.'

'His motives, a sad, sad mystery. Often I've said this to colleagues.'

'Now, I know that those disgusting rumours about the death can still be heard here and there –'

'Totally disgusting. Nothing but rumours.'

'I was going to say, rumours from diseased, vindictive, envy-driven mouths. But one knows how to deal with them, doesn't one – yes, with annihilating contempt. There are people who cannot believe that good and friendly actions, such as yours toward my cousin, should be regarded for what they so sincerely are. They will look for evil, where there is none, only its very reverse. They will allege selfishness where there is only patent *un*selfishness. They will dismiss generosity as deception and hidden viciousness. These perverse slanders are a shaming comment on some members of humankind, Mansel. Your example, though, shows that not all are so negative, thank heaven.'

'My mother believed very thoroughly in kindness towards most, and passed this belief on to my brothers and sisters and me.'

Lionel-Garth took hold of the Jaguar door handle. 'You are robust and morally secure, Mansel, and have the excellent teaching of your mother as well as the present support of your new partner – and perhaps soon-to-be wife – plus your children, Matilda and Laurent. These cumulatively are superb assets. At your wish, and regretfully, I must leave you now in the excellent company of those traditions planted in you as a child, and your present kith and kin. If, however, you should ever need help from outside this admirable team, please be in touch. Thankfulness shall not fade, nor the sense of obligation.'

He did not attempt to shake hands again but went from the Jaguar and made for his own car. Manse thought he seemed slightly crouched, and he walked in a plodding, sort of weary, slow, inner-suffering style. Maybe the regret he'd mentioned was affecting his body, the gross sodding slob. Or it could be exhaustion after that endless fucking slimy spiel with its smelly double meanings. What the hell was the jerk getting at when he said Mansel 'took care of' Denz? 'Taken care of' – everyone knew what that could hint at. 'Taken care of' meant taken out of the scene, that is, killed, because someone had become a pest or superfluous. Lionel-Garth spoke like it referred to the flat in the rectory, and the job. Manse wondered, though, and wondered again. Lionel-Garth had also said Denz *may* of killed hisself. Where the fuck did that 'may' come from then? If there was one thing Manse hated almost as much as treachery it was slipperiness in others –words used to cover things up, not to describe how they are. In fact, he hated that whole last speech by Lionel-Garth, so chummy and reasonable, and stuffed with evil. Why did he have to bring up them rumours about how Denz went under and the paired pistols?

Yes, he said they was rumours and disgusting rumours, but he still had to bring them up, didn't he? What he said was full of bad suggestions and threats but done up as deep admiration and friendship, the sly, dangerous git. When he referred to them rooms given to Denz it was 'at the top of your fine property', like he had been stuck up in the loft out of sight like some old luggage or children's board games, which was what the bastard deserved, anyway.

Naturally, Manse would never ask Naomi about the rotten things Lionel-Garth spoke of. What could he say to her? It would be like, 'Oh, by the way, Naomi, darling, is it true you make a nice little bit of extra on top of consultancy fees, by putting big substances suppliers in touch with cash-rich, crack-head and/or mainline celebs you meet via the rag?' That would be the end of Naomi and him, wouldn't it? To be accused of this, or even just asked about it, she would regard as a full-scale insult. She might think that only someone in dirty trade hisself could imagine such a sickening idea. She'd want to know where such foul info – foul, *false* info – came from, and he would have to explain about Lionel-Garth and his connection with Manse via the late chauffeur, odd-job-man, bodyguard and lodger, Denz.

And, of course, Naomi would also ask how this Lionel-Garth knew about her link with Manse, and how Lionel-Garth could even pretend to have details of her career in London. Shale would not be able to dodge out of admitting he'd been tailed there, including the times he met her at the gallery and in the restaurant and even on the extremely special, joyful, first-fuck trip to Ealing. This would alarm and offend her, and he would look like a total arsehole to have let himself and her get followed and never notice. Manse considered he *was* a total arsehole in this respect.

She'd be sure to wonder what kind of existence she might let herself in for with Shale, especially if Lionel-Garth's reports of her sort of pimping role in the London top-grade drugs commerce was not true, or only slightly true. Would she have to be looking back all the time to see who was tracking where she and Manse went? This would spoil what ought to be a happy union.

He thought around it all quite an amount. He would not mind if she did get some good takings from putting the right people in contact with the right people. 'Pimping' was a stupid word for it. In the general business world it would be regarded as what was known as 'entrepreneurial', and people considered this as not just legit but very constructive and OK indeed. Many a national economy depended on the entrepreneurial side of things. He knew the word because Matilda had been doing the growth of British commerce in history and she said some folk then had been very entrepreneurial, and showed it to him written down.

His own firm was glad of the same kind of go-between help, and paid for it. Lionel-Garth should of known Manse would be aware of what a facilitator was, the gabby, superior sod. But Manse didn't want Naomi to know that he knew about it, if she *was* a facilitator, which, most likely, she wasn't. She had not told him about it – if it *was* true – and he considered it would be rude and unforgivable if

184

he showed he did know. Of course, there might not be anything *to* know, which would make it more upsetting if he asked her about it.

Somebody associated with a celebrity paper would certainly have good openings for entrepreneurial deals and what was termed 'furtherance of trade'. It really delighted Manse to think that when she bought them Pre-Raph posters, it might not be because she was stuck at that dud level owing to lack of funds. No, it could be on account of having super-plenty funds, which was the very opposite. Maybe she thought it safest not to give certain possibly criminal schemers any hint of this wealth. True, Manse hisself went for the originals, and always had. You would not find no prints or posters in *his* property, thank you very much. He realized things was different for him, though. He could call for protection if he needed it, and one of the originals hid a fucking armoury, anyway, very ready, weapons and enough rounds to see off a swarm.

If Lionel-Garth had it correct, them posters of Naomi's really mocked people who regarded them as pathetic, cheapo imitations. They *was* cheapo imitations, but cheapo imitations because cheapo imitations was wise and tactful in the circs, a smart ploy. Manse saw possibilities of a new, interesting side to Naomi, if what Lionel-Garth said about her extra activities turned out right, or even a bit right. Shale had been certain from the start that Naomi was the long-term woman for him and he felt even more certain now.

He could tell the children would be delighted if Naomi became their stepmother and lived all the time at the rectory, except, obviously, for the London business visits, maybe facilitating, or just giving a consult at the paper. Shale knew he didn't need to ask Matilda and Laurent never to mention Carmel or Lowri or Patricia to Naomi. His kids was sharp, and definitely understood about what could be referred to as 'situations' and their tricky aspects, such as the way time changed various factors in someone's life, for instance, Manse's. He would get in touch with the three of them, Carmel, Lowri and Patricia, and thank each one for her good help in the bad times after Syb went, and he would give all of them very decent leaving presents in old notes, as well as the legacies in the will. Obviously, he would hate it for one or more of them to come to the rectory without no invitation and make a fucking to-do about the past, as women sometimes did, yelling and spitting and stating all he'd wanted was shags. Although he could see matters from their angle, it would not be pleasant for Naomi to observe that sort of thing if, by then, she had become his fiancée or even wife and moved in permanently to the rectory which, of course, none of them three never did.

He had let all of them know by many a sign that this definitely could not happen. He would hate to have to threaten them now and hoped the money managed to keep them friendly and far away – happy to recall lovely moments with him, but also to accept them moments was over, over, over, and not coming back. After all, there was plenty of other men about for them, though, admittedly, hardly any would have an ex-rectory with genuine Pre-Raphs on the walls.

If one of them, or more than one, became a nuisance, he'd ask Hubert V.L. Camborne, with, possibly, Quentin Noss, another promising lad from the firm, to go and have a helpful conversation with her, or them – definitely only a conversation at first, but a conversation heavier than he would feel right for him, personally, to start. They had been sweet and very considerate partners on a temporary basis, and he would never be able to forget that, or not for a while. He knew he owed the three a lot and he would like to return this to them in what was known as liquidity, on top of the will mentions, owing to important shifts that was happening. Patricia came from a rough, violent, jaily tribe. Manse would have to be alert. God, families could be such a sodding trouble.

Today, Manse and Naomi were in bed after he returned from the school run. They would often take their breakfasts upstairs and either leave the meals and percolator on side tables while they made love, or have the breakfast first and then make love. He didn't mind at all which order things came in. Some might of been fussy in this matter but Manse, no. The coffee would still be warm, even if not taken till later, and the food was not of the cooked type. If she had Marmite on her breath or streaking a couple of her teeth black-brown, so what? In fact, it could excite him more, reminding of that first time they had it off in Ealing and he could taste and smell some of that fine restaurant lunch still toning up her mouth. And probably his own mouth had also contained a hint or two of that feast on expenses – hers. All right, so they was being watched at their table then, but he didn't know, so that couldn't spoil the feed nor the later full intimacy.

He didn't like Marmite, so she wouldn't get traces of that from him now. But he loved houmous on toast, especially the roasted red pepper kind, and she'd definitely feel some extra garlicky heat and spiciness on her tongue when she prodded it down towards his tonsils. Obviously, she couldn't deep-throat him the way he could deep-throat her, but she wasn't the sort to sulk because of this, so she made the best of it by deep-throating him with her tongue instead. And a tongue could bring back flavours, but a deep-throating dick couldn't, of course. Dicks were very necessary, but they had their limits.

Manse and Naomi made great and long-lasting love this morning and were now into the breakfasts. He said, when his mouth was empty for a spell: 'There's a jeweller in Nash Street who gets a very nice range of stuff in, Naomi. All sorts. You might think a town like this wouldn't have a jeweller's with the kind of top category items that might be usual for jewellers in London, but this jeweller in Nash Street is really pretty OK.'

'Ah', she replied.

'Luckily, I know him quite well, as a matter of fact. He wouldn't never try to sell me phoney items, or dodgy pieces he might be fencing for associates, which could lead to a trace and police bother later, and even to pulling a ring off of someone's finger, to be returned to where it was stolen from, although the ring might be the sign of a lovely relationship.'

'There's hardly any business where the scrupulousness of the proprietor is more crucial than a jeweller's.'

'I'll certainly accept that view,' Shale said. 'Do you feel like a trip there, I wonder? His name's Percy Ardoyne. People giggle at the name Percy now, but it used to be very noble. That's what I mean about him being reliable.'

'Hotspur in Shakespeare was a Percy.'

'Exactly,' Shale replied.

'When would you like to go there?'

'Soon.'

'Today?'

'Today or tomorrow.'

'I'm away tomorrow,' she said.

'Oh?'

'It's a nuisance but I have to pop up to the smoke.'

'Something wrong? A crisis?'

'I wouldn't put it as strongly as that, but I need to be there.'

'To do with the paper?'

'Of course.'

'But not a crisis?'

'Not a full-out crisis.'

'You're needed, though. You personally? To do with one of your contacts? That's what newspaper people call them, isn't it – contacts?'

'It's in my sort of area, yes.'

'These contacts will only deal with you as you? Only you can handle it?'

'Along those lines.'

'There must be all sorts of . . . of aspects to a paper like that,' he said.

'Yes, some.'

'I suppose it reaches out to quite a few in many different kinds of life.'

'Well, we hope so. It's what these papers depend on.'

'I can see that.' He waited for anything more. That was it, though. 'Well, we can go and see Percy later today.'

'Yes, later,' she said. She put her empty coffee cup back on the table and slid down in the bed. To Shale she seemed such a damn mystery, and he loved it – the unknown aspects. She was definitely more than just someone who had to buy poster-prints, and whose eyes rolled back into her head when she fucked. She wouldn't do anal but Manse considered this was only a quirk and would pass. It seemed not natural for someone who loved the Pre-Raphaelites.

Chapter Twenty-Seven

2009

Harpur loathed walking on broken glass. Through his soles these fragments on the street or the floor of a building brought a deeply hellish message. He got one now at the charity shop. To Harpur, the splintering din from such trodden-on bits proclaimed the collapse of order. Windows were civilization. They'd helped man quit the cave and climb to domesticity. They made palaces, conservatories and hospitals possible and banks. They had a kind of flat or curved useful beauty. They let in light and barred weather, dust, smoke, fog, moths, bats, seagulls and some noise. Windows separated inside from outside but also allowed those snug and corporate inside to see outside while remaining inside, and vice versa – a lovely, simple, sophisticated invention. But they were also hopelessly fragile. A sudden smack at any spot on their surface could make the whole translucent caboodle fall to bits, as if the total windowly structure had been a harebrained gamble or con. This shop window had fallen to bits. Civilization and its required orderliness could fall to bits.

Harpur didn't normally go in for such highest-high-flyer philosophizing. He left that to the supremos. Mark Lane, the previous Chief Constable, used to regard any major local crime as the start of universal catastrophe, catastrophe that would be blamed exclusively on him, because it began here, thanks to his slackness and all-round

incompetence. In those days, Iles would mock this obses-
sion – claim that Lane frantically studied the final Bible
book, Revelation, to see if he appeared there in some disguise as the prime cause of the world's end. I am
Apocalypse. Lane was gone from this patch now, but, very
strangely, Iles had turned into that same kind of broad field
worryguts himself. Lately, he'd shown classic symptoms
of dread that some bad situation on the manor proved
general rot was setting in, and by general he meant world-
wide. The shooting and the siege could be classed as bad
situations, or very bad.

And now Harpur found he, too, had begun this kind
of woolly, cosmic theorizing. Perhaps he was due for
promotion. He had found the sight of Iles running, in that
imperturbable, designated way, a sign that goodness on a
universal scale might survive regardless. 'I am not only
Gold. I am alchemy – can by my skill and magic *create*
gold. I will put things to rights.' But these brittle, ruined
glass segments, articulate under Harpur's shoes, said
something so different, didn't they? They said that windows were weakness, and that this weakness might be
symbolic of untreatable social weakness everywhere. He'd
heard of Kristallnacht 1938 – Crystal Night, as it was
prettily, callously, called – when the Nazis went on a spree
smashing the glass fronts of Jewish-owned German shops
in a storm of organized, authorized terror. There would
have been a lot of it underfoot that day. It had signified. It
had signified chaos. Yes. Yes.

Harpur stepped into the shop, as Iles had, and as much
an easy target as Iles would have been. The sun hadn't
gone down yet and in any case all the shop lights were on.
Harpur had heard no further shots, though. Out of sight
behind racked display garments the ACC said: 'Good
evening, folks. I'm Iles. Is he dead?', his tone slightly
muffled by all the shop's hanging, worthy gear

'He might be dead,' a woman said.

'He hasn't moved, not for a couple of minutes,' a man said.

'There was a struggle,' another, older-voiced woman said. 'The pistol went off.'

'We have it,' the man said.

'Put it on the floor and stand away,' Iles said.

'Stand away?' the man said.

'A contingent of my people will be here in a minute,' Iles said. 'They'll be excited and gun-happy. I know these folk. They are admirable and home-loving, but it's best they don't see a man unknown to them with a firearm just now.'

'Right,' he said.

Harpur pushed aside the castored show stand of used jackets and suits and went to stand near Iles. Over by the bric-a-brac display a fair-haired man lay half-curled on the floor. He'd be late twenties or a little older, in a good suit, newer and smarter than any for sale here. He wore brown cowboy boots. A pool of blood had formed on the carpet near his chest and was spreading.

Rockmain arrived, gunless, at the shop. He came in through the front door. A warning bell jangled when he opened it. The sound seemed to Harpur absurdly normal, given how things were here now. Iles said: 'You shouldn't have come, Andrew, dear. You're much too valuable to be put at risk. The country needs your brain and general, measured aplomb. No siege is complete without you.'

'Was this necessary, Gold, really necessary?' Rockmain said.

'Was what necessary?' Iles said.

'The intervention, the potential violence.'

'Ask the people here,' Iles said.

'With respect, they could not see the full picture,' Rockmain said.

'Could you?' Iles said.

'There is a great deal of proven, handed-down wisdom on the conduct of sieges,' Rockmain said.

'This one will be added to it,' Iles said. 'My canter and Doddy-neutralizing will become part of that proven, handed-down wisdom, perhaps a necessary, amending contribution, to demonstrate that wisdom and waiting are not the same.' He turned slightly. 'Ah, here come the boys and girls in bulk and bristling with armament.' Ten officers wearing plain navy dungarees and grey, big-peaked baseball caps rushed into the shop through the window gap and the door. They moved with astonishing quietness. Some carried pistols, others Heckler and Koch sniper rifles or semi-automatic carbines. They fanned out quickly around the shop. White capitals on the caps said POLICE.

Iles raised his voice: 'No shooting, please, my brave and timely ladies and gentlemen. You'll all know me. I am, unmistakably, Iles and Gold. With me is Commander Rockmain, a tactician and discard, short-arsed and runtish but nonetheless on our side. And then we have DCS Harpur, also almost certainly known to all of you as someone occasionally well-intentioned but' – the ACC's voice began to escalate from shouting towards screaming – 'but who, prick-driven, is always ready to get at other men's wives, even, I have to tell you, the wife of someone superior to him in rank, education, taste and breeding, and who had always treated him with the kindness and unpatronizing generosity that I, Iles, am justly known for and –'

Harpur said to the attack group: 'All other personnel standing are hostages and of no danger. Four individuals, three female, one male.'

'That's one of his damn tricks,' Iles said. 'Did you notice it? Of course you noticed it.' He spat in rage on to the carpet twice, dredging hard inside himself to get stuff for the second go. He spoke to the hostages, who stood grouped among the chock-a-block display stands. 'He'll cut into my very reasonable statements, about his obnoxious, sickening, lech behaviour, with some unnecessary, diverting banality to do with the work scene.' Iles did a smarmy, sing-song, contemptuous imitation. '"Four individuals, three female, one male." A brilliant piece of sexing, wouldn't you agree? Does the bugger think you can't see or count? Deviousness? He'll get a bleeding Nobel Prize for it.'

People in the police party had probably heard Iles carry on like this at other times in public, often featuring more vehemence and phlegm, and they listened and watched now without their features under the baseball caps showing much interest. The hostages stared at him, perhaps already disorientated by their hours kept captive here, now subjected to extra rough shock and strain, maybe a slice of that chaos Harpur had forecast to himself. Iles, this time addressing the whole mixed gathering, said with a resounding, loony chuckle: 'I can assure you all, though, that when my wife, Sarah Iles, and I discuss those degrading episodes now – what we refer to jointly, entirely jointly and in total accord, as "the Harpur blip", that's it, "the Harpur blip", an appropriate phrase, isn't it? – yes, when we discuss them now Sarah Iles is amazed that she could ever have regarded him, Harpur, as someone entitled to any kind of relationship with her, and certainly not service-lane knee tremblers or activities in fleapit hotels, municipal parks and bandstands, and backs of cars, no, certainly not any of those. Recalling that time, Sarah Iles and I laugh together in our home at the obvious, hindsight preposterousness of it and –'

'Why do you keep calling her Sarah Iles?' the older woman said. 'If her name is Sarah and she's your wife we would know she must be Sarah Iles.'

'Don't fucking well abuse me with your logic,' Iles replied. 'I came to effect a rescue.'

'No need,' the woman said.

Harpur said: 'What Mr Iles – i.e. Gold – means to indicate, I think, is that our firearms party should withdraw at this point. The siege is effectively over. I believe that was your drift, wasn't it, sir?'

'Thank you, Col,' Iles replied. 'Yes, put up your weapons. The man dying or dead near the trash stall there would obviously have been our boy to blast, but no longer. He does not, repeat not, require further clinching, coup-de-fucking-grâce rounds in the head or anywhere adjacent, thank you.'

Rockmain, fingering one of the tweed display coats, said: 'Do you think, Gold, that someone –'

'The garment's not at all your style, Rockmain,' Iles replied. 'You should go for the subfusc. The subfusc is right up your street, wouldn't you agree, Col?'

'Do you think, Gold, that someone with your type of acute mental variability should be in charge of anything, let alone a life-and-death siege?' Rockmain said.

'I don't imagine you're the first one to ask that kind of question,' Iles said. 'Not by a long chalk.'

'No, most likely not, but what is the answer?' Rockmain said. He unhooked the coat and held it against himself.

'I told you, you'd look rubbish in that,' Iles said. 'But you put things very well. "Variability". That's quite a word, taking into account the context, wouldn't you say, Harpur?'

'But we have to ask whether it amounts to a disabling quality,' Rockmain said. He replaced the coat.

'Ask whom?' Iles replied.

Harpur went over to the man lying face down on the floor and crouched to get a better look at his face. He avoided the blood. This was the kind of absolute ground-level closeness that Iles would usually bag for himself when examining a corpse, or about to be, especially when the ACC was in uniform. He liked to demonstrate that rank didn't get in the way of nitty-gritty policing, particularly when there was blood. Harpur knew he'd better act immediately to beat him to 'John'. Harpur resented having only been second in the gallop and entry to the shop, and with having no part at all in the nulling of Dodd. Also, Harpur felt ashamed for allowing Iles to step first into the place, when the risk of being shot was max. Harpur needed to rebuild himself. Iles was Gold and magnificent in many ways, but Harpur knew he must not let the sod get imperial. Iles adored domination – his – and so there had to be a snaffle bridle on him somehow. Harpur, getting his own nose down to alongside John's bent nose before Iles did, amounted to a decent pick-me-up and triumph. About twenty-nine, yes, slightly aquiline, thin-lipped, blue-grey eyes, both open.

'Do we know him?' Iles said.

'I don't,' Harpur said. He went through his pockets. 'Nothing on him except this other pistol – a Walther. Full chamber.'

'So, a pro,' Iles said.

'Not a very good one if he was after Manse Shale,' Harpur said.

'Not a very good one if he gets scragged by hostages,' Iles said.

'You see, he had defects. He would obviously have capitulated if given a little more time and pressure,' Rockmain said.

'The people here gave him pressure,' Iles said.

'With respect, not the right kind,' Rockmain said.

'Oh, I don't know,' Iles said.

Chapter Twenty-Eight

2008

When Naomi and Manse went to look at Percy Ardoyne's stock of engagement rings in the afternoon, Manse felt pretty happy – yes, obviously he did – this was a fine occasion – but he had to think, also, about Naomi going to London tomorrow, for something to do with the celebrity paper she said, and it certainly might be right. He definitely didn't have nothing to show it wasn't. As he told himself recently, a consultant had to be on the spot sometimes to be consulted. That's what consultants did. Anyone would see this. You couldn't be a consultant if nobody could consult you now and then face-to-face, or via some other body part.

For instance, if you thought of a hospital consultant, well, he needed to be *at* the hospital to do operations and check on piles or brain tumours. Being a celebrity paper's consultant was not exactly like being a hospital consultant and some of Naomi's work could most probably be done by telephone or email. Now and then, though, she would have to get there to explain which pictures ought to go on this or that page, and make sure the crossword puzzle was OK, if they had one, and maybe interview some important star in that grand restaurant. Having quite a feed with vintages could be an important part of a consultant's job.

Just the same, this new trip was bound to give Manse some worry. He'd *always* worried when she went back to

London for a day or two, and maybe he should of worried more. The thing was, what Lionel-Garth had said re facilitating truly troubled Manse. Yes, it might be all rotten guess and flimflam. But if someone or more than one had been watching him and Naomi up there at the gallery and so on, maybe they'd be watching her now when she went on her own to the paper and anywhere else.

All right, it had been easy to get behind Manse and dog him, because they knew where he'd be starting from – the Hackney drink-up and eats after the highly tragic Denz funeral. It might not be as simple as that with Naomi, but they could have a watch on the paper's London offices in case she showed. Or they might even be spying on the house here so as to get with her when she set out. That idea really angered and upset Shale – to have snoopers doing a lurk and sly peep at such a once-religious building as a fucking rectory. This would be terrible disrespect and a sort of insulting sin, in Manse's opinion. He'd kept an eye lately, of course, but he didn't observe nothing troublesome of a surveillance kind.

Anyway, he considered Naomi ought to have someone with her. Joan Fenton, the lawyer, had told him off for not taking a bodyguard when he went to London. Now, because of Naomi's link to him, maybe *she* ought to have a bodyguard herself in London. He could see problems with this which nagged him hard even while they talked to Perce and tried to choose the ring in his shop. Shale had told Naomi that Percy would never offer imitations or heist-hot stones to such a noted customer as hisself, or to anyone connected to him, for example, Naomi, and Manse more or less believed this. Perce would be careful never to offend Manse – never to get up his nose, you could say, because noses did come into this, oh, yes! Perce had to think he might want to get back to nostrilizing coke lines some day, and he would know from not very long ago that Manse could always supply at an honest price, with home delivery if required, due to illness, a collapse or just lying low after some bother.

And Percy would also know that, for customers Manse liked, the stuff was certain to be of through-and-through quality. That had always been one of the things Shale and Ralph Ember agreed on in full. The customers you knew well, and even had a sort of friendship with, you looked after, making sure the commodity you sold them had deep but jaunty character and no over-mix. Regulars who very plainly had good, steady money to spend deserved this, if everything was OK between them and Manse or Ralphy. So, Perce would have to go careful, and no messing now with the ring.

Well, of course, Perce was very interested in Naomi and the engagement, not just because he'd most likely make a very nice sale, but also relating to Manse's changed situation as far as a partner was concerned. Curiosity gave Perce's eyes a real bubbly glint. It was like he'd climbed a mountain and could see from the top a landscape he'd never viewed before on the other side. He knew Syb, naturally, although he hadn't supplied the engagement and weddings rings for her and Manse way back, because his shop wasn't there then. But Shale had often taken her there for Christmas and birthday jewellery, and on anniversaries of the first Liston–Clay fight, 25th February 1964, which Sybil regarded as a very important date, and not just because she got jewellery out of it every year, such as an unbase metal bracelet or necklace.

Manse was in favour of jewellery as how to beat inflation, always a peril regardless of which gang of cruds ran the government. Also, he liked jewellery if he had a lot of cash income to get rid of. To put a whack of it in the bank could make people there wonder where it came from. Or, of course, they'd *know* where it came from, but if it was massive they'd start talking about it. *Heard how much Manse Shale put across the counter today? Go on, have a guess, and then stick a couple of noughts on the end.* This kind of gossip could be harmful, and Manse regarded it as extremely unnecessary. Also, if you had a lot of accounts to spread the funds, someone in the fucking Revenue might wonder about that, too. W.P. Spilsby, known as Cummerbund Spilsby, used to advise him on investments, but Cummerbund went through a big religious experience with visions one afternoon when very close to sober and, they said, later became a friar or something like that in the Persian Gulf or Tasmania, or around there. It might be wrong to call him Cummerbund now, because there wouldn't be no dressing up for him in this new post.

As everyone would expect, Manse had called on his own at Percy's shop a while ago to tell him he and Naomi might be along and wanted to see only true stones, and true stones without no ram-raid or hold-up tasty tales to them, whatever the danger discount. Clearly, this was not the kind of statement you could give over the phone, on account of that sod Iles and the taps he might arrange on Percy's line or Manse's – illegal, but this didn't bother dear fucking Desmond Iles. That's how you got to be an Assistant Chief with gold leaf on your cap, knowing what was legal and what wasn't, and then being able to pick the illegal aspects you could get away with. Of course, Perce went all hurt and said he would never have such articles on his premises, not for any customer, but especially not for Mansel. 'I just thought a word at this juncture might be useful, Perce.'

'Be at ease, Mansel,' Percy had replied.

'Thank you, Perce.'

'Totally at ease, Mansel. It goes without saying.'

'Thank you, Perce. And I don't want no diamond made in a factory – one of them synthetics, as they're called. This diamond got to come out of a mine somewhere, such as South Africa.'

'Undoubtedly, Manse.'

Because of the various factors, Manse would go to 85 per cent in trusting Perce, or even 87. Just the same, Manse wished he could concentrate more on the rings now in the shop, but them anxieties about Naomi's return to London did grab some of his brain. He thought he'd be able to spot a phoney diamond, or other jewel, straight off, even if a truly brilliant fake. This was not the chief trouble, though, was it? Where the jewels came from – that question bothered Manse most. And because some of his mind was switched to thoughts about Naomi's next day plans, he found it hard to remember the full list of gems lifted in recent, successful British hits, and their descriptions in the press.

It would be bad if the police or insurance nigglers came down on Percy for dealing stolen items, and took back stuff he'd sold lately, including Naomi's ring, a splendid token from Manse, her extremely devoted fiancé. He could soon get her a replacement from a different shop, yes, but to have something as serious and joyful as an engagement kicked about and dirtied like that would be inappropriate. He'd noticed the way some very top people used this word, 'inappropriate', to mean bleeding horrible, but they couldn't say that owing to their environment.

Most probably, Naomi would think protection by body-guards a nuisance and not necessary at all, so it would have to be secret, if possible. And the point was he'd *prefer* it to be secret because he'd like to know if the hop to London had another side to it, not just the paper. In the early days when Naomi returned to London on a visit, he used to be afraid she might have someone else up there, a man. He would get nervy and jealous until she returned. London was full of sex. You could feel it hanging about everywhere, whether you went by taxi or bus or tube train, even in Hackney. Why did they need all them taxis except to get people from here to there for sex? They used to have smog. Sex took over. Think of that Fenton piece or her arse-proud secretary, Angelica, with the horny pink pen. And, naturally, there'd be men around who considered they had a right to all the available meat. He'd always worried she might be in this sort of scene, such as – 'Naomi! Splendid! Great to see you again! Feel like another fuck?'

His fear now, though, was not about that kind of carry-on – not to do with leg-over, casual or long-term. No, he wanted to find out if she ran a sort of business sideline, fixing for celebrities to get fixes. He would not be angry with her, if so. In the world of commerce all sorts happened. Trade had to be kept moving at a sweet and strong rate, or things in many areas might seize up. Life was complicated, nobody could deny this, surely, with all sorts of things affecting other sorts of things in them many areas, and so on, and then so on some more. It was known that the Great War, with all the mud and casualties and bayonet charges, started just because some foreign sod got shot on the way to his car in a next-to-nowhere place abroad.

Mansel did reckon he ought to have the full picture of Naomi's career, though, so he could know how to take care of her. No question, it could be a fucking dangerous bit of facilitating she was into if she was. Manse wouldn't be able to tail her hisself. He'd be too easy to recognize. If she noticed him from a side glance or a reflection in a shop window, she'd be disgusted to find her lover could try such smelly tricks. Kibosh for him, most likely. And it wouldn't be no use saying to her in an open, jolly way, 'I'll come with you to London, just for an outing, Naomi,' because, suppose he did go along, she might change her programme, if she regarded some of this as confidential and didn't want him inspecting it.

Manse thought he might tell Hubert V.L. Camborne to get behind her, perhaps with Quentin Noss. They'd both need to be weaponed or the bodyguarding would not add up to much at all, would it? He'd give them something each from behind the Arthur Hughes, including a very decent helping of rounds. If you expected gunfire you had to make sure the gunfire coming from you or yours would be a real gunfire blast which could go on and on until the opposition had enough gunfire holes for the *Guiness Book of Records.*

He would advise Hubert and Quentin they better be always ready to get theirselves to positions near her which would be like a wall against any bullets aimed at Naomi. There'd be a risk bonus of £377 each for this job, plus all private medical costs including surgery and convalescence up to a fortnight in a Majorca four-star if one or both of them got hurt through protecting her. He wouldn't speak to them about possible death from this duty, because it might make them jumpy and less use at the job, their gun arms shaking, like that hopeless jerk Fredo's in *The Godfather* on the movie channel, when he was supposed to be guarding his dad from killers sent by the Turk. But Hubert and Quentin would be sure to know from previous slip-ups that the firm would take on all funeral expenses with a class undertaker, and see women and children all right for at least five and a half years in that unfortunate event.

Shale said: 'Naomi and I talked the other day, Percy, about the way your name goes right back in history and used to belong to truly distinguished families and perhaps still does.'

'Oh, yes,' he said, 'I often feel that link. It's like a responsibility, although in my case only a first name, not the family name.'

'Just the same, it gives like a tone, Perce,' Manse said. 'People will know they are dealing with someone straight and of honour.'

'I hope they would know this anyway,' he said, 'whatever my name.'

'Very true, Perce,' Manse said. 'Many buy their engagement rings online these days, I know. But to me that would never seem right. It's more suitable to go to someone we know and trust. Or that *I* know and trust anyway, and Naomi will agree that anyone I know and trust will be completely worth knowing and trusting. The choice here, on your premises, Perce, seems to have a kind of . . . well, yes, a kind of blessing to it, a blessing from the one who has up till now looked after the ring in his personal shop, like waiting to match this ring to the right person and finger.'

'This is very much how I see it, too, Manse,' Percy said. 'A privilege, the kind of which doesn't come all that often to Nash Street, and is, therefore, the more prized when it does.'

Manse had wanted to give Perce a way to spout something holy like that in front of Naomi, so she might feel OK about buying here. But, of course, she was in the press and people in the press didn't believe a fucking word anyone said, which was why they made up theirselves most of what they put in the paper. 'There's a Mr Percy, or, more like it, *Lord* Percy, in one of the plays by that well-known writer many years ago, William Shakespeare, Naomi tells me,' Manse replied.

'Oh, yes,' he said. 'You read a lot, do you, Naomi, and go to the theatre?'

Obviously, Manse could tell this was Perce doing some digging. Manse didn't mind it too much, although what damn right did Percy have to dig? He was here to flog stuff, that's all. It looked like he definitely believed the name Percy made him special owing to a family way back and William Shakespeare. Manse had the idea Percy felt surprised that someone who was a reader, and even went to the theatre for heavy stuff such as William Shakespeare, would be teaming up with him, Manse Shale – not really a scholar at all, Manse would admit that – and maybe leading to marriage. Perce might think it must be a money thing – she being after Manse's. He wouldn't know Naomi could have plenty of her own through sale of that share in a London paper, and consulting, and perhaps helping trade up there, also in London, through facilitating. Most probably Perce wouldn't even know what facilitating fucking meant. He could do smarmy sale jabber, yes, but facilitating he wouldn't have no idea about.

And he wouldn't know, either, that Manse and Naomi was brought together in a very strong and lovely way by art, and especially the Pre-Raphaelites. He wondered if someone like Perce would be able to understand that. Also, he wondered if someone like Perce had ever *heard* of the Pre-Raphaelites *or* facilitating. Percy thought all the time about prices and profits and shafting the customers, plus perhaps memories of when he used to get himself high and noisy and optimistic through very honest coke. It was a tease, really, kidding him along that he belonged to some greats in history. He was underweight and tall with a face so thin and bony and hard-looking you would think you could cut out fretwork models with it.

'Ah, I see you already have some rings, Naomi,' Perce said. More dig, dig.

'Yes, I'm fond of them,' Naomi said, like that would be enough, thank you, Percy.

'The opal, beautiful. Red on black, so rare,' Percy replied, if you could call it that. He took her right hand and lifted it so he could get a full gawp. It was undoubtedly physical and offensive, or almost. Percy sounded like he wanted to ask her who coughed up for it, the cheeky bastard. *Manse* wanted to ask who coughed up for it, but that was different, clearly – he had a right. This was a woman he allowed to make a home in the rectory and was buying an engagement ring for, although the divorce from Syb still had to be absoluted.

'I like them both equally, the opal *and* the amethyst,' Naomi said. She took her hand back.

'Oh, certainly,' Perce said. 'Most rings carry a story with them, perhaps a precious story, even a *semi*-precious stone like the amethyst.'

'So, what you got in the way of diamonds, then?' Manse replied.

She liked them, the opal and the amethyst, did she, and would she like this engagement ring better than either of them or both? This question gave Manse some torment. His spit turned sour. Spit could be such an indicator, couldn't it? He began to wish they'd gone to another jeweller, one with not so much chat and knowledge.

'Opal, the gemstone of Australia,' Percy said.

'Yes, I believe so,' she said.

Did she have something going with Aussies then in the past – them tanned bodies by surfing so much at Bondi beach? Would she of met someone from there through the paper? Did Australia have any celebs? Or was he someone she knew through facilitating?

'And are you from this area, Naomi?' Percy said.

'London,' she said.

'Ah, the big, big city. People from there often miss it when they move. Do you have to get back now and then to enjoy the flavour again for a while?' Perce said.

Which flavour? Manse would like to know. Was he talking oral, the sod?

'For work occasionally,' Naomi said.

'A business connection?' Perce said.

'So what you got in the way of diamonds, then?' Shale replied.

Percy said: 'I like to chat with a customer, a new customer, such as Naomi so I can make a guess at the kind of jewellery she might prefer. We know about the opal and the amethyst, yes, but now I have to make a judgement on the kind of diamond settings to show her. I don't say I'm infallible at this kind of guesswork, but I do have some experience, some considerable experience. A moment.'

He went to a display, unlocked the glass door and pulled out a tray of rings, with quite a bit of gesture, like a magician getting an egg from some old lady's earhole. He put the tray on the counter in front of Naomi. '*Voilà, madame,*' he said. He stood back, so pleased with his gawky self, and with what he most likely thought was a smile on his razor-wire fucking face, teeth definitely on view, yellow and big and oblong and shaky-looking, like a knacker's-yard horse. 'This is what is known as a triple, Naomi,' he said. 'Isn't it magnificent? This is a ring that via its cluster signals not only the splendid nature of the occasion, but, through the harmonious bringing together of three diamonds, speaks also of the enduring harmony of the relationship, engagement, marriage. They do not compete with one another, are not engaged – engaged! – in rivalry or upstaging, they are three and yet they are one, as though meant for one another, yes, from the moment they were mined.'

'Attractive. But I think I'd prefer a solitaire,' Naomi replied.

Manse really adored her for this. He had an idea 'solitaire' meant one diamond on its own, no tripling up and getting fancy and numerous. The French did quite a bit with jewellery, so words like 'solitaire' was borrowed from them. He would not never of told Naomi a single jewel was what he wanted her to want but now she showed she wanted that he felt truly pleased and did not mind if Perce saw how pleased he was to have that triple idea chucked into the ditch.

He reckoned Percy deserved this because, when he talked about the enduring harmony, he was obviously taking the piss – more or less saying he hoped the thing with Naomi worked and didn't turn out the same as with Sybil, where enduring harmony became a bit fucking scarce, and so did she, as was fairly well known. Although Manse had naturally given Lowri, Carmel and Patricia some jewellery, he never brought them to Percy's shop for it. That would not of seemed at all right because he had been here before with Syb. But to bring Naomi was totally OK because she would be like permanent. She had an undoubted right to go in any shop in the city, either with Manse or on her own, using card or cash.

All right, they had to put up with a lot of bullshit from Percy through coming here, but this was still the best jewellery shop in the town and none of the others would really be good enough for Naomi. For quality, the Nash Street shop was like that terrific restaurant in London she took him to on exes, hers, so coming here was kind of equalling up. Somebody ought to say to Perce, but in a completely helpful, understanding way, that he should try not to smile, or if he did smile not to open his gob so wide in case people got scared some of his teeth might fall out on to a jewels tray. That would be a lovely fucking triple, wouldn't it, not diamonds but Perce-style front gnashers?

'Or a solitaire!' Percy said. 'In my head, when I was guessing at your taste, Naomi, I thought *either* a triple *or* a solitaire, I swear. I'll confess I got it wrong – but not so very, very wrong. Marginally wrong. A solitaire, because it stands alone, unclutteredly magnificent and strongly simple, will tell the world that this is a relationship bound to continue, and, in its unobtrusive but confident fashion, to thrive.'

Manse hated the way he kept on about enduring and continuing, like he didn't believe things between Manse and Naomi *would* endure or continue, so he had to state over and over that they would, like drunks who never stopped telling you they wasn't drunk. But at least Perce didn't start mentioning Syb's name to Naomi and saying he felt sure she and Mansel would last much better, which would obviously mean he *didn't* feel sure of it and neither would anyone else. He knew he had to go delicate if he'd like to sell a pricey ring now, and if he'd like to know Manse would always be there with good gear in case Perce decided to get his habit moving again. Although Perce could be a right prick, Manse always felt a powerful, warm sense of community when entering his shop. Up to a point many people that Manse knew helped one another, and only became cruel and destructive when truly necessary because of a disagreement or for self-defence.

Manse considered the ring Naomi chose looked entirely right on her finger. He didn't think he'd ever seen a ring look more right for the finger it was on. He could tell, too, that Perce saw how wrong the triple would of been on that finger – fussy, common, crowded. She held out her hand in front of him and Shale and Manse muttered, almost to himself, 'Yes, oh, yes, yes.'

Percy said: 'Oh, yes.'

The diamond was square but not in a boxy, pushy, sort of way. The angles of it was nicely rounded off. Sometimes Manse did a bit of imagining and fancy thinking and he decided now that the silver claws holding the stone looked proud to do it. So they bloody should! The gleam off the diamond was a true gleam, steady, superior, pure, full of genuine cost. Manse knew that some referred to this gleam as a diamond's 'fire'. He liked that. This one had plenty of fire. Percy didn't put no price tags on his rings, and Manse thought that was wise, because a man wouldn't want his fiancée's choice influenced by such a grubby matter. When Naomi went over to the shop window to get the light better on the diamond, Perce came closer to Manse and said quietly, 'Seven and a half grand normally, but seven to you, Mansel, for old time's sake and your kind remarks about the history of my name.'

'Six,' Manse replied.

'Six and a half,' Percy said.

'Six two five.'

'Six three,' Percy said.

'Done, and a written, signed affidavit showing where it come from, what's known as provenance, Perce.' This word you noticed a lot in art – the 'provenance' of a picture, meaning its total history, showing it was not a copy – a phoney. That would be nearly the same for the ring, but, instead, Perce had to make clear it had not been nicked in some raid, possibly where the owner or guards was pistol-whipped, or their balls electrocuted to make them cough the code, or even shot dead. He would not

209

want a tainted ring like that on Naomi's finger, nor ripped off of Naomi's finger by police sent by that sod Desmond Iles, who'd get a big giggle from this brand of unpleasantness. One of the things about the ring was, when clients that she might be doing a facilitate with saw it, they would know she was used to bloody good money, so they'd realize her commission had to be something very worthwhile, thank you.

Manse had ten thousand on him in cash. He hadn't known what price ring Naomi might of gone for and he'd needed to be ready. Ten grand was five hundred bills. You couldn't use fifties in this sort of deal. Perce would not take them. Hardly anybody would take them, there was such beautiful duds about. Fifties was worth taking trouble over the illustrations and paper quality. Forgers did, and fifties had become like a dose of the clap – you didn't want one, and definitely not a hundred and twenty-six, which would of been £6,300.

So, he had £10,000 in twenties: four wads spread around different pockets of his suit. The thing was he wouldn't like Perce to see he'd come with £10,000 because that might make him ratty. He'd think he didn't charge enough. He'd believe Manse had expected to pay more but did some very smart beating down just now. All right, the deal was done and Perce couldn't go back on it – wouldn't go back on it, because of the rules and his pride. People as tall as Perce went in a lot for pride, and especially when their name came from history. Next time, though, Percy might fight for a tougher bargain. Manse believed in planning for the future. Although he didn't think he'd be getting engaged ever again, or definitely not for a while, anyway, he'd probably come to Perce for other kinds of jewellery. Most likely Naomi wouldn't want to celebrate the Clay–Liston fight every year, but she might have different crucial dates to remember.

The other point about the cash was, Manse wondered how Naomi would regard it, settling up in note bundles, not by a cheque or card, which would be the way people paid where she came from. They wouldn't flash rolls. Most likely they'd consider that vulgar, like bookies at the course. 'Percy and I will just pop into the little office here, Naomi,' Manse said. 'The paperwork. Guarantees, that sort of thing.'

'Fine.'

She seemed to think this was quite OK. Perhaps Naomi felt that the paying side of today shouldn't get mixed up with the lovely loving and romantic side. Manse could definitely understand that. It was what he meant about not having crude price tickets on these jewels of true, deep affection.

In the office with Perce, he pulled out bills from three pockets and noticed him looking at the one Manse hadn't touched. That was obviously the trouble with notes. A quantity had bulk. Someone who did a lot of cash deals, such as Perce, could manage a rough totting up of what you carried just by a gaze at the tailoring outline. Manse counted out three hundred and fifteen twenties. That still left £1,200 from only them three pockets, which Manse replaced. There would be another £2,500 not handled at all, just folded and unbothered in his left jacket pocket. Perce wouldn't be able to do an exact tally by glance, but he'd know it was more than two grand and less than three five. He didn't look too joyful. Well, fuck him. He used to be a damn good snort customer, fine money and reliable, but now he'd gone clean as clean, the dirty failure. If they all suddenly turned negative like that businesses everywhere would fold. Had he thought of such very serious results of his selfishness? Not at all. Although Shale still kept coming to his shop for purchases, Percy did not do even a whisker of buying from Manse these days. So, yes, fuck him.

'A lovely woman, Manse,' Percy said.

'Thank you, Perce.'

'What she has is dignity, but not a cold dignity. There is warmth present.'

'Warmth is one of her qualities. And dignity, yes.'

'Composure.'

'Certainly.'

'She is evidently familiar with the London scene.'

'She is much respected there.'

'Which particular aspect of the London scene?'

'She has an easy, straightforward way with people which is considerably appreciated in the capital, where so much is to do with appearance for appearance's sake.'

'Well, yes. Does she know the . . . well, the context here?'

'In which respect?'

'Your business.'

'Oh, she's getting used to the rectory now,' Shale replied with some excellent heartiness. 'It's a change from her own place, a flat Ealing way, very comfortable and very nice – I certainly don't look down on flats – but obviously not quite the size of the property here! She loves the high ceilings and cornices and mahogany frame french windows to the garden. Cornices thrill her. I don't think there's many of them around in the Ealing district.'

Perce gathered up the twenties and put them in a desk drawer. He didn't count them. He did have some manners, and, in any case, Manse had counted them aloud as he put the bills on the desk. For Perce to repeat would be a smear. They went out of the office and rejoined Naomi. 'This has been a true delight, Percival,' Manse said. 'I know I speak for Naomi, too.'

'A shared pleasure, I assure you,' Perce replied.

At home, the children were really excited by the ring. They sat close to Naomi to get good gazes at it from all sides. They enjoyed the ways colours seemed to appear and change in the diamond as light hit it from different angles. He knew they would never speak to her about Syb's engagement ring, comparing them. They could feel from inside theirselves without being told that this would be the wrong topic and might hurt Naomi. Syb's was one of them triples, as a matter of fact, though not bought from

212

Perce whose shop wasn't there then. That's what Syb wanted – a triple. Manse had gone along with this. Well, of course. Even when younger he'd believed women should have a say in things, quite a few things – not just rings – because they was entitled to make some choices for theirselves, seeing some of them definitely had brains and might know quite a bit about life. He had thought then, and still did, that Syb was a triply kind of person.

He didn't mean to be rude or make a criticism of her. There had to be some people who the triple suited or they would not have triples in the shops, would they? A triple could be right for Syb, but for Naomi the single stone was just as right. The children used to look at Syb's ring and was fond of it, but they wouldn't say to Naomi something like, 'Our mother had a three-diamond ring, known as a triple, this not being the same as yours, which is a diamond on its own.' The children behaved now like they had never even seen a triple. They talked like a single diamond for a ring was the only sort of ring, and fine. Naomi stayed truly patient with them, letting Laurent and Matilda really take their time admiring.

Manse found it wonderful to watch the three of them on his furniture, so happy with one another. Families could be a fucking pest now and then, such as Denz's brother and cousin, to do with the death, but families could also be terrific, and he considered Naomi was helping get this family back to being a close, loving crew again, despite the children's mother, gone with some roofer or vet or maybe a chef.

Laurent said there was the famed nursery rhyme in which a star twinkled in the sky like a diamond, but also another much more serious poem where the writer stated he, himself, was like an immortal diamond because of his everlasting soul, even if his body wasn't up to much. Matilda knew some history of diamonds, such as India and Brazil in South America, where they first came from, and she mentioned that the Greek word for a diamond meant 'unalterable'.

Manse didn't mind the children going on like that about how a diamond was something that lasted, and had therefore become important and quite thumbs-up for engagements and marriages after. When Perce had talked like that he was just being fucking snide, the snide, hinting sod, remembering Syb. But Manse believed the children felt really pleased that the ring might mean something good. While they talked with Naomi about it, he went to the den room and phoned Hubert. Manse told him to get over to the rectory right away and bring Quentin Noss. Because there might be line tapping he didn't say why, but Hubert would guess it must be urgent. Manse knew the kind of pistol Hubert liked best, but he would have to ask Quentin about *his* favourite.

The children went to bed and soon afterwards Naomi said she'd go upstairs to pack for the journey tomorrow. Manse took the Arthur Hughes off the wall and opened the safe. These days he had two Glock 17s, two Walthers and three Brownings in there, plus plenty of their suitable ammo. He thought Hubert would most likely take the Glock. He said he fancied a weapon used by police because they would pick a gun that really stopped the bugger hit. In a little while he and Quentin Noss arrived. Manse did not regard this as a simple situation, not at all. He told the pair he wanted Naomi protected, to stick with her non-stop, and stay unobserved.

But he would not like them to think he needed to find out on the sly whatever she did when she wasn't at the paper or at her flat in Ealing, although that's what he did want them to find out. He could imagine Hubert and Quentin putting it around that he didn't trust Naomi and had to get her spied on. This could make Manse seem scared and pathetic. And it would be really bad if Perce mentioned here and there about the engagement ring being bought, and these two mentioned here and there that

Manse had to have her followed because he didn't know what she would get up to in London. He *didn't* know what she might get up to in London, but he wouldn't want to seem stupid and cunt-struck – buying a pricey ring for someone who might be giving him the run-around and getting banged undisclosed on the London circuit.

Of course, Hubert and Quentin would think his worries was about some other man up there, or men. He did not tell them about the facilitating. He considered it best to keep that kind of information confidential. It would trouble Manse if he saw they regarded Naomi as some sort of high grade pusher. But that was how they *might* regard it. They would be like Perce and probably not understand the commercial term, 'facilitating'. Manse told them her London office address and the name of the restaurant, plus business, home and mobile numbers. Before her first visit to the rectory she'd given him some photographs of herself to show the children, so she wouldn't seem a stranger. He laid these out on the table for Hubert and Quentin to study, and Hubert borrowed two, one a profile, one head-on.

Quentin took a Browning. He was short, going fast towards gross, with thick-framed glasses. He knew the technical side pretty good and asked Manse now whether the best thing would be to put a trace bug in Naomi's luggage. But that seemed foxy and grim to Manse, especially as she might find it. He said no.

Manse locked the safe and put the Arthur Hughes back. When he went up to bed Naomi was sleeping, and he felt disappointed. He had hoped they could make love, because this was an important day and it would have been a sign that even though she was going to London tomorrow her true life went on here now. However, he thought it would be crude and roughhouse to wake her up. Her left hand was on top of the duvet. The diamond ring made a lovely show in yellowy light from the table lamp.

He guessed she had deliberately settled down like that so he'd see it and feel great about it when he came to bed.

The opal and the amethyst was out of sight under the clothes. Good. Get that fucking Oz opal buried. This was a woman who could sense his thinking, even if she had gone asleep early on this considerable day. He felt a bit ashamed of putting Hubert and Quentin on to such a caring lover, but he didn't cancel their orders. He was glad, though, that he'd refused the bug. Besides, how would it get fitted? He didn't want someone like Quentin wearing them glasses going through private clothing in her case with his fat fingers. Manse had told them fucking strong not to get seen by her. It would be fine as long as she didn't know she had tails sent by Manse.

But it looked like she *did* know she had tails sent by Manse, or, anyway, that she had tails. Manse arranged for Hubert to call a pay phone from a pay phone at exactly 6.30 p.m. next day. He came through to say they'd lost Naomi. 'I think she'd spotted us, Manse. She did all the usual counter moves on the underground, learned from TV espionage tales and Joseph Conrad's *The Secret Agent*, of course.'

'Ah, yes,' Manse said.

'Sit down in a carriage and then exit back on to the platform just before the train goes. All right, we were ready for that one, and only Quentin had got on with her. I'm waiting in case she does the bale out, and I take over. I follow up on the escalator. She immediately goes back down on the one next to it and picks the opposite side platform for a train going the other way. I'm with her. I don't see her looking at me ever, and I didn't see her look at Quentin, either. She's bloody fly, Manse, if you don't mind me saying.'

Manse did, but he only grunted He hated a word like that – 'fly' – stuck on to Naomi. It made her sound like some street con merchant with the three-card trick.

'Yes, an expert,' Hubert said. 'What's her background?'

216

Fuck her background. Just do the job I sent you on, prick. But Manse stayed silent.

Hubert obviously realized he'd get no answer, and in a minute started again with this dismal yarn. 'She gets on the first train to arrive. So do I. She makes like she's about to do another leap. I leap. She stays. The train pulls away.'

So this fucker, Hubert, was *not* so fucking fly, was he? How about fucking 'useless'? How about 'dick-headed'? How about 'a liability', especially if he did some talking where he shouldn't?

'Quentin and I rendezvous by mobile at her office,' Hubert said. 'We can't tell whether she's in there, of course. I phone and ask to be put through to her. The girl says Naomi Gage only rarely comes to the office these days and is not expected this week. It might or might not be true, we couldn't tell. At lunchtime I went into the restaurant you mentioned, said I was looking for a friend, but she wasn't there. We decide we ought to visit the Ealing flat to check if that's where she's gone.

'We get a cab and ask him to take us to a car hire firm. We rent a Focus, in case we need to watch her place – less obvious from a vehicle. There doesn't seem to be anyone in the flat. Hard to be sure, though. It's afternoon and someone in there wouldn't need lights yet. We watch the building for ninety minutes. Nothing. We quit the car and walk to the flat's front door. Quentin is good on locks, as you know, Manse, podge or not. He opens up. This time he wasn't all that clever, though, and there's a little splintering. She might notice. We do a quick but very thorough survey. More nothing.

'Listen, Manse, she has two pictures hanging in that style you like – the Pre-Raphaelites. But , of course, stupid of me, I expect you've seen them there. Quentin says it would be a good notion to take both and then this break-in would only look like an art robbery, not someone being charted, which could lead to awkward inquiries. Obviously, you wouldn't be able to receive the pictures, Manse, because she's living in the rectory and would recognize them. Quentin says he knows someone who will buy high quality art, and not make too many queries about where it came from. It seems an idea – he's bright, greaseball or not – but I tell him any proceeds must go to you, because the art has been lifted in the firm's time.'

Suckholing bastard. 'They're posters,' Manse said. 'The frames are worth more than the pictures. Twenty quid would cover the lot.'

'Posters? Like pop star rubbish for kids' walls?'

'Prints. By the million. Sink them somewhere.'

'Really, Manse?'

'You're not going to take them back and hang them, are you?'

'Quentin will be disappointed.'

'Oh, dear, I'll blub, shall I? When do you think she spotted you?'

'Not sure. Is it important, Manse?'

'Of course it's fucking important. If she noticed she was followed from here she'll know who sent you, won't she?'

'Well, I thought she'd guess that, anyway. Are there other interests who might tail her?'

'That's what I wanted to find out,' Shale said.

When Naomi came home next day, Manse said: 'So how did it go?'

'Great – and many compliments on the ring.'

Chapter Twenty-Nine

2009

There were four statements. Harpur read them again.

1. Mrs Beatrice South, aged fifty-two, of 11 Masterman
Avenue, shop manageress.

*As was usual, I opened the shop at 8.30 a.m. on Wednesday,
3rd June 2009. Mrs Maureen Hyde, a voluntary worker who
helps on three days a week, arrived at 8.35. At about 8.50 the
first customer, a middle-aged man, entered the shop and went to
look at items on the Books, CDs and DVDs shelves. Just after
9 a.m. the shop door was pushed open violently from outside and
a man and a woman came in. The man had a pistol in his right
hand and was holding the woman with his left hand around the
neck. She seemed to be trying to free herself by tugging at his
hand with the fingers of her right hand. But he pulled her with
him into the shop.*

*I thought the man was in his late twenties, the woman older,
early thirties. The man slammed the shop door shut and began
shouting at the four of us in there. It was something like, 'Don't
anyone try anything. You'll be all right.' There was swearing
among these words, which I don't want to repeat here. I now
know the man to have been Lance Stanley Sparks and the woman
Veronica Susan Cleaver.*

*Sparks shouted at us to get to the middle of the shop and keep
still. 'This is loaded,' he said. He put the gun against the
woman's head for a moment. The man customer shouted, 'No,*

219

no, we'll do what you say.' Then Sparks let go of the woman's neck and pushed her towards the centre of the shop. He screamed at the rest of us again to get there, too, and not 'to try anything'. I believe we were all too frightened to 'try anything'. I'm usually reasonably calm, but that morning I felt terrified. I was standing, but feared my legs would go.

It was impossible at the time to know why he acted like this. It was obviously not a robbery. There's not much worth taking in a charity shop. So, it was as though he'd gone mad and unpredictable. Nobody could tell what he might do next. This was the frightening part of it. I wondered whether Sparks and Cleaver knew each other. Maybe this was some kind of lovers' quarrel or a domestic crisis that had spilled into the street, and then into the shop.

There is an alarm button behind the main counter in case of trouble. It links to the police station. But I had been arranging clothes on one of the racks and could not get to it. I thought Sparks must have guessed there'd be an alarm somewhere, which was why he wanted us all in the middle of the shop where he could watch us. I was scared to make a move towards the button and, in any case, my legs felt too weak to take me there. For a couple of minutes I had to hold on to the clothes display stand for support.

Mrs Hyde was behind the counter near the Local History Artefacts display and not far from the button and I tried to signal to her with my eyes that she should get to it and press it. But she was not looking at me, she was looking only at the man with the gun. And after a couple of moments she came out from behind the counter and joined the other two in the middle of the shop. I decided after a little while that my legs would do it and I also went into the middle of the room.

Sparks told us to sit on the floor. He stood behind us with the gun held up across his chest. He could look out over us through the shop window to the street. He seemed to think people would come in pursuit. His breathing was noisy and fast. I could see some of the street from where I sat but there didn't seem to be *any movement out there. The man customer spoke to him – asked him what had happened, what it was all about.*

Sparks sounded in a rage when he answered. I thought the accent sounded like the Midlands or Northern. He said it was about him getting away from trouble, 'very big trouble'. I recall those words –'very big trouble'. The male customer didn't say anything more for a few minutes. (I now know him to be Thomas Ure.) He seemed to realize that if he kept on asking questions Sparks might get more ratty and go wild with the gun. I had an idea that what had happened had something to do with that gun. It was not a fake gun. When he said it was loaded I thought he meant it was still *loaded although some shots had been fired from it. He seemed to believe we could tell what had happened earlier with the gun and might think all his ammunition was gone. I wondered if what had happened was so big and terrible that it took up nearly all his mind, and it was so dominant in his think-ing that he assumed everyone else knew about it, too. Of course, that would be crazy. But he might be crazy, and crazy with a pistol.*

Thomas Ure asked what very big trouble he meant, and said we might be able to help. He said he was sure everyone here would agree with that. I said, 'Certainly.' And Mrs Hyde said, 'Oh, yes.' Veronica Susan Cleaver didn't say anything. She was crying and most probably in shock. All Sparks said with more swearing was yes we were a help, by being hostages. He said nobody would fire into this shop while they knew he had pri-soners in case of hitting them, so we'd better not try anything because we were a weapon, just as the gun was a weapon. The one weapon, his gun, would make sure the other weapon, us, didn't try anything. What he said was 'any fucking thing' but I have cut out most of the swearing. That's how some people talk when they are tense and scared and desperate – they think the swearing makes them sound hard and not easy to beat.

Then he asked if there was a back door to the shop. I didn't know why he asked this – whether he thought he could get out that way and disappear, or whether he feared he could be attacked from that direction. I said yes there was a back door on to a ser-

221

vice lane. I told him I had a key to the door, of course. I hoped he would decide to get out and leave us. I wanted to make it easy for him to go.

But just then we heard cars, a number of cars, driven very fast outside. I could see some of the street through the shop window. Most of the cars and vans were marked police vehicles, and the unmarked ones might have been police, also. I could hear other vehicles at the rear of the shop. Sparks saw and heard, too. 'They're here,' he said. 'All round me.' I wondered then whether Mrs Hyde had been able to press the alarm, after all. But I felt pretty sure she hadn't. There probably would not have been as big a response as this if she had. It appeared that this flock of cars and vans had come because of whatever it was had happened earlier. Sparks had been chased here. I saw a big caravan towed into place in front of the shop.

About a quarter of an hour after this the telephone rang. It was on a shelf near the cash desk. Sparks moved backwards with the pistol pointing at us until he reached the shelf and picked up the receiver. I could tell it must be the police speaking to him. He would not tell them his real name but said to call him John.

The statement broke off here and the interviewing officer had inserted an explanatory note. 'The conversations between Sparks ('John') and the negotiator are as recorded and included in the siege log, and Mrs South's version of the Sparks side of these exchanges has been omitted as superfluous, resuming on the final sentences.'

Towards evening I saw a man emerge suddenly from the police caravan and begin to run up the road towards the shop. He wore civilian clothes. Veronica Cleaver was also looking from the window and when she saw the man she gave a little scream of shock. She said, 'Oh, God, it's Gary. Oh, God, sorry, sorry, sorry, Gary.' They are the sort of words that stick in the mind. I didn't understand them properly. What did she mean – 'sorry'? She did not sound well, but that could have been just the trauma and fear. Very shortly afterwards another man, but in police uniform, came from the caravan and began to pursue the civilian. He ran much faster than 'Gary' and about halfway to the

222

shop caught up with him and threw himself on Gary from behind, the way a buzzard might come down on a rabbit. They both lay there still. It looked to me as though Gary had been knocked unconscious when he hit the ground with the policeman's weight on top of him.

The policeman's uniform didn't look like an ordinary policeman's, but of superior material. I learned later that this was Assistant Chief Constable Iles. It was unusual to see an Assistant Chief Constable chasing someone in the street and flinging himself on to him – Gary James Dodd, as I later discovered. In the shop, Sparks had seen these two men running towards us and he seemed to get very agitated and worried. He was shouting over the telephone about these men being a decoy. He kept on about that.

He yelled at Veronica Cleaver, 'Gary? Who's Gary? Is he police?' He seemed to think that what had happened in the street was to get his attention while other people attacked from the back of the shop. He turned to look that way, swung his gun that way, the phone in his other hand. I believe it was the first time he had pointed the gun away from us. He was standing near Mrs Hyde and she suddenly stood up and hit him on the head with something, a real swinging blow. At first I couldn't see what it was she used.

The blow made him stagger and she hit him again. He dropped the phone and half steadied himself. But Thomas Ure and I both stood and tried to grapple with him and get the gun out of his hand. We had to fight him. Mrs Hyde hit again with the thing in her hand, this time to his jaw. I saw she had picked up from the Local History Artefacts display an old-style, plainclothes officer's pocket truncheon made of lead with a heavy rounded tip and a wrist strap. It was thought to have been used to deal with a street riot during a factory strike in 1901. I felt Sparks go weak but he would not let go of the gun. We still tried to get it free and Veronica Cleaver joined us now.

We must have struggled with him for more than a minute. Mrs Hyde kept striking him and as he tried to twist away from us the gun went off, the sound muffled by clothes, his and ours, but very clearly a gunshot. All strength went from his body and he slid out of our grips towards the ground. Mrs Hyde hit him once more as he fell, in the genitals this time, but I think he was already dead. She didn't seem to believe this, though, and moved around so she could get at his head again.

When Mrs Hyde stood up she had accidentally pushed one of the full, wheeled display stands and it rolled forward and into the front window bringing it down. Very shortly after this, and the struggle and gunshot, Assistant Chief Constable Iles and other police arrived from the front and back of the shop. Veronica Cleaver ran from the front door towards Gary James Dodd who still lay unmoving on the ground. Coming in the other direction – that is, towards us – I saw four people, a male and a female police officer, a man and a young girl. I now know the man to be Mr Mansel Shale and the girl, his daughter, Matilda. Mr Shale's name is, of course, well known in the city owing to the type of business he runs, but I wasn't certain I had ever seen him before. Matilda was crying. She held Shale's arm as they walked. He himself looked very distressed, though at the time I did not know why. As well as his name being familiar, I thought I recognized Mr Shale as someone who had recently donated some Pre-Raphaelite posters, but, as I've said, I wasn't certain.

They passed Veronica Cleaver and Dodd. I saw a crowd of watchers behind police tape near what seemed to be the caravan incident room. Another man ducked under the tape and ran to talk to Veronica Cleaver. She seemed embarrassed or angry with him. Two paramedics came with a stretcher and took Dodd away to an ambulance. Veronica Cleaver went with them. The other man returned to the crowd and I lost sight of him.

Shale and the policeman entered the shop. Shale's daughter waited outside in the street with the woman police sergeant. I think Shale had been brought there to see whether he could identify the gunman – Lance Stanley Sparks. He still lay where he had fallen, face down. Assistant Chief Constable Iles bent and took a handful of Sparks' hair so as to pull his head back and make his face visible. Shale bent forward and looked at it very briefly. He said: 'No.' Assistant Chief Constable Iles asked him *whether he was sure and Shale straightened up and turned away. He said he'd never seen the man before.*

2. Mrs Maureen Hyde, aged seventy-nine, of 23A Frame Street, widow.

Luckily I had read my horoscope for the day before going to the shop. I don't remember all the words exactly but I know it warned me of a possibly unexpected 'and not necessarily or entirely pleasant' interruption to the normal course of things. Therefore, I tried to remain close to the Local History Artefacts tray where a small truncheon made of lead was on show as well as a knuckle-duster, both of which were apparently used by the police during a riot at the beginning of last century. We have had trouble in the shop previously from openly defiant thieves and rough, misbehaving child gangs, and I wondered if the horoscope referred to such intrusions. I thought it would be irresponsible if I did not prepare myself to deal with troublemakers, because, this being a charity shop, its good work for unfortunates should be protected in every available fashion.

I felt that since the truncheon and knuckle-duster had not been bought yet and were therefore present, they had, as it were, been allocated by Destiny, as foreseen in the horoscope, to deal with the interruption mentioned. I had decided that if either the truncheon or the knuckle-duster became bloodied during some incident, they could easily be washed under a cold tap and then returned to the Local History Artefacts tray for sale utterly unstained. During the 1950s I was in the Women's Royal Army Corps and we learned some unarmed combat, such as the weak spots on an attacker's body if male, particularly the temple and genitals. I met my future husband in the army.

When the man I now know to be L.S. Sparks came into the shop, with the woman I now know to be Veronica Susan Cleaver, I felt no fear because I saw at once that his arrival had been fore-seen in my horoscope and I realized I would be able to deal with him, owing to mental preparedness and physical preparedness also – that is, my nearness to the truncheon and knuckle-duster. He was shouting and screaming the fuck, bastards and cunt words, as would be expected in this type of crisis, and I could tell it was all based on weakness.

These are words that do have meanings, but they are not used for their meanings in this type of occasion, only to frighten and abuse. I had the idea even then that the gunman had done something terrible before reaching the shop and he knew he would soon be called to account for it. Of course, I know now what he had done. I thought of the Bible verse, 'Be sure your sins will find you out', and I picked up the truncheon and hid it in the sleeve of my woolly, with the strap around my wrist. I did not take the knuckle-duster because it would have been too obvious, and I was not trained in the WRAC to give upper-cuts, which is the best punch with a knuckle-duster.

It was important for me to keep the truncheon hidden because he told us all to get into the middle of the shop away from the counters. I think he realized there might be an alarm bell there. In fact, there was an alarm bell there, but I thought it best not to go for it because he would have noticed and maybe shot at me, so that having the truncheon would have been useless. I also thought that if I pressed the bell the police station might send someone around when they could, but it would be only one or two officers and unarmed. That's what usually happened when we have rung the bell previously. This would be no good against a man with a gun or guns. Occasionally, they didn't even have anyone at all to send around at once and we would have to wait as much as an hour.

Although Mrs South was trying to give me an eye signal to press the bell, I ignored her and considered it best to hang on until Sparks was distracted somehow and then really wham him with the cosh. In the WRAC we were trained to sum up all aspects of a situation and then arrive at a plan, with the objective very clear. Here the objective would be to flatten Sparks as soon as there was a chance. So I went out from behind the counter and joined the others in the middle of the shop. Veronica Cleaver looked very, very bad.

This time, Harpur skimmed the central parts of Maureen Hyde's statement. He knew they chimed pretty well with

Beatrice South's version, except that Mrs Hyde claimed to have been going for Sparks' temple, not his jaw, with one of her hits, and said that launching the display stand against the window had been deliberate, not an accident. Her army training had told her to maximize chaos in this kind of set-to, so as to further confuse the enemy, 'like the fireships at Cadiz,' she said. In none of the statements – South's, Hyde's, Ure's or Cleaver's – was it clear how Sparks' pistol had gone off. Nobody mentioned getting a finger on the trigger. Would Mrs Hyde have been trained to go for the enemy's gun, as well as to clobber him thoroughly at the temple and balls? Her right hand would probably have been wielding the cosh. And her left? She didn't mention it. And none of the others spoke of getting a hand on the gun, either. So, did Sparks do himself, maybe unintentionally in the struggle, maybe not? At the end of her statement, Mrs Hyde described Veronica Cleaver's rush towards Dodd, still prone on the ground.

This seemed to show true worry and love for him. She had cried out strangely when he first began running from the police caravan, speaking his name, Gary, saying she was sorry. She said it several times. I didn't know what she meant. While she was attending to Dodd on the ground another man seemed to ignore the cordon tape and come to talk to her. But she looked as though she really didn't want this, whoever he was. I had seen something like this when I was in the WRAC. A man was hurt during an exercise on Salisbury Plain and his girlfriend, who was also in the exercise, came running to see if he was all right. Then another soldier came and tried to pull her away from the one on the ground. He got up, although hurt, and there was a sort of fight, the three of them, until an officer came. This didn't happen with Veronica Cleaver, because the man on the ground didn't recover. But she looked as though she wanted the other man to get lost. And he did. In both these episodes it was like the woman had been carrying on a bit, and suddenly there's too many men around. But I don't suppose this is relevant to the siege and so on.

No.

3. Thomas Ure, fifty-two, of The Old Water Mill, Kaletree, private means.

I visit charity shops from time to time in order to ascertain whether what I would regard as unsuitable material is on sale there, with particular reference to books, CDs and DVDs. By 'unsuitable' I mean of a sexual, violent or perverted kind. I know very well that I cannot prevent the sale of such material in commercial emporia, but I feel that for shops devoted to charitable work some sort of protest should be made. If I come across examples of this kind of degraded and degrading work, I draw the attention of the shop manageress to it. I do not in any respect damage the items on the spot, but, having spoken to the manageress, I offer to pay for the offending articles as long as I can have an assurance that they will be withdrawn and possibly destroyed. I certainly do not wish to take such dubious goods with me.

I do not care to think of folk in, say, the poorer areas of Ethiopia, receiving benefits from a charity shop which have in fact been paid for by the sale of improper stock. On the morning of 3rd June I had come across in the charity shop a copy of a book called Torch *by someone called David Craig which, on a quick perusal, I deemed not to be right for purchase here. I was about to take the book to the manageress, who was attending to clothes on hangers, when the door was very abruptly thrust open from outside and a man holding a gun came in, dragging after him a protesting woman.*

The man was shouting words which indicated, I thought, an uncommon degree of stress for a customer in a charity shop, such as 'fuck', ' twats', ' cunt' and 'bastards'. This sudden event seemed to mirror some of the speech in books, CDs, and DVDs, which I consider not altogether right for a charity shop's shelves. But this was a man actually using these terms as parlance and I could not at first see how to deal with it. This was acutely different from words on a page or spoken via electronic means by actors. I wanted to help him and said so.

Ure's description of what followed also tallied with Mrs South's and Mrs Hyde's, and Harpur skipped again. At the end, Ure's statement said:

228

Although it was comparatively easy in charity shops to complain about unsavoury exhibits for sale, I came to see that someone uttering gross language and with a gun in his hand – this, I think, was the important matter, I mean the gun in his hand – in those circumstances I decided that physical remedy was probably necessary and I was content to help the manageress and the lady with the truncheon in restraining the intruder, though death seemed excessive. This is often the trouble with guns. They go off.

4. Veronica Susan Cleaver, aged thirty-two, of 9 Larch Lane, IT consultant.

I had parked my car in a multi-storey and was walking towards the shops in Scourton Road on Wednesday, 3rd June at about 9 a.m. This was not a part of the town where I normally shopped, but a colleague had said there were bargains to be had here. I became aware of a man running towards me. Two police officers in uniform were chasing him and shouting at him to stop. He was carrying a pistol in his right hand. The policemen also had guns. I was so startled and afraid that I think I froze for a minute. I hoped he and the police officers would run past me. I have not been well lately and find it difficult to cope with stress episodes.

The man with the gun, who, I have since learned, was called Sparks, did not pass me, however, but when he was very close shouted to me to get into the charity shop. I obviously did not want to go in there if he meant to come in there also. I stood still. He grabbed me, by the shoulder at first, and stood behind me with the gun against the back of my neck and he screamed at the two officers chasing him to stop or he would shoot me. They did stop. They were yelling at him to let me go, but he didn't.

The two policemen got down and lay on the road, their guns pointing towards him, but they did not fire. I think they must have withdrawn to the cordon later. Sparks moved his hand from my shoulder. Instead, he took hold of me around the neck, so breathing became difficult. He kicked the door of the charity shop open and pulled me inside after him, then he kicked the door shut.

Her statement described the events in the shop, without much difference from the other three statements. She hadn't taken part in the fight with Sparks because she felt so weak and numbed by his attack on her. She concluded:

I had recognized my partner, Gary James Dodd, making his way from the police caravan towards the shop and then brought down by the man I have learned since was Assistant Chief Constable Iles. I realized Gary must have heard of the siege somehow and come to find me, if he could. As soon as Sparks fell, seeming unconscious or possibly dead from a gunshot wound, I left the shop and hurried to where Gary still lay. He seemed to be coming round and was able to speak my name. I was hugely relieved. Just then a stretcher party came and I went with them and Gary to an ambulance and the hospital.

Chapter Thirty

2009

Not very long after the wedding* and honeymoon, Manse set off to London to see Joan Fenton again and check over the most recent amendments to his will and sign it. The divorce settlement with Sybil had been done OK, he thought – on the generous side, as Manse had always wanted. He hated meanness, even towards someone like Syb, who hadn't behaved at all proper, in his opinion. Anyway, now his new wife, Naomi, had to be properly looked after in some vital changed clauses.

Hubert drove him in one of the firm's Audis. Manse had wanted to leave him behind to do the school run with Matilda and Laurent, but Naomi insisted real hard that this had to be her duty. Although it worried him, he agreed. He could understand her thinking. She was their stepmother now and very keen to make this obvious. It was official, yes, but she also required people to recognize it, see it as normal, accept it. This seemed to Manse very lovable and strong.

He left the Jaguar for her so that up at the school they would know this was undoubtedly the new Mrs Shale, who absolutely had a right to drive this car and to be in charge of the children. Never would Manse have allowed Carmel or Patricia or Lowri to of ferried Matilda and

* See *Hotbed*

Laurent in the Jag. It would not of been correct. Their role was not to drive the children to school. He had an idea Carmel, Patricia and Lowri would of recognized this theirselves. For Naomi, another thing about driving the children was it showed she was settling down much more here. She seemed to of almost given up going to London. Maybe the consultancy didn't matter so much to her now. Shale wondered, too, whether the 'facilitating' had never really happened – just made up by that sod Lionel-Garth to bring trouble and nerviness. To Manse in these days and weeks and months, Naomi, Matilda, Laurent and himself seemed a true family, a happy household.

Naomi certainly deserved to be big in his will, even though she'd automatically get a good sackful if he went because a wife had certain entitlements via quite a law or two. The rotten idea that he could get snuffed at any time still hung about. It was even worse lately. Them two, Egremont Lake and Lionel-Garth Field, had been quiet since he saw them at the rectory or up near Bracken Collegiate, but that might not mean much. Why had one or other of them done that tracking and tracing? Perhaps Joan Fenton had been right when she said he ought to have a bodyguard always. It was definitely sensible to get the will tied up and neat.

He'd had Ralphy Ember as his best man for the wedding, but that might not mean much either. Always there was this pressure to get monopoly. Manse felt it often. And he guessed Ralph did, too. It could be dangerous. One reason he'd asked Ralph to be best man was that he'd have to stand close to Shale in church for some of the service. If Ember had been thinking the ceremony would put Manse nice and exposed and easy to blast by gunmen smuggled into the congregation, he'd have to ditch that plan because he might get hit hisself.

Manse and Hubert left early and would of been in London with at least an hour to spare, if they hadn't turned back. The appointment with Fenton was at noon. Manse asked Quentin Noss to keep in touch by mobile and let him know any developments on the patch. The call came at just after ten thirty. Noss said: 'Manse, something bad, very bad.'

In the evening at the rectory Manse had three visitors and a phone call. Ralph Ember arrived first. 'I didn't know whether to come or not – whether it would be intrusive, Manse. But Margaret said I should.'

Hi, Ralph. Matilda told me Laurent thought you sent the hired fucking murderer of my wife and child. He believed you wanted all the trade for yourself and your firm. However, I don't consider you stupid enough to pick the sort of bungler who kills two lovely people by mistake. But Manse did not say this. 'Hi, Ralph. I'm glad you did come. Thank you, and thank Margaret.'

'And your daughter?' Ember said.

'They've given her a sedative. She's with her aunty.' If Matilda saw you she'd probably gob in your fucking face. But he didn't say this last bit either.

'Terrible for her.'

'Yes.' They went into the den room. Shale poured claret.

'Half a family wiped out,' Ember said.

'Yes.'

'And for what?'

'A mystery,' Shale said.

'Have you thought about the Lake family?'

'The Lake family? Why?'

'That death of Denzil.'

'His suicide?'

'Well, yes, his suicide,' Ember said. 'We all know that's what it was, of course, but does the family accept this?'

'But why shouldn't they, Ralph?'

'Well, yes, but you know what some people are like. He came from a rough dynasty, I heard. Hackney?'

'That way, yes.'

233

'Might they want to settle things?' Ember said.

'Settle? Which things?'

'It's been a long while since the death, but what's that saying about revenge? A dish best eaten cold. Have you had any dealings with those folk? Could they be secretly determined to get you?'

'They must know I was as distressed as any of them by what happened to Denz. We was very close, you know.'

'Certainly,' Ember said. 'That, too – his death – must have been an appalling shock for you.'

'Appalling,' Manse said. 'A true shock.'

'Yes.'

Iles and Harpur called while Ember was still there. Shale poured more wine. Iles said: 'You're brave, Manse. It would break me, a wonderful woman, a wonderful child.'

'You'll probably know we got an identification pretty quickly,' Harpur said. 'Lance Stanley Sparks.'

'No, I've never heard the name,' Shale said.

'Ralph?' Iles said.

'No, how would I?' Ember said.

'Sparks – an up-and-coming general duties villain operating in mainly Manchester,' Harpur said. 'Sometimes Liverpool and Nottingham. We put out a picture of him and had a more or less instant response from West Midlands police. They'd had a tip he might be offering himself as a freelance executioner at ten grand a pop and were working on it. Obviously, he hadn't properly learned the trade yet. And so the terrible mistakes, Manse. He saw what he'd been conditioned to see – the Jaguar.'

'Not that we'd have wanted him to get it right, and wipe you out, as commissioned, Manse, of course,' Iles said. 'A few of these youngsters try to come on too fast. He'd convinced someone he could do it. But you've definitely no knowledge of him, Ralph? You keep in touch, don't you?'

'In touch with what?' Ember said.

'That's one of your strengths,' Iles replied, 'keeping in touch with many.'

'We wondered about the Lakes,' Harpur said.

'What about them?' Manse said.

'A revenge situation?' Iles said. 'But mucked up by some novice shooter. He's been told a Jag and the likely time so just blazes away, thinking it's you.'

'Revenge for what?' Ember asked. 'Do you mean the death of Denzil? Surely everyone knows he took his own life. If I were Mansel I'd feel very hurt at that kind of questioning. Very hurt and resentful.'

'You're known to be sensitive, Ralph,' Iles said.

'Disgraceful innuendo against Mansel,' Ember replied.

'Naomi – the London connections, Manse,' Harpur said. 'Might she have run into dangerous folk up there? Excuse us for all the questions so soon after the tragedy, but we need to see which way inquiries should go. Is it possible she was the target after all, not you? The boy killed simply because he was there.'

'She worked as consultant on a celebrity paper,' Shale said.

'Yes, we know that. It's the kind of job where people can run into all sorts of other people,' Iles said.

'Which sorts of other people?' Shale said.

'Yes, all sorts of people,' Iles replied.

'Smear and then extra smear,' Ember said. 'That's always your method.'

When they'd gone, Ember said: 'Maybe Naomi did have some troublesome links through the job, Manse.'

'What sort of troublesome links?' Shale said.

'I do understand your touchiness on this, Manse. She was such a lovely woman. It's difficult to imagine any darker side to her life.'

'Well fucking don't.'

Ember stood. 'You'll want to rest, Manse. Please call at any time if you feel the need of company. This house will seem very large and lonely now, although you have Matilda.'

235

Not long after Ember had left, the phone rang and a man said, 'Excuse me, this is something of an exploratory call. I've just seen on television news about the terrible shooting of a lady called Naomi Shale and her stepson. I am hoping, trusting, it is not the Naomi we used to have dealings with in London. We knew her then as Naomi Gage, a charming, very helpful person. She has not been among us recently, and I'd heard she went away to get married in your part of the world. So, you see my concern and why I make this rather, well, rather *wide* inquiry. I do hope I'm wrong.'

'What dealings?'

'Yes, dealings, you know. There are some very ruthless individuals connected to this kind of dealing. I won't spell it out. One needs to be very judicious on the phone. Perhaps you know something about this trade, indeed. Possibly that is what brought you together.'

'The Pre-Raphaelites. How did you get this number?'

'Please do tell me I'm wrong, and this Naomi Shale is not our Naomi Gage.'

'What dealings? Facilitating?'

'So, I'm *not* wrong. Oh, God. Such a loss. I grieve with you.'

Afterwards, Manse dialled 1471. 'You were called at 2132. The caller withheld their number.' Only the other day when Laurent had used 1471, after he answered a ring on the phone and got silence from the other end, he'd told Manse that this announcement by British Telecom was not good grammar. 'It shouldn't be "withheld *their* number" but *his* or *her* number.' In this case, his. Yes, only the other day.